ANATOLE FRANCE

PENGUIN ISLAND

MODERN LIBRARY
NEW YORK

Library of Congress Cataloging in Publication Data

France, Anatole, 1844-1924.
Penguin Island.

Translation of: L'Île des pingouins.
I. Title.
PQ2254.I4E5 1984   843'.8   84-4657
ISBN 0-394-60516-0

CONTENTS

BOOK I

THE BEGINNINGS

BOOK II

THE ANCIENT TIMES

BOOK III

THE MIDDLE AGES AND THE RENAISSANCE

CONTENTS

BOOK VII

MODERN TIMES

BOOK VIII

FUTURE TIMES

INTRODUCTION

THERE are certain works of art plainly marked as works. of thoroughly matured outlook and experienced craftsman- ship. They may not always be the most reputed or the most likable thing that the artist has given us, but they represent him as a graduate of life, no longer a pupil; as a master of his art, not a journeyman. *Cymbeline* is such a work, and *Brahms' Fourth Symphony; Penguin Island* is unmistakably another. The doubter may suggest that this is only an *ex post facto* judgment—if we have the dates, obviously the late works are the mature ones But this is not necessarily true, for a painter, a writer, a composer, must have solid intel- lectual qualities to be capable of this sort of development. An artist without those qualities may go out on a flare of "inspiration" and outlive in his physical life his whole achieve- ment as an artist. The question is not one of years, but of capacity to add continuously and surely to one's intellectual capital, and to utilize that capital to advantage.

It seems to go without saying that the quality of a work of this sort is somewhat more profound than that of the more obviously enjoyable sort; and this in spite of whatever irony and mental airiness may serve for its outer garment. And, too, works which bear the marks of the mould of their creator's thinking mind may appeal least to those who know the quality and variety of that mind in its more instantly agreeable—in other words, its more popular—aspects.

But *Penguin Island* has the rather unusual quality of being both mature and diverting. It is a work conceived in amiable irony, gracious, and filled with the pleasantries (sometimes malicious, and sometimes devilish) that are an inseparable part of one of the most genial of modern literary personalities. The book is a satire, of course, but satire with an admirable difference; for France falls certainly within that elect group whose comedy, as Meredith puts it, "awakens thoughtful laughter."

This is in some degree an inheritance from the French literary tradition. French satire is something of delicate point and excellently disinterested humor, free from the heavy puritanical savagery that frequently animates the English. In the hands of Dryden and Pope satire was a marketable thing that nursed partisanships and fed private grudges. With Swift, though infinitely more social, it reflected the bitterness of a wry brain over personal defeat. With Voltaire, on the other hand, satire was a passionless, amused, reflective, and consistent mode of comment upon the social paradox; something fluid, simple, and, though significant, always fascinating. As a satirist Anatole France is Voltaire's intellectual heir. His mind is just as responsively tuned to the social sense of his own age; his spirit is much the same; and the actual mechanism of his satire is interestingly reminiscent of Voltaire. That is not to say, however, that France is without a satiric character of his own, but merely to note in passing that his cosmopolitan mind, like Voltaire's, is still thoroughly a Frenchman's, sensitive, alert, volatile, schooled in a classic tradition of wit, yet steadily honest and critical.

The most conspicuous point of difference between Voltaire and France, perhaps, lies in the fact that Voltaire, true to his century, is a philosophic satirist, and his first concern is with systems of thought. France, equally the child of his age, is in the main a satirist of institutions, and his great concern is with systems of polity and social control. This difference, at least so far as it affects France, may seem rather broadly stated, but we are now speaking of him only as a satirist. There is a great body of his writing in which there is no large or consistent satiric intention, though most of it has generally a satiric edge.

If we look back, however, over all but France's very earliest apprentice years—the years of *Sylvestre Bonnard* and *My Friend's Book*—we shall find that there is one matter in which he shows a persistent and thoughtful interest, though variously expressed and variously accented: the faith of men in regulative systems, and their pathetic willingness to subordinate to these systems their instincts and their interests. And two phases of institutionalism interest France above others—the translation of religious impulses into formulas and ascetic practices, and the subjection of society to that consummate student of human weaknesses—the politician, or to put it more broadly, the "natural leader." This is the moving idea of almost all of France's writing. It underlies those early parodies of religious legend in *Balthasar* and *The Well of St. Claire*. But in these the idea is shadowy, the humor studiously thin; they bear a visible relation, however, to the mould of thought and the manner of his more impressive fictions. They are not, after all, apprentice work, though they might be likened to charcoal studies for "big pieces." But the art of these little stories is somewhat too fragile, too literary, to be altogether good; and upon the reader who doesn't know his *Golden Legend* or his *Patroologia* their perfection of pattern is likely to be lost. Yet the skill shown in these things is not wasted; France has perfected in them the disarming manner, studied discreet understatement, and these achievements are carried over, with a broadened satirical intent and a sharpening of character and incident, into the superb *Thaïs* and the engaging *Queen Pedauque*. These developments from the earlier spirit and manner have the mass, the strength, the consequence that the shorter pieces, for all their nicety, are without. And for France's literary repute this is a rather important consideration. The studio-piece may be in its very nature a fatal temptation to a writer of as accomplished virtuosity as France. But where the mind settles upon some impelling conception, as France's does in *Thaïs* or *Penguin Island*, the veneer of literary amenity and the bibelot manner disappear, and a somewhat disembodied art takes on flesh and blood. The improvement in command touches every aspect of his work. In *Thaïs* he shows a previously unsuspected force and concentration. He steps instantly from the world of bourgeois gentility into a world of what he himself does not hesitate to call "animal realities." His somewhat finical humor shows a Rabelaisian relish, and a meandering wit begins to move with assured artistic purpose. And this power, from this point on, is never lost. It takes an even more trenchant edge in his political satire—as in *Penguin Island*. And it appears with a poignant ambiguity where it touches the conflict of private relations with moral controls. In *A Mummer's Tale* (*Histoire Comique*) and *The Red Lily* his social piety (something he undeniably possesses) and his tolerant amusement are like twin sisters, hardly to be told apart.

France was forty-six when *Thaïs* appeared. In sensuous fervor it is a young man's book, in ironic understanding an old man's. But in it his spirit is at once and finally clear. His knowledge not merely of the obscurer suggestions of historical fact, but of the persistently human "human nature" which defies the salutary social device and the moral sanction, is what furnishes the stuff of the most significant volumes of these later years. But the interest of the thing is focused upon the personal problem in *Thaïs*. In *Penguin Island* it throws its light upon an entire panorama of history.

France himself is credited with the remark that "all great authors write badly." If we take this to imply a certain indifference to the canons of "form" and "taste," then it is a saving judgment for himself. His most suave writing is likely to be inconsequential; his most spirited, reckless. *Penguin Island* is boldly imagined, somewhat feebly oriented; and like all France's work when it contains the *arrière pensée* of social criticism, its power depends more upon the force of its high incidents than upon actual artistic integrity. France has never written a first-rate novel; he himself would scarcely have ventured to call most of his longer narratives novels. But that is merely a way of saying that his strongest and most characteristic works move in a free medium which in itself furnishes an important part of their interest.

In *Penguin Island* there is a very simple idea—the humorously interpretive handling of history in a chain of episodes illustrating the origins and the expansion of custom and law. The intention here, attached though it is to a definite aim, is one with France's unmoral and unromantic attitude toward all social matters of discussion. Nor is this attitude merely negative; it is a positive dissent from every form of organized idolatry. He does not deny a meaning in history, but he questions persistently that cheerful and fallacious reading of history as a route-map of steady progress toward perfect human relations. Yet the skeptical student of history must be, at least potentially, a really informed historian. France was in fact that, and more. His scholarship is at every point adequate, and in many respects profound. That quite amazing erudition which bubbles constantly to the surface of his recorded conversations appears in *Penguin Island* as a solid conversancy with what has animated European culture through a multitude of social and intellectual changes. The moral truth of his narrative, however, lies in no parade of records, but in an unfailing ear for the mood and tone of highly varying social conditions, and in a searching eye for the dominant prejudices of any period. It is a rare discrimination that can skim the essential from the vast and disturbed surface of beliefs and happenings that we call cultural history.

But this *penchant* of France's for the historical point of view works with the symbolic rather than the literal fact; or it may be truer to say that it chooses the symbolic, and not the literal, fact. Of course so inexplicit a representation of historical background outrages the academic historian's sense of propriety. He feels that the method is so colored by underlying convictions and distorted by whimsicalities that it can be only irresponsible and partisan. Yet while there is a substantial truth in this view of the matter, the fact remains that France was an intelligent traveler not only of the highways of history, but of its bye-roads, and that his interpretive attitude reveals at least a clear and equitable view of social institutions. Here again he is like Voltaire—in his intentness upon disentangling the human element in history from the intellectual, and in his smiling refusal to attach tragic seriousness to the failures which prove our collective humanity. His views of social origins are simple, like Voltaire's, and his tests of both people and institutions are (like Voltaire's) the primary virtues. It is natural, then, that the historic instance should be contrived for his purpose—as in his portrait of The Holy Mael or his account of the invention of clothes in Penguinia; but the symbolic truth of the personality or the event is irrefragable—animated as it is by that backward-looking prophecy which discovers the actual social intention beneath the clutter of facts.

France's historical outlook, then, is consistent; consistent with itself and with his intelligent, if somewhat doctrinal, social philosophy. And his burlesque method, his amused pose of scholarly accuracy, is a fair and relevant comment upon unprofitable learning. Above all he is interested in that phenomenon that he handled fancifully and aggressively in his earlier parodies—the legendary process actively and persistently at work in all history, ancient and modern—the overlaying of the significance of social evidence by superstition, popular idolatry, institutionalism, partisan convictions, what not.

Behind this screen of imaginative play with an invented but nevertheless thoroughly representative history there is, then, a clear social logic and a profound conviction. Indirection, comic stress, are vehicles. Irony is the garb of an acute sympathy. In France there is no misanthropy. His sense of the weakness of man under his own institutions, of his docile submission to the dominating mind, of his desperate but distracted urge for spiritual freedom, reflects precisely the same friendly pity that one discovers in the personal instance in his characters of *Sylvestre Bonnard* and *M. Bergeret*. France is not an atheist; he understands religion and is drawn to its beauties and its precepts. He is likewise not an anarchist— he believes in both political and economic control. His social philosophy is collectivist. But his skepticism breeds a spirited scorn for acts and expedients and enterprises that are with‧ out virtue unless individual will and discretion can displace collective credulity and spinelessness.

But France's manner disturbs the mind into understanding; it does not seduce it or belabor it with reason. Its cunning ambiguity challenges thought—and by the same token not infrequently baffles the unthinking. His mental, and also his emotional range, is immense, but his perceptions are so much the artist's, and his mental attack so distinctly that of a man alert to the preciousness of an idea, that even when his manner seems most Socratic he is bringing the mind not to an easy resting-place, but to some precarious see-saw of incongruous claims. And he is acutely conscious of both the comedy and the tragedy of the eternal dilemmas. Paradoxes are for him symbols of life as a whole. Life's consistency lies in the universality of its inconsistencies. Truth is found in the very contrast of extremes, not in the impossible "safe middle ground" of the average-minded. Mental life is mental motion—the swing of the pendulum (to borrow Shaw's figure) between the angelic and the diabolic temper, and we might add between the rational and the irrational, the simple and the complex, and any and all other extremes of merely momentary mental rest.

Therefore what seems at times in France a humorous duplicity—even a calculated betrayal of the reader's trust by some twist of ludicrous or excruciating doubt in a narrative that is pursued with the air of truth—is really not so much literary trickery as it is the manifestation of his absorbed interest in the eternal mixture of truth and untruth. So even the visions of ascetics, the fabrications of historians, the rationalizations of politicians, have for him their discoverable explanations, in aspects of human nature that are just as definitely human as the virtues to which in our traditional morality they stand opposed. But France's "will to believe" is all on the side of the virtues—not the canonical virtues, but the virtues that repose in an understanding of both the reasoning and the emotional nature. And the student of these virtues must be concerned less with formulated beliefs, with social poses, with "acts of grace," than with the wish and the will to understand the complicated thing called life and the complex beings who live it.

Hence the strain in France that has been called "pessimistic" and "cynical." His view of life in his more definitely social fictions, such as *The Gods are Athirst, Penguin Island,* and *The Revolt of the Angels,* certainly carries no brave affirmation of the creed of Dr. Pangloss. Yet can a laughing pessimist be a pessimist; or a generous and sympathetic cynic a cynic? What interests and concerns France in these narratives is social experience as the solvent of social character, the finding of life in the losing of it, the heroic but pathetic struggle of man to refashion his man's destiny. And France's air of unconcern is no sign of indifference to the import or the outcome of the struggle. His urbanity is the wise man's armor against life's cruelest wounds—those which reach the unprotected emotions. And the conclusion of *Penguin Island* is no counsel of despair, but a challenge to the social urge to justify itself through an intelligence that is at once more intent and more cautious than history has commonly shown it to be.

H. R. STEEVES.

COLUMBIA UNIVERSITY,
September, 1932.

BOOK 1

THE BEGINNINGS

I

LIFE OF SAINT MAËL

MAËL, a scion of a royal family of Cambria, was sent in his ninth year to the Abbey of Yvern so that he might there study both sacred and profane learning. At the age of fourteen he renounced his patrimony and took a vow to serve the Lord. His time was divided, according to the rule, between the singing of hymns, the study of grammar, and the meditation of eternal truths.

A celestial perfume soon disclosed the virtues of the monk throughout the cloister, and when the blessed Gal, the Abbot of Yvern, departed from this world into the next, young Maël succeeded him in the government of the monastery. He established therein a school, an infirmary, a guest-house, a forge, work-shops of all kinds, and sheds for building ships, and he compelled the monks to till the lands in the neighbourhood. With his own hands he cultivated the garden of the Abbey, he worked in metals, he instructed the novices, and his life was gently gliding along like a stream that reflects the heaven and fertilizes the fields

At the close of the day this servant of God was accustomed to seat himself on the cliff, in the place that is to-day still called St. Maël's chair. At his feet the rocks bristling with green seaweed and tawny wrack seemed like black dragons as they faced the foam of the waves with their monstrous breasts. He watched the sun descending into the ocean like a red Host whose glorious blood gave a purple tone to the clouds and to the summits of the waves. And the holy man saw in this the image of the mystery of the Cross, by which the divine blood has clothed the earth with a royal purple.

3

In the offing a line of dark blue marked the shores of the island of Gad, where St. Bridget, who had been given the veil by St. Malo, ruled over a convent of women.

Now Bridget, knowing the merits of the venerable Maël, begged from him some work of his hands as a rich present. Maël cast a hand-bell of bronze for her and, when it was finished, he blessed it and threw it into the sea. And the bell went ringing towards the coast of Gad, where St. Bridget, warned by the sound of the bell upon the waves, received it piously, and carried it in solemn procession with singing of psalms into the chapel of the convent.

Thus the holy Maël advanced from virtue to virtue. He had already passed through two-thirds of the way of life, and he hoped peacefully to reach his terrestrial end in the midst of his spiritual brethren, when he knew by a certain sign that the Divine wisdom had decided otherwise, and that the Lord was calling him to less peaceful but not less meritorious labours.

II

THE APOSTOLICAL VOCATION OF SAINT MAËL

ONE day as he walked in meditation to the furthest point of a tranquil beach, for which rocks jutting out into the sea formed a rugged dam, he saw a trough of stone which floated like a boat upon the waters.

It was in a vessel similar to this that St. Guirec, the great St. Columba, and so many holy men from Scotland and from Ireland had gone forth to evangelize Armorica. More recently still, St. Avoye having come from England, ascended the river Auray in a mortar made of rose-coloured granite into which children were afterwards placed in order to make them strong; St. Vouga passed from Hibernia to Cornwall on a rock whose fragments, preserved at Penmarch, will cure of fever such pilgrims as place these splinters on their heads. St. Samson entered the Bay of St. Michael's Mount in a granite vessel which will one day be called St. Samson's basin. It is because of these facts that when he saw the stone trough the holy Maël understood that the Lord intended him for the apostolate of the pagans who still peopled the coast and the Breton islands.

He handed his ashen staff to the holy Budoc, thus investing him with the government of the monastery. Then, furnished with bread, a barrel of fresh water, and the book of the Holy Gospels, he entered the stone trough which carried him gently to the island of Hœdic.

This island is perpetually buffeted by the winds. In it some poor men fished among the clefts of the rocks and laboriously cultivated vegetables in gardens full of sand and

5

pebbles that were sheltered from the wind by walls of barren
stone and hedges of tamarisk. A beautiful fig-tree raised itself
in a hollow of the island and thrust forth its branches far
and wide. The inhabitants of the island used to worship it.

And the holy Maël said to them: "You worship this tree
because it is beautiful. Therefore you are capable of feeling
beauty. Now I come to reveal to you the hidden beauty."
And he taught them the Gospel. And after having instructed
them, he baptized them with salt and water.

The islands of Morbihan were more numerous in those
times than they are to-day. For since then many have been
swallowed up by the sea. St. Maël evangelized sixty of them.
Then in his granite trough he ascended the river Auray. And
after sailing for three hours he landed before a Roman house.
A thin column of smoke went up from the roof. The holy
man crossed the threshold on which there was a mosaic representing a dog with its hind legs outstretched and its lips drawn
back. He was welcomed by an old couple, Marcus Combabus
and Valeria Moerens, who lived there on the products of
their lands. There was a portico round the interior court
the columns of which were painted red, half their height
upwards from the base. A fountain made of shells stood against
the wall and under the portico there rose an altar with a
niche in which the master of the house had placed some little
idols made of baked earth and whitened with whitewash.
Some represented winged children, others Apollo or Mercury,
and several were in the form of a naked woman twisting her
hair. But the holy Maël, observing those figures, discovered
among them the image of a young mother holding a child
upon her knees.

Immediately pointing to that image he said:

"That is the Virgin, the mother of God. The poet Virgil
foretold her in Sibylline verses before she was born and,
in angelical tones he sang *Jam redit et virgo*. Throughout
heathendom prophetic figures of her have been made, like
that which you, O Marcus, have placed upon this altar.

And without doubt it is she who has protected your modest household. Thus it is that those who faithfully observe the natural law prepare themselves for the knowledge of revealed truths."

Marcus Combabus and Valeria Moerens, having been instructed by this speech, were converted to the Christian faith. They received baptism together with their young freedwoman, Caelia Avitella, who was dearer to them than the light of their eyes. All their tenants renounced paganism and were baptized on the same day.

Marcus Combabus, Valeria Moerens, and Caelia Avitella led thenceforth a life full of merit. They died in the Lord and were admitted into the canon of the saints.

For thirty-seven years longer the blessed Maël evangelized the pagans of the inner lands. He built two hundred and eighteen chapels and seventy-four abbeys.

Now on a certain day in the city of Vannes, where he was preaching the Gospel, he learned that the monks of Yvern had in his absence declined from the rule of St. Gal. Immediately, with the zeal of a hen who gathers her brood, he repaired to his erring children. He was then towards the end of his ninety-seventh year; his figure was bent, but his arms were still strong, and his speech was poured forth abundantly like winter snow in the depths of the valleys.

Abbot Budoc restored the ashen staff to St. Maël and informed him of the unhappy state into which the Abbey had fallen. The monks were in disagreement as to the date on which the festival of Easter ought to be celebrated. Some held for the Roman calendar, others for the Greek calendar, and the horrors of a chronological schism distracted the monastery.

There also prevailed another cause of disorder. The nuns of the island of Gad, sadly fallen from their former virtue, continually came in boats to the coast of Yvern. The monks received them in the guest-house and from this there arose scandals which filled pious souls with desolation.

Having finished his faithful report, Abbot Budoc concluded in these terms:

"Since the coming of these nuns the innocence and peace of the monks are at an end."

"I readily believe it," answered the blessed Maël. "For woman is a cleverly constructed snare by which we are taken even before we suspect the trap. Alas! the delightful attraction of these creatures is exerted with even greater force from a distance than when they are close at hand. The less they satisfy desire the more they inspire it. This is the reason why a poet wrote this verse to one of them:

When present I avoid thee, but when away I find thee.

Thus we see, my son, that the blandishments of carnal love have more power over hermits and monks than over men who live in the world. All through my life the demon of lust has tempted me in various ways, but his strongest temptations did not come to me from meeting a woman, however beautiful and fragrant she was. They came to me from the image of an absent woman. Even now, though full of days and approaching my ninety-eighth year, I am often led by the Enemy to sin against chastity, at least in thought. At night when I am cold in my bed and my frozen old bones rattle together with a dull sound I hear voices reciting the second verse of the third Book of the Kings: 'Wherefore his servants said unto him, Let there be sought for my lord the king a young virgin: and let her stand before the king, and let her cherish him, and let her lie in thy bosom, that my lord the king may get heat,' and the devil shows me a girl in the bloom of youth who says to me: 'I am thy Abishag; I am thy Shunamite. Make, O my lord, room for me in thy couch.'

"Believe me," added the old man, "it is only by the special aid of Heaven that a monk can keep his chastity in act and in intention."

Applying himself immediately to restore innocence and peace to the monastery, he corrected the calendar according to the calculations of chronology and astronomy and he compelled all the monks to accept his decision; he sent the women who had declined from St. Bridget's rule back to their convent; but far from driving them away brutally, he caused them to be led to their boat with singing of psalms and litanies.

"Let us respect in them," he said, "the daughters of Bridget and the betrothed of the Lord. Let us beware lest we imitate the Pharisees who affect to despise sinners. The sin of these women and not their persons should be abased, and they should be made ashamed of what they have done and not of what they are, for they are all creatures of God."

And the holy man exhorted his monks to obey faithfully the rule of their order.

"When it does not yield to the rudder," said he to them, "the ship yields to the rock."

III

THE TEMPTATION OF SAINT MAËL

THE blessed Maël had scarcely restored order in the Abbey of Yvern before he learned that the inhabitants of the island of Hœdic, his first catechumens and the dearest of all to his heart, had returned to paganism, and that they were hanging crowns of flowers and fillets of wool to the branches of the sacred fig-tree.

The boatman who brought this sad news expressed a fear that soon those misguided men might violently destroy the chapel that had been built on the shore of their island.

The holy man resolved forthwith to visit his faithless children, so that he might lead them back to the faith and prevent them from yielding to such sacrilege. As he went down to the bay where his stone trough was moored, he turned his eyes to the sheds, then filled with the noise of saws and of hammers, which, thirty years before, he had erected on the fringe of that bay for the purpose of building ships.

At that moment, the Devil, who never tires, went out from the sheds and, under the appearance of a monk called Samson, he approached the holy man and tempted him thus:

"Father, the inhabitants of the island of Hœdic commit sins unceasingly. Every moment that passes removes them farther from God. They are soon going to use violence towards the chapel that you have raised with your own venerable hands on the shore of their island. Time is pressing. Do you not think that your stone trough would carry you more quickly towards them if it were rigged like a boat and furnished with a rudder, a mast, and a sail, for then you would be driven by

the wind? Your arms are still strong and able to steer a
small craft. It would be a good thing, too, to put a sharp
stem in front of your apostolic trough. You are much too
clear-sighted not to have thought of it already."

"Truly time is pressing," answered the holy man. "But
to do as you say, Samson, my son, would it not be to make
myself like those men of little faith who do not trust the
Lord? Would it not be to despise the gifts of Him who has
sent me this stone vessel without rigging or sail?"

This question, the Devil, who is a great theologian, answered by another.

"Father, is it praiseworthy to wait, with our arms folded,
until help comes from on high, and to ask everything from
Him who can do all things, instead of acting by human prudence and helping ourselves?"

"It certainly is not," answered the holy Maël, "and to
neglect to act by human prudence is tempting God."

"Well," urged the Devil, "is it not prudence in this case
to rig the vessel?"

"It would be prudence if we could not attain our end in
any other way."

"Is your vessel then so very speedy?"

"It is as speedy as God pleases."

"What do you know about it? It goes like Abbot Budoc's
mule. It is a regular old tub. Are you forbidden to make it
speedier?"

"My son, clearness adorns your words, but they are unduly
over-confident. Remember that this vessel is miraculous."

"It is, father. A granite trough that floats on the water
like a cork is a miraculous trough. There is not the slightest
doubt about it. What conclusion do you draw from that?"

"I am greatly perplexed. Is it right to perfect so miraculous
a machine by human and natural means?"

"Father, if you lost your right foot and God restored it to
you, would not that foot be miraculous?"

"Without doubt, my son."

"Would you put a shoe on it?"

"Assuredly."

"Well, then, if you believe that one may cover a miraculous foot with a natural shoe, you should also believe that we can put natural rigging on a miraculous boat. That is clear. Alas! Why must the holiest persons have their moments of weakness and despondency? The most illustrious of the apostles of Brittany could accomplish works worthy of eternal glory ... But his spirit is tardy and his hand is slothful. Farewell then, father! Travel by short and slow stages and when at last you approach the coast of Hœdic you will see the smoking ruin of the chapel that was built and consecrated by your own hands. The pagans will have burned it and with it the deacon you left there. He will be as thoroughly roasted as a black pudding."

"My trouble is extreme," said the servant of God, drying with his sleeve the sweat that gathered upon his brow. "But tell me, Samson, my son, would not rigging this stone trough be a difficult piece of work? And if we undertook it might we not lose time instead of gaining it?"

"Ah! father," exclaimed the Devil, "in one turning of the hour-glass the thing would be done. We shall find the necessary rigging in this shed that you have formerly built here on the coast and in those store-houses abundantly stocked through your care. I will myself regulate all the ship's fittings. Before being a monk I was a sailor and a carpenter and I have worked at many other trades as well. Let us to work."

Immediately he drew the holy man into an outhouse filled with all things needful for fitting out a boat.

"That for you, father!"

And he placed on his shoulders the sail, the mast, the gaff, and the boom.

Then, himself bearing a stem and a rudder with its screw

and tiller, and seizing a carpenter's bag full of tools, he ran to the shore, dragging the holy man after him by his habit. The latter was bent, sweating, and breathless, under the burden of canvas and wood.

IV

ST. MAËL'S NAVIGATION ON THE OCEAN
OF ICE

THE Devil, having tucked his clothes up to his arm-pits,
dragged the trough on the sand, and fitted the rigging in less
than an hour.

As soon as the holy Maël had embarked, the vessel, with all
its sails set, cleft through the waters with such speed that the
coast was almost immediately out of sight. The old man steered
to the south so as to double the Land's End, but an irresistible
current carried him to the south-west. He went along the
southern coast of Ireland and turned sharply towards the
north. In the evening the wind freshened. In vain did Maël
attempt to furl the sail. The vessel flew distractedly towards
the fabulous seas.

By the light of the moon the immodest sirens of the North
came around him with their hempen-coloured hair, raising
their white throats and their rose-tinted limbs out of the sea;
and beating the water into foam with their emerald tails, they
sang in cadence:

> Whither go'st thou, gentle Maël,
> In thy trough distracted?
> All distended is thy sail
> Like the breast of Juno
> When from it gushed the Milky Way.

For a moment their harmonious laughter followed him beneath the stars, but the vessel fled on, a hundred times more
swiftly than the red ship of a Viking. And the petrels, surprised
in their flight, clung with their feet to the hair of the holy man.
Soon a tempest arose full of darkness and groanings, and

the trough, driven by a furious wind, flew like a sea-mew through the mist and the surge.

After a night of three times twenty-four hours the darkness was suddenly rent and the holy man discovered on the horizon a shore more dazzling than diamond. The coast rapidly grew larger, and soon by the glacial light of a torpid and sunken sun, Maël saw, rising above the waves, the silent streets of a white city, which, vaster than Thebes with its hundred g/.tes, extended as far as the eye could see the ruins of its forum built of snow, its palaces of frost, its crystal arches, and its iridescent obelisks.

The ocean was covered with floating ice-bergs around which swam men of the sea of a wild yet gentle appearance. And Leviathan passed by hurling a column of water up to the clouds.

Moreover, on a block of ice which floated at the same rate as the stone trough there was seated a white bear holding her little one in her arms, and Maël heard her murmuring in a low voice this verse of Virgil, *Incipe parve puer*.

And full of sadness and trouble, the old man wept.

The fresh water had frozen and burst the barrel that contained it. And Maël was sucking pieces of ice to quench his thirst, and his food was bread dipped in dirty water. His beard and his hair were broken like glass. His habit was covered with a layer of ice and cut into him at every movement of his limbs. Huge waves rose up and opened their foaming jaws at the old man. Twenty times the boat was filled by masses of sea. And the ocean swallowed up the book of the Holy Gospels which the apostle guarded with extreme care in a purple cover marked with a golden cross.

Now on the thirtieth day the sea calmed. And lo! with a frightful clamour of sky and waters a mountain of dazzling whiteness advanced towards the stone vessel. Maël steered to avoid it, but the tiller broke in his hands. To lessen the speed of his progress towards the rock he attempted to reef the sails, but when he tried to knot the reef-points the wind pulled

them away from him and the rope seared his hands. He s;
three demons with wings of black skin having hooks at the
ends, who, hanging from the rigging, were puffing with thei.
breath against the sails.

Understanding from this sight that the Enemy had governed him in all these things, he guarded himself by making
the sign of the Cross. Immediately a furious gust of wind
filled with the noise of sobs and howls struck the stone trough,
carried off the mast with all the sails, and tore away the rudder
and the stem.

The trough was drifting on the sea, which had now grown
calm. The holy man knelt and gave thanks to the Lord who
had delivered him from the snares of the demon. Then he
recognised, sitting on a block of ice, the mother bear who
had spoken during the storm. She pressed her beloved child to
her bosom, and in her hand she held a purple book marked
with a golden cross. Hailing the granite trough, she saluted
the holy man with these words:

"Pax tibi Maël"

And she held out the book to him.

The holy man recognised his evangelistary, and, full of astonishment, he sang in the tepid air a hymn to the Creator and
His creation.

V

THE BAPTISM OF THE PENGUINS

AFTER having drifted for an hour the holy man approached a narrow strand, shut in by steep mountains. He went along the coast for a whole day and a night, passing around the reef which formed an insuperable barrier. He discovered in this way that it was a round island in the middle of which rose a mountain crowned with clouds. He joyfully breathed the fresh breath of the moist air. Rain fell, and this was so pleasant that the holy man said to the Lord:

"Lord, this is the island of tears, the island of contrition."

The strand was deserted. Worn out with fatigue and hunger, he sat down on a rock in the hollow of which there lay some yellow eggs, marked with black spots, and about as large as those of a swan. But he did not touch them, saying:

"Birds are the living praises of God. I should not like a single one of these praises to be lacking through me."

And he munched the lichens which he tore from the crannies of the rocks.

The holy man had gone almost entirely round the island without meeting any inhabitants, when he came to a vast amphitheatre formed of black and red rocks whose summits became tinged with blue as they rose towards the clouds, and they were filled with sonorous cascades.

The reflection from the polar ice had hurt the old man's eyes, but a feeble gleam of light still shone through his swollen eyelids. He distinguished animated forms which filled the rocks, in stages, like a crowd of men on the tiers of an amphitheatre. And at the same time, his ears, deafened by the continual noises of the sea, heard a feeble sound of voices.

Thinking that what he saw were men living under the natural
law, and that the Lord had sent him to teach them the Divine
law, he preached the gospel to them.

Mounted on a lofty stone in the midst of the wild circus:

"Inhabitants of this island," said he, "although you be of
small stature, you look less like a band of fishermen and
mariners than like the senate of a judicious republic. By your
gravity, your silence, your tranquil deportment, you form on
this wild rock an assembly comparable to the Conscript Fathers at Rome deliberating in the temple of Victory, or rather,
to the philosophers of Athens disputing on the benches of the
Areopagus. Doubtless you possess neither their science nor
their genius, but perhaps in the sight of God you are their
superiors. I believe that you are simple and good. As I went
round your island I saw no image of murder, no sign of
carnage, no enemies' heads or scalps hung from a lofty pole
or nailed to the doors of your villages. You appear to me to
have no arts and not to work in metals. But your hearts are
pure and your hands are innocent, and the truth will easily
enter into your souls."

Now what he had taken for men of small stature but of
grave bearing were penguins whom the spring had gathered
together, and who were ranged in couples on the natural steps
of the rock, erect in the majesty of their large white bellies.
From moment to moment they moved their winglets like arms,
and uttered peaceful cries. They did not fear men, for they
did not know them, and had never received any harm from
them; and there was in the monk a certain gentleness that
reassured the most timid animals and that pleased these penguins extremely. With a friendly curiosity they turned towards
him their little round eyes lengthened in front by a white oval
spot that gave something odd and human to their appearance.

Touched by their attention, the holy man taught them the
Gospel.

"Inhabitants of this island, the early day that has just risen
over your rocks is the image of the heavenly day that rises

in your souls. For I bring you the inner light; I bring you the light and heat of the soul. Just as the sun melts the ice of your mountains so Jesus Christ will melt the ice of your hearts."

Thus the old man spoke. As everywhere throughout nature voice calls to voice, as all which breathes in the light of day loves alternate strains, these penguins answered the old man by the sounds of their throats. And their voices were soft, for it was the season of their loves.

The holy man, persuaded that they belonged to some idolatrous people and that in their own language they gave adherence to the Christian faith, invited them to receive baptism.

"I think," said he to them, "that you bathe often, for all the hollows of the rocks are full of pure water, and as I came to your assembly I saw several of you plunging into these natural baths. Now purity of body is the image of spiritual purity."

And he taught them the origin, the nature, and the effects of baptism.

"Baptism," said he to them, "is Adoption, New Birth, Regeneration, Illumination."

And he explained each of these points to them in succession.

Then, having previously blessed the water that fell from the cascades and recited the exorcisms, he baptized those whom he had just taught, pouring on each of their heads a drop of pure water and pronouncing the sacred words.

And thus for three days and three nights he baptized the birds.

VI

AN ASSEMBLY IN PARADISE

WHEN the baptism of the penguins was known in Paradise, it caused neither joy nor sorrow, but an extreme surprise. The Lord himself was embarrassed. He gathered an assembly of clerics and doctors, and asked them whether they regarded the baptism as valid.

"It is void," said St. Patrick.

"Why is it void?" asked St. Gal, who had evangelized the people of Cornwall and had trained the holy Maël for his apostolical labours.

"The sacrament of baptism," answered St. Patrick, "is void when it is given to birds, just as the sacrament of marriage is void when it is given to a eunuch."

But St. Gal replied:

"What relation do you claim to establish between the baptism of a bird and the marriage of a eunuch? There is none at all. Marriage is, if I may say so, a conditional, a contingent sacrament. The priest blesses an event beforehand; it is evident that if the act is not consummated the benediction remains without effect. That is obvious. I have known on earth, in the town of Antrim, a rich man named Sadoc, who, living in concubinage with a woman, caused her to be the mother of nine children. In his old age, yielding to my reproofs, he consented to marry her, and I blessed their union. Unfortunately Sadoc's great age prevented him from consummating the marriage. A short time afterwards he lost all his property, and Germaine (that was the name of the woman), not feeling herself able to endure poverty, asked for the annulment of a marriage which was no reality. The Pope granted her request, for it was just. So much for marriage. But baptism is conferred without restrictions or reserves of any kind. There is no doubt about it, what the penguins have received is a sacrament."

Called to give his opinion, Pope St. Damasus expressed himself in these terms:

"In order to know if a baptism is valid and will produce its result, that is to say, sanctification, it is necessary to consider who gives it and not who receives it. In truth, the sanctifying virtue of this sacrament results from the exterior act by which it is conferred, without the baptized person co-operating in his own sanctification by any personal act; if it were otherwise it would not be administered to the newly born. And there is no need, in order to baptize, to fulfill any special condition; it is not necessary to be in a state of grace; it is sufficient to have the intention of doing what the Church does, to pronounce the consecrated words and to observe the prescribed forms. Now we cannot doubt that the venerable Maël has observed these conditions. Therefore the penguins are baptized."

"Do you think so?" asked St. Guénolé. "And what then do you believe that baptism really is? Baptism is the process of regeneration by which man is born of water and of the spirit, for having entered the water covered with crimes, he goes out of it a neophyte, a new creature, abounding in the fruits of righteousness; baptism is the seed of immortality; baptism is the pledge of the resurrection; baptism is the burying with Christ in His death and participation in His departure from the sepulchre. That is not a gift to bestow upon birds. Reverend Fathers, let us consider. Baptism washes away original sin; now the penguins were not conceived in sin. It removes the penalty of sin; now the penguins have not sinned. It produces grace and the gift of virtues, uniting Christians to Jesus Christ, as the members to the body, and it is obvious to the senses that penguins cannot acquire the virtues of confessors, of virgins, and of widows, or receive grace and be united to—"

St. Damasus did not allow him to finish.

"That proves," said he warmly, "that the baptism was useless; it does not prove that it was not effective."

"But by this reasoning," said St. Guénolé, "one might baptize in the name of the Father, of the Son, and of the Holy Ghost, by aspersion or immersion, not only a bird or a quadru· ped, but also an inanimate object, a statue, a table, a chair, etc. That animal would be Christian, that idol, that table would be Christian! It is absurd!"

St. Augustine began to speak. There was a great silence.

"I am going," said the ardent bishop of Hippo, "to show you, by an example, the power of formulas. It deals, it is true, with a diabolical operation. But if it be established that formulas taught by the Devil have effect upon unintelligent animals or even on inanimate objects, how can we longer doubt that the effect of the sacramental formulas extends to the minds of beasts and even to inert matter?

"This is the example. There was during my lifetime in the town of Madaura, the birthplace of the philosopher Apuleius, a witch who was able to attract men to her chamber by burning a few of their hairs along with certain herbs upon her tripod, pronouncing at the same time certain words. Now one day when she wished by this means to gain the love of a young man, she was deceived by her maid, and instead of the young man's hairs, she burned some hairs pulled from a leather bottle, made out of a goatskin that hung in a tavern. During the night the leather bottle, full of wine, capered through the town up to the witch's door. This fact is undoubted. And in sacraments as in enchantments it is the form which operates. The effect of a divine formula cannot be less in power and extent than the effect of an infernal formula."

Having spoken in this fashion the great St. Augustine sat down amidst applause.

One of the blessed, of an advanced age and having a melancholy appearance, asked permission to speak. No one knew him. His name was Probus, and he was not enrolled in the canon of the saints.

"I beg the company's pardon," said he, "I have no halo, and I gained eternal blessedness without any eminent distinction. But after what the great St. Augustine has just told you I believe it right to impart a cruel experience, which I had, relative to the conditions necessary for the validity of a sacrament. The bishop of Hippo is indeed right in what he said. A sacrament depends on the form; its virtue is in its form; its vice is in its form. Listen, confessors and pontiffs, to my woeful story. I was a priest in Rome under the rule of the Emperor Gordianus. Without desiring to recommend myself to you for any special merit, I may say that I exercised my priesthood with piety and zeal. For forty years I served the church of St. Modestus-beyond-the-Walls. My habits were regular. Every Saturday I went to a tavern-keeper called Barjas, who dwelt with his wine-jars under the Porta Capena, and from him I bought the wine that I consecrated daily throughout the week. During that long space of time I never failed for a single morning to consecrate the holy sacrifice of the mass. However, I had no joy, and it was with a heart oppressed by sorrow that, on the steps of the altar I used to ask, 'Why art thou so heavy, O my soul, and why art thou so disquieted within me?' The faithful whom I invited to the holy table gave me cause for affliction, for having, so to speak, the Host that I administered still upon their tongues, they fell again into sin just as if the sacrament had been without power or efficacy. At last I reached the end of my earthly trials, and falling asleep in the Lord, I awoke in this abode of the elect. I learned then from the mouth of the angel who brought me here, that Barjas, the tavern-keeper of the Porta Capena, had sold for wine a decoction of roots and barks in which there was not a single drop of the juice of the grape. I had been unable to transmute this vile brew into blood, for it was not wine, and wine alone is changed into the blood of Jesus Christ. Therefore all my consecrations were invalid, and unknown to us, my faithful and myself had for forty years been deprived of the sacrament and were in fact in a state of excommunication. This revelation threw me into a stupor which overwhelms me even to-day in this abode of bliss. I go all through Paradise without ever meeting a single one of those Christians whom formerly I admitted to the holy table in the basilica of the blessed Modestus. Deprived of the bread of angels, they easily gave way to the most abominable vices, and they have all gone to hell. It gives me some satisfaction to think that Barjas, the tavern-keeper, is damned. There is in these things a logic worthy of the author of all logic. Nevertheless my unhappy example proves that it is sometimes inconvenient that form should prevail over essence in the sacraments, and I humbly ask, Could not eternal wisdom remedy this?"

"No," answered the Lord. "The remedy would be worse than the disease. It would be the ruin of the priesthood if essence prevailed over form in the laws of salvation."

"Alas! Lord," sighed the humble Probus. "Be persuaded by my humble experience; as long as you reduce your sacraments to formulas your justice will meet with terrible obstacles."

"I know that better than you do," replied the Lord. "I see in a single glance both the actual problems which are difficult, and the future problems which will not be less difficult. Thus I can foretell that when the sun will have turned round the earth two hundred and forty times more . . ."

"Sublime language," exclaimed the angels.

"And worthy of the creator of the world," answered the pontiffs.

"It is," resumed the Lord, "a manner of speaking in accordance with my old cosmogony and one which I cannot give up without losing my immutability. . . .

"After the sun, then, will have turned another two hundred and forty times round the earth, there will not be a single cleric left in Rome who knows Latin. When they sing their litanies in the churches people will invoke Orichel, Roguel, and Totichel, and, as you know, these are devils and not angels. Many robbers desiring to make their communions, but fearing that before obtaining pardon they would be forced to give up the things they had robbed to the Church, will make their confessions to travelling priests, who, ignorant of both Italian and Latin, and only speaking the *patois* of their village, will go through cities and towns selling the remission of sins for a base price, often for a bottle of wine. Probably we shall not be inconvenienced by those absolutions as they will want contrition to make them valid, but it may be that their baptisms will cause us some embarrassment. The priests will become so ignorant that they will baptize children *in nomine patria et filia et spirita sancta,* as Louis de Potter will take a pleasure in relating in the third volume of his 'Philosophical, Political, and Critical History of Christianity.' It will be an arduous question to decide on the validity of such baptisms; for even if in my sacred writings I tolerate a Greek less elegant than Plato's and a scarcely Ciceronian Latin, I cannot possibly admit a piece of pure *patois* as a liturgical formula. And one shudders when one thinks that millions of new-born babes will be baptized by this method. But let us return to our penguins."

"Your divine words, Lord, have already led us back to them," said St. Gal. "In the signs of religion and the laws of salvation form necessarily prevails over essence, and the validity of a sacrament solely depends upon its form. The whole question is whether the penguins have been baptized with the proper forms. Now there is no doubt about the answer."

The fathers and the doctors agreed, and their perplexity became only the more cruel.

"The Christian state," said St. Cornelius, "is not without serious inconveniences for a penguin. In it the birds are obliged to work out their own salvation. How can they succeed? The habits of birds are, in many points, contrary to the commandments of the Church, and the penguins have no reason for changing theirs. I mean that they are not intelligent enough to give up their present habits and assume better."

"They cannot," said the Lord; "my decrees prevent them."

"Nevertheless," resumed St. Cornelius, "in virtue of their baptism their actions no longer remain indifferent. Henceforth they will be good or bad, susceptible of merit or of demerit."

"That is precisely the question we have to deal with," said the Lord.

"I see only one solution," said St. Augustine. "The penguins will go to hell."

"But they have no soul," observed St. Irenaeus.

"It is a pity," sighed Tertullian.

"It is indeed," resumed St. Gal. "And I admit that my disciple, the holy Maël, has, in his blind zeal, created great theological difficulties for the Holy Spirit and introduced disorder into the economy of mysteries."

"He is an old blunderer," cried St. Adjutor of Alsace, shrugging his shoulders.

But the Lord cast a reproachful look on Adjutor.

"Allow me to speak," said he; "the holy Maël has not intuitive knowledge like you, my blessed ones. He does not see me. He is an old man burdened by infirmities; he is half deaf and three parts blind. You are too severe on him. However, I recognise that the situation is an embarrassing one."

"Luckily it is but a passing disorder," said St. Irenaeus. "The penguins are baptized, but their eggs are not, and the evil will stop with the present generation."

"Do not speak thus, Irenaeus my son," said the Lord. "There are exceptions to the laws that men of science lay down on the earth because they are imperfect and have not an exact application to nature. But the laws that I establish are perfect and suffer no exception. We must decide the fate of the baptized penguins without violating any divine law, and in a manner comformable to the decalogue as well as to the commandments of my Church."

"Lord," said St. Gregory Nazianzen, "give them an im-mortal soul."

"Alas! Lord, what would they do with it," sighed Lactantius. "They have not tuneful voices to sing your praises. They would not be able to celebrate your mysteries."

"Without doubt," said St. Augustine, "they would not observe the divine law."

"They could not," said the Lord.

"They could not," continued St. Augustine. "And if, Lord, in your wisdom, you pour an immortal soul into them, they will burn eternally in hell in virtue of your adorable decrees. Thus will the transcendent order, that this old Welshman has disturbed, be re-established."

"You propose a correct solution to me, son of Monica," said the Lord, "and one that accords with my wisdom. But it does not satisfy my mercy. And, although in my essence I am im-mutable, the longer I endure, the more I incline to mildness. This change of character is evident to anyone who reads my two Testaments."

As the discussion continued without much light being thrown upon the matter and as the blessed showed a disposition to keep repeating the same thing, it was decided to consult St. Catherine of Alexandria. This is what was usually done in such cases. St. Catherine while on earth had confounded fifty very learned doctors. She knew Plato's philosophy in addition to the Holy Scriptures, and she also possessed a knowledge of rhetoric.

VII

AN ASSEMBLY IN PARADISE

(*Continuation and End*)

St. Catherine entered the assembly, her head encircled by a crown of emeralds, sapphires, and pearls, and she was clad in a robe of cloth of gold. She carried at her side a blazing wheel, the image of the one whose fragments had struck her persecutors.

The Lord having invited her to speak, she expressed herself in these terms:

"Lord, in order to solve the problem you deign to submit to me I shall not study the habits of animals in general nor those of birds in particular. I shall only remark to the doctors, confessors, and pontiffs gathered in this assembly that the separation between man and animal is not complete since there are monsters who proceed from both. Such are chimeras—half nymphs and half serpents; such are the three Gorgons and the Capripeds; such are the Scyllas and the Sirens who sing in the sea. These have a woman's breast and a fish's tail. Such also are the Centaurs, men down to the waist and the remainder horses. They are a noble race of monsters. One of them, as you know, was able, guided by the light of reason alone, to direct his steps towards eternal blessedness, and you sometimes see his heroic bosom prancing on the clouds. Chiron, the Centaur, deserved for his works on the earth to share the abode of the blessed; he it was who gave Achilles his education; and that young hero, when he left the Centaur's hands, lived for two years, dressed as a young girl, among the daughters of King Lycomedes. He shared their games and their bed without allowing any suspicion to arise that he was not a young virgin like them. Chiron, who taught him such good morals, is, with the Emperor Trajan, the only righteous man who obtained celestial glory by following the law of nature. And yet he was but half human.

"I think I have proved by this example that, to reach eternal blessedness, it is enough to possess some parts of humanity, always on the condition that they are noble. And what Chiron, the Centaur, could obtain without having been regenerated by baptism, would not the penguins deserve too if they became half penguins and half men? That is why, Lord, I entreat you to give old Maël's penguins a human head and breast so that they can praise you worthily. And grant them also an immortal soul—but one of small size."

Thus Catherine spoke, and the fathers, doctors, confessors, and pontiffs heard her with a murmur of approbation.

But St. Anthony, the Hermit, arose and stretching two red and knotty arms towards the Most High:

"Do not so, O Lord God," he cried, "in the name of your holy Paraclete, do not so!"

He spoke with such vehemence that his long white beard shook on his chin like the empty nose-bag of a hungry horse.

"Lord, do not so. Birds with human heads exist already. St. Catherine has told us nothing new."

"The imagination groups and compares; it never creates," replies St. Catherine drily.

"They exist already," continued St. Anthony, who would listen to nothing. "They are called harpies, and they are the most obscene animals in creation. One day as I was having supper in the desert with the Abbot St. Paul, I placed the table outside my cabin under an old sycamore tree. The harpies came and sat in its branches; they deafened us with their shrill cries and cast their excrement over all our food. The clamour of the monsters prevented me from listening to the teaching of the Abbot St. Paul, and we ate birds' dung with our bread and lettuces. Lord, it is impossible to believe that harpies could give thee worthy praise.

"Truly in my temptations I have seen many hybrid beings, not only women-serpents and women-fishes, but beings still more confusedly formed such as men whose bodies were made out of a pot, a bell, a clock, a cupboard full of food and crockery, or even out of a house with doors and windows through which people engaged in their domestic tasks could be seen. Eternity would not suffice were I to describe all the monsters that assailed me in my solitude, from whales rigged like ships to a shower of red insects which changed the water of my fountain into blood. But none were as disgusting as the harpies whose offal polluted the leaves of my sycamore."

"Harpies," observed Lactantius, "are female monsters with birds' bodies. They have a woman's head and breast. Their forwardness, their shamelessness, and their obscenity proceed from their female nature as the poet Virgil demonstrated in his 'Æneid.' They share the curse of Eve."

"Let us not speak of the curse of Eve," said the Lord. "The second Eve has redeemed the first."

Paul Orosius, the author of a universal history that Bossuet was to imitate in later years, arose and prayed to the Lord:

"Lord, hear my prayer and Anthony's. Do not make any more monsters like the Centaurs, Sirens, and Fauns, whom the Greeks, those collectors of fables, loved. You will derive no satisfaction from them. Those species of monsters have pagan inclinations and their double nature does not dispose them to purity of morals."

The bland Lactantius replied in these terms:

"He who has just spoken is assuredly the best historian in Paradise, for Herodotus, Thucydides, Polybius, Livy, Velleius Paterculus, Cornelius Nepos, Suetonius, Manetho, Diodorus Siculus, Dion Cassius, and Lampridius are deprived of the sight of God, and Tacitus suffers in hell the torments that are reserved for blasphemers. But Paul Orosius does not know heaven as well as he knows the earth, for he does not seem to bear in mind that the angels, who proceed from man and bird, are purity itself."

"We are wandering," said the Eternal. "What have we to do with all those centaurs, harpies, and angels? We have to deal with penguins."

"You have spoken to the point, Lord," said the chief of the fifty doctors, who, during their mortal life had been confounded by the Virgin of Alexandria, "and I dare express the opinion that, in order to put an end to the scandal by which heaven is now stirred, old Maël's penguins should, as St. Catherine who confounded us has proposed, be given half of a human body with an eternal soul proportioned to that half."

At this speech there arose in the assembly a great noise of private conversations and disputes of the doctors. The Greek fathers argued with the Latins concerning the substance, nature, and dimensions of the soul that should be given to the penguins.

"Confessors and pontiffs," exclaimed the Lord, "do not imitate the conclaves and synods of the earth. And do not bring into the Church Triumphant those violences that trouble the Church Militant. For it is but too true that in all the councils held under the inspiration of my spirit, in Europe, in Asia, and in Africa, fathers have torn the beards and scratched the eyes of other fathers. Nevertheless they were infallible, for I was with them."

Order being restored, old Hermas arose and slowly uttered these words:

"I will praise you, Lord, for that you caused my mother, Saphira, to be born amidst your people, in the days when the dew of heaven refreshed the earth which was in travail with its Saviour. And I will praise you, Lord, for having granted to me to see with my mortal eyes the Apostles of your divine Son. And I will speak in this illustrious assembly because you have willed that truth should proceed out of the mouths of the humble, and I will say: 'Change these penguins

to men. It is the only determination conformable to your justice and your mercy.' "

Several doctors asked permission to speak, others began to
do so. No one listened, and all the confessors were tumultuously shaking their palms and their crowns.

The Lord, by a gesture of his right hand, appeased the
quarrels of his elect.

"Let us not deliberate any longer," said he. "The opinion
broached by gentle old Hermas is the only one conformable
to my eternal designs. These birds will be changed into men.
I foresee in this several disadvantages. Many of those men
will commit sins they would not have committed as penguins.
Truly their fate through this change will be far less enviable
than if they had been without this baptism and this incorpora-
tion into the family of Abraham. But my foreknowledge must
not encroach upon their free will.

"In order not to impair human liberty, I will be ignorant of
what I know, I will thicken upon my eyes the veils I have
pierced, and in my blind clear-sightedness I will let myself be
surprised by what I have foreseen."

And immediately calling the archangel Raphael:

"Go and find the holy Maël," said he to him; "inform him
of his mistake and tell him, armed with my Name, to change
these penguins into men."

VIII

METAMORPHOSIS OF THE PENGUINS

THE archangel, having gone down into the Island of the Penguins, found the holy man asleep in the hollow of a rock surrounded by his new disciples. He laid his hand on his shoulder and, having waked him, said in a gentle voice:

"Maël, fear not!"

The holy man, dazzled by a vivid light, inebriated by a delicious odour, recognised the angel of the Lord, and prostrated himself with his forehead on the ground.

The angel continued:

"Maël, know thy error, believing that thou wert baptizing children of Adam thou hast baptized birds; and it is through thee that penguins have entered into the Church of God."

At these words the old man remained stupefied.

And the angel resumed:

"Arise, Maël, arm thyself with the mighty Name of the Lord, and say to these birds, 'Be ye men!'"

And the holy Maël, having wept and prayed, armed himself with the mighty Name of the Lord and said to the birds:

"Be ye men!"

Immediately the penguins were transformed. Their foreheads enlarged and their heads grew round like the dome of St. Maria Rotunda in Rome. Their oval eyes opened more widely on the universe; a fleshy nose clothed the two clefts of their nostrils; their beaks were changed into mouths, and from their mouths went forth speech; their necks grew short and thick; their wings became arms and their claws legs; a restless soul dwelt within the breast of each of them.

However, there remained with them some traces of their

first nature. They were inclined to look sideways; they balanced themselves on their short thighs; their bodies were covered with fine down.

And Maël gave thanks to the Lord, because he had incorporated these penguins into the family of Abraham.

But he grieved at the thought that he would soon leave the island to come back no more, and that perhaps when he was far away the faith of the penguins would perish for want of care like a young and tender plant.

And he formed the idea of transporting their island to the coasts of Armorica.

"I know not the designs of eternal Wisdom," said he to himself. "But if God wills that this island be transported, who could prevent it?"

And the holy man made a very fine cord about forty feet long out of the flax of his stole. He fastened one end of the cord round a point of rock that jutted up through the sand of the shore and, holding the other end of the cord in his hand, he entered the stone trough.

The trough glided over the sea and towed Penguin Island behind it; after nine days' sailing it approached the Breton coast, bringing the island with it.

BOOK II

THE ANCIENT TIMES

I

THE FIRST CLOTHES

ONE day St. Maël was sitting by the seashore on a warm stone that he found. He thought it had been warmed by the sun and he gave thanks to God for it, not knowing that the Devil had been resting on it. The apostle was waiting for the monks of Yvern who had been commissioned to bring a freight of skins and fabrics to clothe the inhabitants of the island of Alca.

Soon he saw a monk called Magis coming ashore and carrying a chest upon his back. This monk enjoyed a great reputation for holiness.

When he had drawn near to the old man he laid the chest on the ground and wiping his forehead with the back of his sleeve, he said:

"Well, father, you wish then to clothe these penguins?"

"Nothing is more needful, my son," said the old man. "Since they have been incorporated into the family of Abraham these penguins share the curse of Eve, and they know that they are naked, a thing of which they were ignorant before. And it is high time to clothe them, for they are losing the down that remained on them after their metamorphosis."

"It is true," said Magis as he cast his eyes over the coast where the penguins were to be seen looking for shrimps, gathering mussels, singing, or sleeping, "they are naked. But do you not think, father, that it would be better to leave them naked? Why clothe them? When they wear clothes and are under the moral law they will assume an immense pride, a vile hypocrisy, and an excessive cruelty."

"Is it possible, my son," sighed the old man, "that you un-

derstand so badly the effects of the moral law to which even
the heathen submit?"

"The moral law," answered Magis, "forces men who are
beasts to live otherwise than beasts, a thing that doubtless
puts a constraint upon them, but that also flatters and re-
assures them; and as they are proud, cowardly, and covetous
of pleasure, they willingly submit to restraints that tickle their
vanity and on which they found both their present security
and the hope of their future happiness. That is the principle
of all morality.... But let us not mislead ourselves. My companions are unloading their cargo of stuffs and skins on the
island. Think, father, while there is still time! To clothe the
penguins is a very serious business. At present when a penguin desires a penguin he knows precisely what he desires and
his lust is limited by an exact knowledge of its object. At this
moment two or three couples of penguins are making love
on the beach. See with what simplicity! No one pays any attention and the actors themselves do not seem to be greatly
preoccupied. But when the female penguins are clothed, the
male penguin will not form so exact a notion of what it is
that attracts him to them. His indeterminate desires will fly
out into all sorts of dreams and illusions; in short, father,
he will know love and its mad torments. And all the time the
female penguins will cast down their eyes and bite their lips,
and take on airs as if they kept a treasure under their clothes!
... what a pity!

"The evil will be endurable as long as these people remain
rude and poor; but only wait for a thousand years and you
will see, father, with what powerful weapons you have endowed the daughters of Alca. If you will allow me, I can give
you some idea of it beforehand. I have some old clothes in
this chest. Let us take at hazard one of these female penguins
to whom the male penguins give such little thought, and let
us dress her as well as we can.

"Here is one coming towards us. She is neither more beautiful nor uglier than the others; she is young. No one looks

at her. She strolls indolently along the shore, scratching her
back and with her finger at her nose as she walks. You cannot
help seeing, father, that she has narrow shoulders, clumsy
breasts, a stout figure, and short legs. Her reddish knees
pucker at every step she takes, and there is, at each of her
joints, what looks like a little monkey's head. Her broad and
sinewy feet cling to the rock with their four crooked toes,
while the great toes stick up like the heads of two cunning
serpents. She begins to walk, all her muscles are engaged in
the task, and, when we see them working, we think of her
as a machine intended for walking rather than as a machine intended for making love, although visibly she is
both, and contains within herself several other pieces of
machinery besides. Well, venerable apostle, you will see what
I am going to make of her."

With these words the monk, Magis, reached the female
penguin in three bounds, lifted her up, carried her in his arms
with her hair trailing behind her, and threw her, overcome
with fright, at the feet of the holy Maël.

And whilst she wept and begged him to do her no harm,
he took a pair of sandals out of his chest and commanded her
to put them on.

"Her feet," observed the old man, "will appear smaller when
squeezed in by the woollen cords. The soles, being two fingers
high, will give an elegant length to her legs and the weight
they bear will seem magnified."

As the penguin tied on her sandals she threw a curious
look towards the open coffer, and seeing that it was full of
jewels and finery, she smiled through her tears.

The monk twisted her hair on the back of her head and
covered it with a chaplet of flowers. He encircled her wrist
with golden bracelets and making her stand upright, he passed
a large linen band beneath her breasts, alleging that her
bosom would thereby derive a new dignity and that her sides
would be compressed to the greater glory of her hips.

He fixed this band with pins, taking them one by one out of his mouth.

"You can tighten it still more," said the penguin.

When he had, with much care and study, enclosed the soft parts of her bust in this way, he covered her whole body with a rose-coloured tunic which gently followed the lines of her figure.

"Does it hang well?" asked the penguin.

And bending forward with her head on one side and her chin on her shoulder, she kept looking attentively at the appearance of her toilet.

Magis asked her if she did not think the dress a little long, but she answered with assurance that it was not—she would hold it up.

Immediately, taking the back of her skirt in her left hand, she drew it obliquely across her hips, taking care to disclose a glimpse of her heels. Then she went away, walking with short steps and swinging her hips.

She did not turn her head, but as she passed near a stream she glanced out of the corner of her eye at her own reflection.

A male penguin, who met her by chance, stopped in surprise, and retracing his steps began to follow her. As she went along the shore, others coming back from fishing went up to her, and after looking at her, walked behind her. Those who were lying on the sand got up and joined the rest.

Unceasingly, as she advanced, fresh penguins, descending from the paths of the mountain, coming out of clefts of the rocks, and emerging from the water, added to the size of her retinue.

And all of them, men of ripe age with vigorous shoulders and hairy breasts, agile youths, old men shaking the multitudinous wrinkles of their rosy and white-haired skins, or dragging their legs thinner and drier than the juniper staff that served them as a third leg, hurried on, panting and emitting an acrid odour and hoarse gasps. Yet she went on peacefully and seemed to see nothing.

"Father," cried Magis, "notice how each one advances with his nose pointed towards the centre of gravity of that young damsel now that the centre is covered by a garment. The sphere inspires the meditations of geometers by the number of its properties. When it proceeds from a physical and living nature it acquires new qualities, and in order that the interest of that figure might be fully revealed to the penguins it was necessary that, ceasing to see it distinctly with their eyes, they should be led to represent it to themselves in their minds. I myself feel at this moment irresistibly attracted towards that penguin. Whether it be because her skirt gives more importance to her hips, and that in its simple magnificence it invests them with a synthetic and general character and allows only the pure idea, the divine principle, of them to be seen, whether this be the cause I cannot say, but I feel that if I embraced her I would hold in my hands the heaven of human pleasure. It is certain that modesty communicates an invincible attraction to women. My uneasiness is so great that it would be vain for me to try to conceal it."

He spoke, and, gathering up his habit, he rushed among the crowd of penguins, pushing, jostling, trampling, and crushing, until he reached the daughter of Alca, whom he seized and suddenly carried in his arms into a cave that had been hollowed out by the sea.

Then the penguins felt as if the sun had gone out. And the holy Maël knew that the Devil had taken the features of the monk, Magis, in order that he might give clothes to the daughter of Alca. He was troubled in spirit, and his soul was sad. As with slow steps he went towards his hermitage he saw the little penguins of six and seven years of age tightening their waists with belts made of sea-weed and walking along the shore to see if anybody would follow them.

II

THE FIRST CLOTHES

(*Continuation and End*)

THE holy Maël felt a profound sadness that the first clothes put upon a daughter of Alca should have betrayed the penguin modesty instead of helping it. He persisted, none the less, in his design of giving clothes to the inhabitants of the miraculous island. Assembling them on the shore, he distributed to them the garments that the monks of Yvern had brought. The male penguins received short tunics and breeches, the female penguins long robes. But these robes were far from creating the effect that the former one had produced. They were not so beautiful, their shape was uncouth and without art, and no attention was paid to them since every woman had one. As they prepared the meals and worked in the fields they soon had nothing but slovenly bodices and soiled petticoats.

The male penguins loaded their unfortunate consorts with work until they looked like beasts of burden. They knew nothing of the troubles of the heart and the disorders of passion. Their habits were innocent. Incest, though frequent, was a sign of rustic simplicity and if drunkenness led a youth to commit some such crime he thought nothing more about it the day afterwards.

III

SETTING BOUNDS TO THE FIELDS AND
THE ORIGIN OF PROPERTY

THE island did not preserve the rugged appearance that it
had formerly, when in the midst of floating icebergs it sheltered a population of birds within its rock amphitheatre. Its
snow-clad peak had sunk down into a hill from the summit of
which one could see the coasts of Armorica eternally covered
with mist, and the ocean strewn with sullen reefs like monsters
half raised out of its depths.

Its coasts were now very extensive and clearly defined and
its shape reminded one of a mulberry leaf. It was suddenly
covered with coarse grass, pleasing to the flocks, and with
willows, ancient fig-trees, and mighty oaks. This fact is at-
tested by the Venerable Bede and several other authors
worthy of credence.

To the north the shore formed a deep bay that in after years
became one of the most famous ports in the universe. To the
east, along a rocky coast beaten by a foaming sea, there
stretched a deserted and fragrant heath. It was the Beach of
Shadows, and the inhabitants of the island never ventured on
it for fear of the serpents that lodged in the hollows of the
rocks and lest they might encounter the souls of the dead who
resembled livid flames. To the south, orchards and woods
bounded the languid Bay of Divers. On this fortunate shore
old Maël built a wooden church and a monastery. To the
west, two streams, the Clange and the Surelle, watered the
fertile valleys of Dalles and Dombes.

Now one autumn morning, as the blessed Maël was walking
in the valley of Clange in company with a monk of Yvern

called Bulloch, he saw bands of fierce-looking men loaded with stones passing along the roads. At the same time he heard in all directions cries and complaints mounting up from the valley towards the tranquil sky.

And he said to Bulloch:

"I notice with sadness, my son, that since they became men the inhabitants of this island act with less wisdom than formerly. When they were birds they only quarrelled during the season of their love affairs. But now they dispute all the time; they pick quarrels with each other in summer as well as in winter. How greatly have they fallen from that peaceful majesty which made the assembly of the penguins look like the Senate of a wise republic!

"Look towards Surelle, Bulloch, my son. In yonder pleasant valley a dozen men penguins are busy knocking each other down with the spades and picks that they might employ better in tilling the ground. The women, still more cruel than the men, are tearing their opponents' faces with their nails. Alas! Bulloch, my son, why are they murdering each other in this way?"

"From a spirit of fellowship, father, and through forethought for the future," answered Bulloch. "For man is essentially provident and sociable. Such is his character and it is impossible to imagine it apart from a certain appropriation of things. Those penguins whom you see are dividing the ground among themselves."

"Could they not divide it with less violence?" asked the aged man. "As they fight they exchange invectives and threats. I do not distinguish their words, but they are angry ones, judging from the tone."

"They are accusing one another of theft and encroachment," answered Bulloch. "That is the general sense of their speech."

At that moment the holy Maël clasped his hands and sighed deeply.

"Do you see, my son," he exclaimed, "that madman who

with his teeth is biting the nose of the adversary he has overthrown and that other one who is pounding a woman's head
with a huge stone?"

"I see them," said Bulloch. "They are creating law; they
are founding property; they are establishing the principles of
civilization, the basis of society, and the foundations of the
State."

"How is that?" asked old Maël.

"By setting bounds to their fields. That is the origin of all
government. Your penguins, O Master, are performing the
most august of functions. Throughout the ages their work
will be consecrated by lawyers, and magistrates will confirm
it."

Whilst the monk, Bulloch, was pronouncing these words a
big penguin with a fair skin and red hair went down into the
valley carrying a trunk of a tree upon his shoulder. He went
up to a little penguin who was watering his vegetables in the
heat of the sun, and shouted to him:

"Your field is mine!"

And having delivered himself of this stout utterance he
brought down his club on the head of the little penguin, who
fell dead upon the field that his own hands had tilled.

At this sight the holy Maël shuddered through his whole
body and poured forth a flood of tears.

And in a voice stifled by horror and fear he addressed this
prayer to heaven:

"O Lord, my God, O thou who didst receive young Abel's
sacrifices, thou who didst curse Cain, avenge, O Lord, this
innocent penguin sacrificed upon his own field and make the
murderer feel the weight of thy arm. Is there a more odious
crime, is there a graver offence against thy justice, O Lord,
than this murder and this robbery?"

"Take care, father," said Bulloch gently, "that what you
call murder and robbery may not really be war and conquest,
those sacred foundations of empires, those sources of all
human virtues and all human greatness. Reflect, above all,

that in blaming the big penguin you are attacking property
in its origin and in its source. I shall have no trouble in showing you how. To till the land is one thing, to possess it is another, and these two things must not be confused; as regards
ownership the right of the first occupier is uncertain and
badly founded. The right of conquest, on the other hand, rests
on more solid foundations. It is the only right that receives
respect since it is the only one that makes itself respected.
The sole and proud origin of property is force. It is born and
preserved by force. In that it is august and yields only to a
greater force. That is why it is correct to say that he who
possesses is noble. And that big red man, when he knocked
down a labourer to get possession of his field, founded at that
moment a very noble house upon this earth. I congratulate
him upon it."

Having thus spoken, Bulloch approached the big penguin,
who was leaning upon his club as he stood in the blood-stained
furrow:

"Lord Greatauk, dreaded Prince," said he, bowing to the
ground, "I come to pay you the homage due to the founder
of legitimate power and hereditary wealth. The skull of the
vile Penguin you have overthrown will, buried in your field,
attest for ever the sacred rights of your posterity over this
soil that you have ennobled. Blessed be your sons and your
sons' sons! They shall be Greatauks, Dukes of Skull, and they
shall rule over this island of Alca."

Then raising his voice and turning towards the holy Maël:

"Bless Greatauk, father, for all power comes from God."

Maël remained silent and motionless, with his eyes raised
towards heaven; he felt a painful uncertainty in judging the
monk Bulloch's doctrine. It was, however, the doctrine destined to prevail in epochs of advanced civilization. Bulloch
can be considered as the creator of civil law in Penguinia.

IV

THE FIRST ASSEMBLY OF THE ESTATES
OF PENGUINIA

"BULLOCH, my son," said old Maël, "we ought to make a census of the Penguins and inscribe each of their names in a book."

"It is a most urgent matter," answered Bulloch, "there can be no good government without it."

Forthwith, the apostle, with the help of twelve monks, proceeded to make a census of the people.

And old Maël then said:

"Now that we keep a register of all the inhabitants, we ought, Bulloch, my son, to levy a just tax so as to provide for public expenses and the maintenance of the Abbey. Each ought to contribute according to his means. For this reason, my son, call together the Elders of Alca, and in agreement with them we shall establish the tax."

The Elders, being called together, assembled to the number of thirty under the great sycamore in the courtyard of the wooden monastery. They were the first Estates of Penguinia. Three-fourths of them were substantial peasants of Surelle and Clange. Greatauk, as the noblest of the Penguins, sat upon the highest stone.

The venerable Maël took his place in the midst of his monks and uttered these words:

"Children, the Lord when he pleases grants riches to men and he takes them away from them. Now I have called you together to levy contributions from the people so as to provide for public expenses and the maintenance of the monks. I consider that these contributions ought to be in proportion to the wealth of each. Therefore he who has a hundred oxen will give ten; he who has ten will give one."

When the holy man had spoken, Morio, a labourer at Anis-on-the-Clange, one of the richest of the Penguins, rose up and said:

"O Father Maël, I think it right that each should contribute to the public expenses and to the support of the Church. For my part I am ready to give up all that I possess in the interest of my brother Penguins, and if it were necessary I would even cheerfully part with my shirt. All the elders of the people are ready, like me, to sacrifice their goods, and no one can doubt their absolute devotion to their country and their creed. We have, then, only to consider the public interest and to do what it requires. Now, father, what it requires, what it demands, is not to ask much from those who possess much, for then the rich would be less rich and the poor still poorer. The poor live on the wealth of the rich and that is the reason why that wealth is sacred. Do not touch it, to do so would be an uncalled for evil. You will get no great profit by taking from the rich, for they are very few in number; on the contrary you will strip yourself of all your resources and plunge the country into misery. Whereas if you ask a little from each inhabitant without regard to his wealth, you will collect enough for the public necessities and you will have no need to enquire into each citizen's resources, a thing that would be regarded by all as a most vexatious measure. By taxing all equally and easily you will spare the poor, for you will leave them the wealth of the rich. And how could you possibly proportion taxes to wealth? Yesterday I had two hundred oxen, to-day I have sixty, to-morrow I shall have a hundred. Clunic has three cows, but they are thin; Nicclu has only two, but they are fat. Which is the richer, Clunic or Nicclu? The signs of opulence are deceitful. What is certain is that everyone eats and drinks. Tax people according to what they consume. That would be wisdom and it would be justice."

Thus spoke Morio amid the applause of the Elders.

"I ask that this speech be graven on bronze," cried the monk, Bulloch. "It is spoken for the future; in fifteen hundred years the best of the Penguins will not speak otherwise."

The Elders were still applauding when Greatauk, his hand on the pommel of his sword, made this brief declaration:

"Being noble, I shall not contribute; for to contribute is ignoble. It is for the rabble to pay."

After this warning the Elders separated in silence.

As in Rome, a new census was taken every five years; and by this means it was observed that the population increased rapidly. Although children died in marvellous abundance and plagues and famines came with perfect regularity to devastate entire villages, new Penguins, in continually greater numbers, contributed by their private misery to the public prosperity.

V

THE MARRIAGE OF KRAKEN AND ORBEROSIA

DURING these times there lived in the island of Alca a Penguin whose arm was strong and whose mind was subtle. He was called Kraken, and had his dwelling on the Beach of Shadows whither the inhabitants never ventured for fear of serpents that lodged in the hollows of the rocks and lest they might encounter the souls of Penguins that had died without baptism. These, in appearance like livid flames, and uttering doleful groans, wandered night and day along the deserted beach. For it was generally believed, though without proof, that among the Penguins that had been changed into men at the blessed Maël's prayer, several had not received baptism and returned after their death to lament amid the tempests. Kraken dwelt on this savage coast in an inaccessible cavern. The only way to it was through a natural tunnel a hundred feet long, the entrance of which was concealed by a thick wood. One evening as Kraken was walking through this deserted plain he happened to meet a young and charming woman Penguin. She was the one that the monk Magis had clothed with his own hands and thus was the first to have worn the garments of chastity. In remembrance of the day when the astonished crowd of Penguins had seen her moving gloriously in her robe tinted like the dawn, this maiden had received the name of Orberosia.*

At the sight of Kraken she uttered a cry of alarm and darted forward to escape from him. But the hero seized her by

* "Orb, poetically, a globe when speaking of the heavenly bodies By extension any species of globular body."—*Littré*.

the garments that floated behind her, and addressed her in these words:

"Damsel, tell me thy name, thy family and thy country."

But Orberosia kept looking at Kraken with alarm.

"Is it you, I see, sir," she asked him, trembling, "or is it not rather your troubled spirit?"

She spoke in this way because the inhabitants of Alca, having no news of Kraken since he went to live on the Beach of Shadows, believed that he had died and descended among the demons of night.

"Cease to fear, daughter of Alca," answered Kraken. "He who speaks to thee is not a wandering spirit, but a man full of strength and might. I shall soon possess great riches."

And young Orberosia asked:

"How dost thou think of acquiring great riches, O Kraken, since thou art a child of the Penguins?"

"By my intelligence," answered Kraken.

"I know," said Orberosia, "that in the time that thou dwelt among us thou wert renowned for thy skill in hunting and fishing. No one equalled thee in taking fishes in a net or in piercing with thy arrows the swift-flying birds."

"It was but a vulgar and laborious industry, O maiden. I have found a means of gaining much wealth for myself without fatigue. But tell me who thou art?"

"I am called Orberosia," answered the young girl.

"Why art thou so far away from thy dwelling and in the night?"

"Kraken, it was not without the will of Heaven."

"What meanest thou, Orberosia?"

"That Heaven, O Kraken, placed me in thy path, for what reason I know not."

Kraken beheld her for a long time in silence.

Then he said with gentleness:

"Orberosia, come into my house; it is that of the bravest and most ingenious of the sons of the Penguins. If thou art willing to follow me, I will make thee my companion."

Then casting down her eyes, she murmured:

"I will follow thee, master."

It is thus that the fair Orberosia became the consort of the hero Kraken. This marriage was not celebrated with songs and torches because Kraken did not consent to show himself to the people of the Penguins; but hidden in his cave he planned great designs.

VI

THE DRAGON OF ALCA

> "We afterwards went to visit the cabinet
> of natural history. . . . The caretaker showed
> us a sort of packet bound in straw that he
> told us contained the skeleton of a dragon;
> a proof, added he, that the dragon is not a
> fabulous animal."—*Memoirs of Jacques
> Casanova*, Paris, 1843. Vol. IV., pp. 404, 405.

IN the meantime the inhabitants of Alca practised the
labours of peace. Those of the northern coast went in boats to
fish or to search for shell-fish. The labourers of Dombes cultivated oats, rye, and wheat. The rich Penguins of the valley of
Dalles reared domestic animals, while those of the Bay of
Divers cultivated their orchards. Merchants of Port-Alca carried on a trade in salt fish with Armorica and the gold of the
two Britains, which began to be introduced into the island,
facilitated exchange. The Penguin people were enjoying the
fruit of their labours in perfect tranquillity when suddenly a
sinister rumour ran from village to village. It was said everywhere that a frightful dragon had ravaged two farms in the
Bay of Divers.

A few days before, the maiden Orberosia had disappeared.
Her absence had at first caused no uneasiness because on
several occasions she had been carried off by violent men who
were consumed with love. And thoughtful people were not
astonished at this, reflecting that the maiden was the most
beautiful of the Penguins. It was even remarked that she sometimes went to meet her ravishers, for none of us can escape his
destiny. But this time, as she did not return, it was feared that
the dragon had devoured her. The more so as the inhabitants

of the valley of Dalles soon knew that the dragon was not a fable told by the women around the fountains. For one night the monster devoured out of the village of Anis six hens, a sheep, and a young orphan child called little Elo. The next morning nothing was to be found either of the animals or of the child.

Immediately the Elders of the village assembled in the public place and seated themselves on the stone bench to take counsel concerning what it was expedient to do in these terrible circumstances.

Having called all those Penguins who had seen the dragon during the disastrous night, they asked them:

"Have you not noticed his form and his behaviour?"

And each answered in his turn:

"He has the claws of a lion, the wings of an eagle, and the tail of a serpent."

"His back bristles with thorny crests."

"His whole body is covered with yellow scales."

"His look fascinates and confounds. He vomits flames."

"He poisons the air with his breath."

"He has the head of a dragon, the claws of a lion, and the tail of a fish."

And a woman of Anis, who was regarded as intelligent and of sound judgment and from whom the dragon had taken three hens, deposed as follows:

"He is formed like a man. The proof is that I thought he was my husband, and I said to him, 'Come to bed, you old fool.'"

Others said:

"He is formed like a cloud."

"He looks like a mountain."

And a little child came and said:

"I saw the dragon taking off his head in the barn so that he might give a kiss to my sister Minnie."

And the Elders also asked the inhabitants:

"How big is the dragon?"

And it was answered:

"As big as an ox."

"Like the big merchant ships of the Bretons."

"He is the height of a man."

"He is higher than the fig-tree under which you are sitting."

"He is as large as a dog."

Questioned finally on his colour, the inhabitants said:

"Red."

"Green."

"Blue."

"Yellow."

"His head is bright green, his wings are brilliant orange tinged with pink, his limbs are silvery grey, his hind-quarters and his tail are striped with brown and pink bands, his belly bright yellow spotted with black."

"His colour? He has no colour."

"He is the colour of a dragon."

After hearing this evidence the Elders remained uncertain as to what should be done. Some advised to watch for him, to surprise him and overthrow him by a multitude of arrows. Others, thinking it vain to oppose so powerful a monster by force, counselled that he should be appeased by offerings.

"Pay him tribute," said one of them who passed for a wise man. "We can render him propitious to us by giving him agreeable presents, fruits, wine, lambs, a young virgin."

Others held for poisoning the fountains where he was accustomed to drink or for smoking him out of his cavern.

But none of these counsels prevailed. The dispute was lengthy and the Elders dispersed without coming to any resolution.

VII

THE DRAGON OF ALCA

(*Continuation*)

DURING all the month dedicated by the Romans to their false god Mars or Mavors, the dragon ravaged the farms of Dalles and Dombes. He carried off fifty sheep, twelve pigs, and three young boys. Every family was in mourning and the island was full of lamentations. In order to remove the scourge, the Elders of the unfortunate villages watered by the Clange and the Surelle resolved to assemble and together go and ask the help of the blessed Maël.

On the fifth day of the month whose name among the Latins signifies opening, because it opens the year, they went in procession to the wooden monastery that had been built on the southern coast of the island. When they were introduced into the cloister they filled it with their sobs and groans. Moved by their lamentations, old Maël left the room in which he devoted himself to the study of astronomy and the meditation of the Scriptures, and went down to them, leaning on his pastoral staff. At his approach, the Elders, prostrating themselves, held out to him green branches of trees and some of them burnt aromatic herbs.

And the holy man, seating himself beside the cloistral fountain under an ancient fig-tree, uttered these words:

"O my sons, offspring of the Penguins, why do you weep and groan? Why do you hold out those suppliant boughs towards me? Why do you raise towards heaven the smoke of those herbs? What calamity do you expect that I can avert from your heads? Why do you beseech me? I am ready to give my life for you. Only tell your father what it is you hope from him.

To these questions the chief of the Elders answered:

"O Maël, father of the sons of Alca, I will speak for all. A horrible dragon is laying waste our lands, depopulating our cattle-sheds, and carrying off the flower of our youth. He has devoured the child Elo and seven young boys; he has mangled the maiden Orberosia, the fairest of the Penguins, with his teeth. There is not a village in which he does not emit his poisoned breath and which he has not filled with desolation. A prey to this terrible scourge, we come, O Maël, to pray thee, as the wisest, to advise us concerning the safety of the inhabitants of this island lest the ancient race of Penguins be extinguished."

"O chief of the Elders of Alca," replied Maël, "thy words fill me with profound grief, and I groan at the thought that this island is the prey of a terrible dragon. But such an occurrence is not unique, for we find in books several tales of very fierce dragons. The monsters are oftenest found in caverns, by the brinks of waters, and, in preference, among pagan peoples. Perhaps there are some among you who, although they have received holy baptism and been incorporated into the family of Abraham, have yet worshipped idols, like the ancient Romans, or hung up images, votive tablets, fillets of wool, and garlands of flowers on the branches of some sacred tree. Or perhaps some of the women Penguins have danced round a magic stone and drunk water from the fountains where the nymphs dwell. If it be so, I believe, O Penguins, that the Lord has sent this dragon to punish all for the crimes of some, and to lead you, O children of the Penguins, to exterminate blasphemy, superstition, and impiety from amongst you. For this reason I advise, as a remedy against the great evil from which you suffer, that you carefully search your dwellings for idol-

atry, and extirpate it from them. I think it would be also effica-
cious to pray and do penance."

Thus spoke the holy Maël. And the Elders of the Penguin
people kissed his feet and returned to their villages with renewed hope.

VIII

THE DRAGON OF ALCA

(*Continuation*)

FOLLOWING the counsel of the holy Maël the inhabitants of Alca endeavoured to uproot the superstitions that had sprung up amongst them. They took care to prevent the girls from dancing with incantations round the fairy tree. Young mothers were sternly forbidden to rub their children against the stones that stood upright in the fields so as to make them strong. An old man of Dombes who foretold the future by shaking grains of barley on a sieve, was thrown into a well.

However, each night the monster still raided the poultry-yards and the cattle-sheds. The frightened peasants barricaded themselves in their houses. A woman with child who saw the shadow of a dragon on the road through a window in the moon-light, was so terrified that she was brought to bed before her time.

In those days of trial, the holy Maël meditated unceasingly on the nature of dragons and the means of combating them. After six months of study and prayer he thought he had found what he sought. One evening as he was walking by the sea with a young monk called Samuel, he expressed his thought to him in these terms:

"I have studied at length the history and habits of dragons, not to satisfy a vain curiosity, but to discover examples to follow in the present circumstances. For such, Samuel, my son, is the use of history.

"It is an invariable fact that dragons are extremely vigilant. They never sleep, and for this reason we often find them employed in guarding treasures. A dragon guarded at Colchis the golden fleece that Jason conquered from him. A dragon watched over the golden apples in the garden of the Hesperides. He was killed by Hercules and transformed into a star by Juno. This fact is related in some books, and if it be true, it was done by magic, for the gods of the pagans are in reality demons. A dragon prevented barbarous and ignorant men from drinking at the fountain of Castalia. We must also remember the dragon of Andromeda, which was slain by Perseus. But let us turn from these pagan fables, in which error is always mixed with truth. We meet dragons in the histories of the glorious archangel Michael, of St. George, St. Philip, St. James the Great, St. Patrick, St. Martha, and St. Margaret. And it is in such writings, since they are worthy of full credence, that we ought to look for comfort and counsel.

"The story of the dragon of Silena affords us particularly precious examples. You must know, my son, that on the banks of a vast pool close to that town there dwelt a dragon who sometimes approached the walls and poisoned with his breath all who dwelt in the suburbs. And that they might not be devoured by the monster, the inhabitants of Silena delivered up to him one of their number every morning. The victim was chosen by lot, and after a hundred others, the lot fell upon the king's daughter.

"Now St. George, who was a military tribune, as he passed through the town of Silena, learned that the king's daughter had just been given to the fierce beast. He immediately mounted his horse, and, armed with his lance, rushed to encounter the dragon, whom he reached just as the monster was about to devour the royal virgin. And when St. George had overthrown the dragon, the king's daughter fastened her girdle round the beast's neck and he followed her like a dog led on a leash.

"That is an example for us of the power of virgins over dragons. The history of St. Martha furnishes us with a still more certain proof. Do you know the story, Samuel, my son?"

"Yes, father," answered Samuel.

And the blessed Maël went on:

"There was in a forest on the banks of the Rhone, between Arles and Avignon, a dragon half quadruped and half fish, larger than an ox, with sharp teeth like horns and huge wings at his shoulders. He sank the boats and devoured their passengers. Now St. Martha, at the entreaty of the people, approached this dragon, whom she found devouring a man. She put her girdle round his neck and led him easily into the town.

"These two examples lead me to think that we should have recourse to the power of some virgin so as to conquer the dragon who scatters terror and death through the island of Alca.

"For this reason, Samuel my son, gird up thy loins and go, I pray thee, with two of thy companions, into all the villages of this island, and proclaim everywhere that a virgin alone shall be able to deliver the island from the monster that devastates it.

"Thou shalt sing psalms and canticles and thou shalt say:

" 'O sons of the Penguins, if there be among you a pure virgin, let her arise and go, armed with the sign of the cross, to combat the dragon!' "

Thus the old man spake, and Samuel promised to obey him. The next day he girded up his loins and set out with two of his companions to proclaim to the inhabitants of Alca that a virgin alone would be able to deliver the Penguins from the rage of the dragon.

IX

THE DRAGON OF ALCA

(*Continuation*)

ORBEROSIA loved her husband, but she did not love him alone. At the hour when Venus lightens in the pale sky, whilst Kraken scattered terror through the villages, she used to visit in his moving hut, a young shepherd of Dalles called Marcel, whose pleasing form was invested with inexhaustible vigour. The fair Orberosia shared the shepherd's aromatic couch with delight, but far from making herself known to him, she took the name of Bridget, and said that she was the daughter of a gardener in the Bay of Divers. When regretfully she left his arms she walked across the smoking fields towards the Coast of Shadows, and if she happened to meet some belated peasant she immediately spread out her garments like great wings and cried:

"Passer-by, lower your eyes, that you may not have to say, 'Alas! alas! woe is me, for I have seen the angel of the Lord.'"

The villagers tremblingly knelt with their faces to the ground. And several of them used to say that angels, whom it would be death to see, passed along the roads of the island in the night time.

Kraken did not know of the loves of Orberosia and Marcel, for he was a hero, and heroes never discover the secrets of their wives. But though he did not know of these loves, he reaped the benefit of them. Every night he found his companion more good-humoured and more beautiful, exhaling pleasure and perfuming the nuptial bed with a delicious odour of fennel and vervain. She loved Kraken with a love that never became importunate or anxious, because she did not rest its whole weight on him alone.

This lucky infidelity of Orberosia was destined soon to save the hero from a great peril and to assure his fortune and his glory for ever. For it happened that she saw passing in the twilight a neatherd from Belmont, who was goading on his oxen, and she fell more deeply in love with him than she had ever been with the shepherd Marcel. He was hunch-backed; his shoulders were higher than his ears; his body was supported by legs of different lengths; his rolling eyes flashed from beneath his matted hair. From his throat issued a hoarse voice and strident laughter; he smelt of the cow-shed. However, to her he was beautiful. "A plant," Gnatho says, "has been loved by one, a stream by another, a beast by a third."

Now, one day, as she was sighing within the neatherd's arms in a village barn, suddenly the blasts of a trumpet, with sounds and footsteps, fell upon her ears; she looked through the window and saw the inhabitants collected in the market-place round a young monk, who, standing upon a rock, uttered these words in a distinct voice:

"Inhabitants of Belmont. Abbot Maël, our venerable father, informs you through my mouth that neither by strength nor skill in arms shall you prevail against the dragon; but the beast shall be overcome by a virgin. If, then, there be among you a perfectly pure virgin, let her arise and go towards the monster; and when she meets him let her tie her girdle round his neck and she shall lead him as easily as if he were a little dog."

And the young monk, replacing his hood upon his head, departed to carry the proclamation of the blessed Maël to other villages.

Orberosia sat in the amorous straw, resting her head in her hand and supporting her elbow upon her knee, meditating on what she had just heard.

Although, so far as Kraken was concerned, she feared the power of a virgin much less than the strength of armed men, she did not feel reassured by the proclamation of the blessed Maël. A vague but sure instinct ruled her mind and warned her that Kraken could not henceforth be a dragon with safety.

She said to the neatherd:

"My own heart, what do you think about the dragon?"

The rustic shook his head.

"It is certain that dragons laid waste the earth in ancient times and some have been seen as large as mountains. But they come no longer, and I believe that what has been taken for a dragon is not one at all, but pirates or merchants who have carried off the fair Orberosia and the best of the children of Alca in their ships. But if one of those brigands attempts to rob me of my oxen, I will either by force or craft find a way to prevent him from doing me any harm."

This remark of the neatherd increased Orberosia's apprehensions and added to her solicitude for the husband whom she loved.

X

THE DRAGON OF ALCA

(*Continuation*)

THE days passed by and no maiden arose in the island to combat the monster. And in the wooden monastery old Maël, seated on a bench in the shade of an old fig-tree, accompanied by a pious monk called Regimental, kept asking himself anxiously and sadly how it was that there was not in Alca a single virgin fit to overthrow the monster.

He sighed and brother Regimental sighed too. At that moment old Maël called young Samuel, who happened to pass through the garden, and said to him:

"I have meditated anew, my son, on the means of destroying the dragon who devours the flower of our youth, our flocks, and our harvests. In this respect the story of the dragons of St. Riok and of St. Pol de Leon seems to me particularly instructive. The dragon of St. Riok was six fathoms long; his head was derived from the cock and the basilisk, his body from the ox and the serpent; he ravaged the banks of the Elorn in the time of King Bristocus. St. Riok, then aged two years, led him by a leash to the sea, in which the monster drowned himself of his own accord. St. Pol's dragon was sixty feet long and not less terrible. The blessed apostle of Leon bound him with his stole and allowed a young noble of great purity of life to lead him. These examples prove that in the eyes of God a chaste young man is as agreeable as a chaste girl. Heaven makes no distinction between them. For this reason, my son, if you believe what I say, we will both go to the Coast of Shadows; when we reach the dragon's cavern we will call the monster in a loud voice, and when he comes forth I will tie my stole round his neck and you will lead him to the sea, where he will not fail to drown himself."

At the old man's words Samuel cast down his head and did not answer.

"You seem to hesitate, my son," said Maël.

Brother Regimental, contrary to his custom, spoke without being addressed.

"There is at least cause for some hesitation," said he. "St. Riok was only two years old when he overcame the dragon. Who says that nine or ten years later he could have done as much? Remember, father, that the dragon who is devastating our island has devoured little Elo and four or five other young boys. Brother Samuel is not so presumptuous as to believe that at nineteen years of age he is more innocent than they were at twelve and fourteen.

"Alas!" added the monk, with a groan, "who can boast of being chaste in this world, where everything gives the example and model of love, where all things in nature, animals, and plants, show us the caresses of love and advise us to share them? Animals are eager to unite in their own fashion, but the various marriages of quadrupeds, birds, fishes, and reptiles are far from equalling in lust the nuptials of the trees. The greater extremes of lewdness that the pagans have imagined in their fables are outstripped by the simple flowers of the field, and, if you knew the irregularities of lilies and roses you would take those chalices of impurity, those vases of scandal, away from your altars."

"Do not speak in this way, Brother Regimental," answered old Maël. "Since they are subject to the law of nature, animals and plants are always innocent. They have no souls to save, whilst man—"

"You are right," replied Brother Regimental, "it is quite a different thing. But do not send young Samuel to the dragon —the dragon might devour him. For the last five years Samuel is not in a state to show his innocence to monsters. In the year of the comet, the Devil in order to seduce him, put in his path a milkmaid, who was lifting up her petticoats to cross a ford. Samuel was tempted, but he overcame the temptation. The Devil, who never tires, sent him the image of that young girl in a dream. The shade did what the reality was unable to accomplish, and Samuel yielded. When he awoke he moistened his couch with his tears, but alas! repentance did not give him back his innocence."

As he listened to this story Samuel asked himself how his secret could be known, for he was ignorant that the Devil had borrowed the appearance of Brother Regimental, so as to trouble the hearts of the monks of Alca.

And old Maël remained deep in thought and kept asking himself in grief:

"Who will deliver us from the dragon's tooth? Who will preserve us from his breath? Who will save us from his look?"

However, the inhabitants of Alca began to take courage. The labourers of Dombes and the neatherds of Belmont swore that they themselves would be of more avail than a girl against the ferocious beast, and they exclaimed as they stroked the muscles on their arms, "Let the dragon come!" Many men and women had seen him. They did not agree about his form and his figure, but all now united in saying that he was not as big as they had thought, and that his height was not much greater than a man's. The defence was organised; towards nightfall watches were stationed at the entrances of the villages ready to give the alarm; and during the night companies armed with pitchforks and scythes protected the paddocks in which the animals were shut up. Indeed, once in the village of Anis some plucky labourers surprised him as he was scaling Morio's wall, and, as they had flails, scythes, and pitchforks, they fell upon him and pressed him hard. One of them, a very quick and courageous man, thought to have run him through with his pitchfork; but he slipped in a pool and so let him escape. The others would certainly have caught him had they not waited to pick up the rabbits and fowls that he dropped in his flight.

Those labourers declared to the Elders of the village that the monster's form and proportions appeared to them human enough except for his head and his tail, which were, in truth, terrifying.

XI

THE DRAGON OF ALCA

(*Continuation*)

On that day Kraken came back to his cavern sooner than usual. He took from his head his sealskin helmet with its two bull's horns and its visor trimmed with terrible hooks. He threw on the table his gloves that ended in horrible claws—they were the beaks of sea-birds. He unhooked his belt from which hung a long green tail twisted into many folds. Then he ordered his page, Elo, to help him off with his boots and, as the child did not succeed in doing this very quickly, he gave him a kick that sent him to the other end of the grotto.

Without looking at the fair Orberosia, who was spinning, he seated himself in front of the fireplace, on which a sheep was roasting, and he muttered:

"Ignoble Penguins.... There is no worse trade than a dragon's."

"What does my master say?" asked the fair Orberosia.

"They fear me no longer," continued Kraken. "Formerly everyone fled at my approach. I carried away hens and rabbits in my bag; I drove sheep and pigs, cows, and oxen before me. To-day these clod-hoppers keep a good guard; they sit up at night. Just now I was pursued in the village of Anis by doughty labourers armed with flails and scythes and pitchforks. I had to drop the hens and rabbits, put my tail under my arm, and run as fast as I could. Now I ask you, is it seemly for a dragon of Cappadocia to run away like a robber with his tail under his arm? Further, incommoded as I was by crests horns, hooks, claws, and scales, I barely escaped a brute who ran half an inch of his pitchfork into my left thigh."

As he said this he carefully ran his hand over the insulted part, and, after giving himself up for a few moments to bitter meditation:

"What idiots those Penguins are! I am tired of blowing flames in the faces of such imbeciles. Orberosia, do you hear me?"

Having thus spoken the hero raised his terrible helmet in his hands and gazed at it for a long time in gloomy silence. Then he pronounced these rapid words:

"I have made this helmet with my own hands in the shape of a fish's head, covering it with the skin of a seal. To make it more terrible I have put on it the horns of a bull and I have given it a boar's jaws; I have hung from it a horse's tail dyed vermilion. When in the gloomy twilight I threw it over my shoulders no inhabitant of this island had courage to withstand its sight. Women and children, young men and old men fled distracted at its approach, and I carried terror among the whole race of Penguins. By what advice does that insolent people lose its earlier fears and dare to-day to behold these horrible jaws and to attack this terrible crest?"

And throwing his helmet on the rocky soil:

"Perish, deceitful helmet!" cried Kraken. "I swear by all the demons of Armor that I will never bear you upon my head again."

And having uttered this oath he stamped upon his helmet, his gloves, his boots, and upon his tail with its twisted folds.

"Kraken," said the fair Orberosia, "will you allow your servant to employ artifice to save your reputation and your goods? Do not despise a woman's help. You need it, for all men are imbeciles."

"Woman," asked Kraken, "what are your plans?"

And the fair Orberosia informed her husband that the monks were going through the villages teaching the inhabitants the best way of combating the dragon; that, according to their instructions, the beast would be overcome by a virgin, and that if a maid placed her girdle around the dragon's neck she could lead him as easily as if he were a little dog.

"How do you know that the monks teach this?" asked Kraken.

"My friend," answered Orberosia, "do not interrupt a serious subject by frivolous questions. . . . 'If, then,' added the monks, 'there be in Alca a pure virgin, let her arise!' Now, Kraken, I have determined to answer their call. I will go and find the holy Maël and I will say to him: 'I am the virgin destined by Heaven to overthrow the dragon.'"

At these words Kraken exclaimed: "How can you be that pure virgin? And why do you want to overthrow me, Orberosia? Have you lost your reason? Be sure that I will not allow myself to be conquered by you!"

"Can you not try and understand me before you get angry?" sighed the fair Orberosia with deep though gentle contempt.

And she explained the cunning designs that she had formed.

As he listened, the hero remained pensive. And when she ceased speaking:

"Orberosia, your cunning is deep," said he. "And if your plans are carried out according to your intentions I shall derive great advantages from them. But how can you be the virgin destined by heaven?"

"Don't bother about that," she replied, "and come to bed."

The next day in the grease-laden atmosphere of the cavern, Kraken plaited a deformed skeleton out of osier rods and covered it with bristling, scaly, and filthy skins. To one extremity of the skeleton Orberosia sewed the fierce crest and the hideous mask that Kraken used to wear in his plundering expeditions, and to its other end she fastened the tail with twisted folds which the hero was wont to trail behind him. And when the work was finished they showed little Elo and the other five children who waited on them how to get inside this machine, how to make it walk, how to blow horns and burn tow in it so as to send forth smoke and flames through the dragon's mouth.

XII

THE DRAGON OF ALCA

(Continuation)

ORBEROSIA, having clothed herself in a robe made of coarse
stuff and girt herself with a thick cord, went to the monastery
and asked to speak to the blessed Maël. And because women
were forbidden to enter the enclosure of the monastery the old
man advanced outside the gates, holding his pastoral cross in
his right hand and resting his left on the shoulder of Brother
Samuel, the youngest of his disciples.

He asked:

"Woman, who art thou?"

"I am the maiden Orberosia."

At this reply Maël raised his trembling arms to heaven.

"Do you speak truth, woman? It is a certain fact that
Orberosia was devoured by the dragon. And yet I see Orberosia
and hear her. Did you not, O my daughter, while within the
dragon's bowels arm yourself with the sign of the cross and
come uninjured out of his throat? That is what seems to me
the most credible explanation."

"You are not deceived, father," answered Orberosia. "That
is precisely what happened to me. Immediately I came out
of the creature's bowels I took refuge in a hermitage on the
Coast of Shadows. I lived there in solitude, giving myself up
to prayer and meditation, and performing unheard of austerities, until I learnt by a revelation from heaven that a maid
alone could overcome the dragon, and that I was that maid."

"Show me a sign of your mission," said the old man.

"I myself am the sign," answered Orberosia.

"I am not ignorant of the power of those who have placed a seal upon their flesh," replied the apostle of the Penguins. "But are you indeed such as you say?"

"You will see by the result," answered Orberosia.

The monk Regimental drew near:

"That will," said he, "be the best proof. King Solomon has said: 'Three things are hard to understand and a fourth is impossible: they are the way of a serpent on the earth, the way of a bird in the air, the way of a ship in the sea, and the way of a man with a maid.' I regard such matrons as nothing less than presumptuous who claim to compare themselves in these matters with the wisest of kings. Father, if you are led by me you will not consult them in regard to the pious Orberosia. When they have given their opinion you will not be a bit farther on than before. Virginity is not less difficult to prove than to keep. Pliny tells us in his history that its signs are either imaginary or very uncertain.* One who bears upon her the fourteen signs of corruption may yet be pure in the eyes of the angels, and, on the contrary, another who has been pronounced pure by the matrons who inspected her may know that her good appearance is due to the artifices of a cunning perversity. As for the purity of this holy girl here, I would put my hand in the fire in witness of it."

He spoke thus because he was the Devil. But old Maël did not know it. He asked the pious Orberosia:

"My daughter, how would you proceed to conquer so fierce an animal as he who devoured you?"

The virgin answered:

"To-morrow at sunrise, O Maël, you will summon the people together on the hill in front of the desolate moor that extends to the Coast of Shadows, and you will take care that no man of the Penguins remains less than five hundred paces from those rocks so that he may not be poisoned by the monster's breath. And the dragon will come out of the rocks and I will

* We have vainly sought for this phrase in Pliny's "Natural History."
—*Editor*.

put my girdle round his neck and lead him like an obedient dog."

"Ought you not to be accompanied by a courageous and pious man who will kill the dragon?" asked Maël.

"It will be as thou sayest, venerable father. I shall deliver the monster to Kraken, who will slay him with his flashing sword. For I tell thee that the noble Kraken, who was believed to be dead, will return among the Penguins and he shall slay the dragon. And from the creature's belly will come forth the little children whom he has devoured."

"What you declare to me, O virgin," cried the apostle, "seems wonderful and beyond human power."

"It is," answered the virgin Orberosia. "But learn, O Maël, that I have had a revelation that as a reward for their deliverance, the Penguin people will pay to the knight Kraken an annual tribute of three hundred fowls, twelve sheep, two oxen, three pigs, one thousand eight hundred bushels of corn, and vegetables according to their season; and that, moreover, the children who will come out of the dragon's belly will be given and committed to the said Kraken to serve him and obey him in all things. If the Penguin people fail to keep their engagements a new dragon will come upon the island more terrible than the first. I have spoken."

XIII

THE DRAGON OF ALCA

(*Continuation and End*)

THE people of the Penguins were assembled by Maël and they spent the night on the Coast of Shadows within the bounds which the holy man had prescribed in order that none among the Penguins should be poisoned by the monster's breath.

The veil of night still covered the earth when, preceded by a hoarse bellowing, the dragon showed his indistinct and monstrous form upon the rocky coast. He crawled like a serpent and his writhing body seemed about fifteen feet long. At his appearance the crowd drew back in terror. But soon all eyes were turned towards the virgin Orberosia, who, in the first light of the dawn, clothed in white, advanced over the purple heather. With an intrepid though modest gait she walked towards the beast, who, uttering awful bellowings, opened his flaming throat. An immense cry of terror and pity arose from the midst of the Penguins. But the virgin, unloosing her linen girdle, put it round the dragon's neck and led him on the leash like a faithful dog amid the acclamations of the spectators.

She had walked over a long stretch of the heath when Kraken appeared armed with a flashing sword. The people, who believed him dead, uttered cries of joy and surprise. The hero rushed towards the beast, turned him over on his back, and with his sword cut open his belly, from whence came forth in their shirts, with curling hair and folded hands, little Elo and the five other children whom the monster had devoured.

Immediately they threw themselves on their knees before the virgin Orberosia, who took them in her arms and whispered into their ears:

"You will go through the villages saying: 'We are the poor little children who were devoured by the dragon, and we came out of his belly in our shirts.' The inhabitants will give you abundance of all that you can desire. But if you say anything else you will get nothing but cuffs and whippings. Go!"

Several Penguins, seeing the dragon disembowelled, rushed forward to cut him to pieces, some from a feeling of rage and vengeance, others to get the magic stone called dragonite, that is engendered in his head. The mothers of the children who had come back to life ran to embrace their little ones. But the holy Maël kept them back, saying that none of them were holy enough to approach a dragon without dying.

And soon little Elo and the five other children came towards the people and said:

"We are the poor little children who were devoured by the dragon and we came out of his belly in our shirts."

And all who heard them kissed them and said:

"Blessed children, we will give you abundance of all that you can desire."

And the crowd of people dispersed, full of joy, singing hymns and canticles.

To commemorate this day on which Providence delivered the people from a cruel scourge, processions were established in which the effigy of a chained dragon was led about.

Kraken levied the tribute and became the richest and most powerful of the Penguins. As a sign of his victory and so as to inspire a salutary terror, he wore a dragon's crest upon his head and he had a habit of saying to the people:

"Now that the monster is dead I am the dragon."

For many years Orberosia bestowed her favours upon neatherds and shepherds, whom she thought equal to the gods. But when she was no longer beautiful she consecrated herself to the Lord.

At her death she became the object of public veneration, and was admitted into the calendar of the saints and adopted as the patron saint of Penguinia.

Kraken left a son, who, like his father, wore a dragon's crest, and he was for this reason surnamed Draco. He was the founder of the first royal dynasty of the Penguins.

BOOK III

THE MIDDLE AGES AND THE RENAISSANCE

BRIAN THE GOOD AND QUEEN GLAMORGAN

THE kings of Alca were descended from Draco, the son of Kraken, and they wore on their heads a terrible dragon's crest, as a sacred badge whose appearance alone inspired the people with veneration, terror, and love. They were perpetually in conflict either with their own vassals and subjects or with the princes of the adjoining islands and continents.

The most ancient of these kings has left but a name. We do not even know how to pronounce or write it. The first of the Draconides whose history is known was Brian the Good, renowned for his skill and courage in war and in the chase.

He was a Christian and loved learning. He also favoured men who had vowed themselves to the monastic life. In the hall of his palace where, under the sooty rafters, there hung the heads, pelts, and horns of wild beasts, he held feasts to which all the harpers of Alca and of the neighbouring islands were invited, and he himself used to join in singing the praises of the heroes. He was just and magnanimous, but inflamed by so ardent a love of glory that he could not restrain himself from putting to death those who had sung better than himself.

The monks of Yvern having been driven out by the pagans who ravaged Brittany, King Brian summoned them into his kingdom and built a wooden monastery for them near his palace. Every day he went with Queen Glamorgan, his wife, into the monastery chapel and was present at the religious ceremonies and joined in the hymns.

Now among these monks there was a brother called Oddoul, who, while still in the flower of his youth, had adorned

81

himself with knowledge and virtue. The devil entertained a great grudge against him, and attempted several times to lead him into temptation. He took several shapes and appeared to him in turn as a war-horse, a young maiden, and a cup of mead. Then he rattled two dice in a dice-box and said to him:

"Will you play with me for the kingdoms of the world against one of the hairs of your head?"

But the man of the Lord, armed with the sign of the Cross, repulsed the enemy. Perceiving that he could not seduce him, the devil thought of an artful plan to ruin him. One summer night he approached the queen, who slept upon her couch, showed her an image of the young monk whom she saw every day in the wooden monastery, and upon this image he placed a spell. Forthwith, like a subtle poison, love flowed into Glamorgan's veins, and she burned with an ardent desire to do as she listed with Oddoul. She formed unceasing pretexts to have him near her. Several times she asked him to teach reading and singing to her children.

"I entrust them to you," said she to him. "And I will follow the lessons you will give them so that I myself may learn also. You will teach both mother and sons at the same time."

But the young monk kept making excuses. At times he would say that he was not a learned enough teacher, and on other occasions that his state forbade him all intercourse with women. This refusal inflamed Glamorgan's passion. One day as she lay pining upon her couch, her malady having become intolerable, she summoned Oddoul to her chamber. He came in obedience to her orders, but remained with his eyes cast down towards the threshold of the door. With impatience and grief she resented his not looking at her.

"See," said she to him, "I have no more strength, a shadow is on my eyes. My body is both burning and freezing."

And as he kept silence and made no movement, she called him in the voice of entreaty:

"Come to me, come!"

With outstretched arms to which passion gave more length, she endeavoured to seize him and draw him towards her.

But he fled away, reproaching her for her wantonness.

Then, incensed with rage and fearing that Oddoul might divulge the shame into which she had fallen, she determined to ruin him so that he might not ruin her.

In a voice of lamentation that resounded throughout all the palace she called for help, as if, in truth, she were in some great danger. Her servants rushed up and saw the young monk fleeing and the queen pulling back the sheets upon her couch. They all cried out together. And when King Brian, attracted by the noise, entered the chamber, Glamorgan, showing him her dishevelled hair, her eyes flooded with tears, and her bosom that in the fury of her love she had torn with her nails, said:

"My lord and husband, behold the traces of the insults I have undergone. Driven by an infamous desire Oddoul has approached me and attempted to do me violence."

When he heard these complaints and saw the blood, the king, transported with fury, ordered his guards to seize the young monk and burn him alive before the palace under the queen's eyes.

Being told of the affair, the Abbot of Yvern went to the king and said to him:

"King Brian, know by this example the difference between a Christian woman and a pagan. Roman Lucretia was the most virtuous of idolatrous princesses, yet she had not the strength to defend herself against the attacks of an effeminate youth, and, ashamed of her weakness, she gave way to despair, whilst Glamorgan has successfully withstood the assaults of a criminal filled with rage, and possessed by the most terrible of demons." Meanwhile Oddoul, in the prison of the palace, was waiting for the moment when he should be burned alive. But God did not suffer an innocent to perish. He sent to him an angel, who, taking the form of one of the queen's servants called Gudrune, took him out of the prison and led him into the very room where the woman whose appearance he had taken dwelt.

And the angel said to young Oddoul:

"I love thee because thou art daring."

And young Oddoul, believing that it was Gudrune herself, answered with downcast looks:

"It is by the grace of the Lord that I have resisted the violence of the queen and braved the anger of that powerful woman."

And the angel asked:

"What? Hast thou not done what the queen accuses thee of?"

"In truth no, I have not done it," answered Oddoul, his hand on his heart.

"Thou hast not done it?"

"No, I have not done it. The very thought of such an action fills me with horror."

"Then," cried the angel, "what art thou doing here, thou impotent creature?" *

And she opened the door to facilitate the young man's escape. Oddoul felt himself pushed violently out. Scarcely had he gone down into the street than a chamber-pot was poured over his head; and he thought:

"Mysterious are thy designs, O Lord, and thy ways past finding out."

* The Penguin chronicler who relates the fact employs the expression, *Species inductilis.* I have endeavoured to translate it literally.

II

DRACO THE GREAT

(*Translation of the Relics of St. Orberosia*)

THE direct posterity of Brian the Good was extinguished about the year 900 in the person of Collic of the Short Nose. A cousin of that prince, Bosco the Magnanimous, succeeded him, and took care, in order to assure himself of the throne, to put to death all his relations. There issued from him a long line of powerful kings.

One of them, Draco the Great, attained great renown as a man of war. He was defeated more frequently than the others. It is by this constancy in defeat that great captains are recognised. In twenty years he burned down more than a hundred thousand hamlets, market towns, unwalled towns, villages, walled towns, cities, and universities. He set fire impartially to his enemies' territory and to his own domains. And he used to explain his conduct by saying:

"War without fire is like tripe without mustard: it is an insipid thing."

His justice was rigorous. When the peasants whom he made prisoners were unable to raise the money for their ransoms he had them hanged from a tree, and if any unhappy woman came to plead for her destitute husband he dragged her by the hair at his horse's tail. He lived like a soldier without effeminacy. It is satisfactory to relate that his manner of life was pure. Not only did he not allow his kingdom to decline from its hereditary glory, but, even in his reverses he valiantly supported the honour of the Penguin people.

Draco the Great caused the relics of St. Orberosia to be transferred to Alca.

85

The body of the blessed saint had been buried in a grotto on the Coast of Shadows at the end of a scented heath. The first pilgrims who went to visit it were the boys and girls from the neighbouring villages. They used to go there in the evening, by preference in couples, as if their pious desires naturally sought satisfaction in darkness and solitude. They worshipped the saint with a fervent and discreet worship whose mystery they seemed jealously to guard, for they did not like to publish too openly the experiences they felt. But they were heard to murmur one to another words of love, delight, and rapture with which they mingled the name of Orberosia. Some would sigh that there they forgot the world; others would say that they came out of the grotto in peace and calm; the young girls among them used to recall to each other the joys with which they had been filled in it.

Such were the marvels that the virgin of Alca performed in the morning of her glorious eternity; they had the sweetness and indefiniteness of the dawn. Soon the mystery of the grotto spread like a perfume throughout the land; it was a ground of joy and edification for pious souls, and corrupt men endeavoured, though in vain, by falsehood and calumny, to divert the faithful from the springs of grace that flowed from the saint's tomb. The Church took measures so that these graces should not remain reserved for a few children, but should be diffused throughout all Penguin Christianity. Monks took up their quarters in the grotto, they built a monastery, a chapel, and a hostelry on the coast, and pilgrims began to flock thither.

As if strengthened by a longer sojourn in heaven, the blessed Orberosia now performed still greater miracles for those who came to lay their offerings on her tomb. She gave hopes to women who had been hitherto barren, she sent dreams to reassure jealous old men concerning the fidelity of the young wives whom they had suspected without cause, and she protected the country from plagues, murrains, famines, tempests, and dragons of Cappadocia.

But during the troubles that desolated the kingdom in the

time of King Collic and his successors, the tomb of St. Orberosia was plundered of its wealth, the monastery burned down,
and the monks dispersed. The road that had been so long
trodden by devout pilgrims was overgrown with furze and
heather, and the blue thistles of the sands. For a hundred
years the miraculous tomb had been visited by none save
vipers, weasels, and bats, when, one day the saint appeared to
a peasant of the neighbourhood, Momordic by name.

"I am the virgin Orberosia," said she to him; "I have chosen
thee to restore my sanctuary. Warn the inhabitants of the
country that if they allow my memory to be blotted out, and
leave my tomb without honour and wealth, a new dragon will
come and devastate Penguinia."

Learned churchmen held an inquiry concerning this appari-
tion, and pronounced it genuine, and not diabolical but truly
heavenly, and in later years it was remarked that in France, in
like circumstances, St. Foy and St. Catherine had acted in
the same way and made use of similar language.

The monastery was restored and pilgrims flocked to it anew.
The virgin Orberosia worked greater and greater miracles.
She cured divers hurtful maladies, particularly club-foot,
dropsy, paralysis, and St. Guy's disease. The monks who kept
the tomb were enjoying an enviable opulence, when the saint,
appearing to King Draco the Great, ordered him to recognise
her as the heavenly patron of the kingdom and to transfer her
precious remains to the cathedral of Alca.

In consequence, the odoriferous relics of that virgin were
carried with great pomp to the metropolitan church and placed
in the middle of the choir in a shrine made of gold and enamel
and ornamented with precious stones.

The chapter kept a record of the miracles wrought by the
blessed Orberosia.

Draco the Great, who had never ceased to defend and exalt
the Christian faith, died fulfilled with the most pious sentiments and bequeathed his great possessions to the Church.

III

QUEEN CRUCHA

TERRIBLE disorders followed the death of Draco the Great.
That prince's successors have often been accused of weakness,
and it is true that none of them followed, even from afar, the
example of their valiant ancestor.

His son, Chum, who was lame, failed to increase the territory of the Penguins. Bolo, the son of Chum, was assassinated
by the palace guards at the age of nine, just as he was ascend-
ing the throne. His brother Gun succeeded him. He was only
seven years old and allowed himself to be governed by his
mother, Queen Crucha.

Crucha was beautiful, learned, and intelligent; but she was
unable to curb her own passions.

These are the terms in which the venerable Talpa expresses
himself in his chronicle regarding that illustrious queen:

"In beauty of face and symmetry of figure Queen Crucha
yields neither to Semiramis of Babylon nor to Penthesilea,
queen of the Amazons; nor to Salome, the daughter of Hero-
dias. But she offers in her person certain singularities that
will appear beautiful or uncomely according to the contradictory opinions of men and the varying judgments of the
world. She has on her forehead two small horns which she
conceals in the abundant folds of her golden hair; one of her
eyes is blue and one is black; her neck is bent towards the left
side; and, like Alexander of Macedon, she has six fingers on
her right hand, and a stain like a little monkey's head upon
her skin.

"Her gait is majestic and her manner affable. She is magnificent in her expenses, but she is not always able to rule desire by reason.

"One day, having noticed in the palace stables, a young groom of great beauty, she immediately fell violently in love with him, and entrusted to him the command of her armies. What one must praise unreservedly in this great queen is the abundance of gifts that she makes to the churches, monasteries, and chapels in her kingdom, and especially to the holy house of Beargarden, where, by the grace of the Lord, I made my profession in my fourteenth year. She has founded masses for the repose of her soul in such great numbers that every priest in the Penguin Church is, so to speak, transformed into a taper lighted in the sight of heaven to draw down the divine mercy upon the august Crucha."

From these lines and from some others with which I have enriched my text the reader can judge of the historical and literary value of the "Gesta Penguinorum." Unhappily, that chronicle suddenly comes to an end at the third year of Draco the Simple, the successor of Gun the Weak. Having reached that point of my history, I deplore the loss of an agreeable and trustworthy guide.

During the two centuries that followed, the Penguins remained plunged in blood-stained disorder. All the arts perished. In the midst of the general ignorance, the monks in the shadow of their cloister devoted themselves to study, and copied the Holy Scriptures with indefatigable zeal. As parchment was scarce, they scraped the writing off old manuscripts in order to transcribe upon them the divine word. Thus throughout the breadth of Penguinia Bibles blossomed forth like roses on a bush.

A monk of the order of St. Benedict, Ermold the Penguin, had himself alone defaced four thousand Greek and Latin manuscripts so as to copy out the Gospel of St. John four thousand times. Thus the masterpieces of ancient poetry and eloquence were destroyed in great numbers. Historians are unanimous in recognising that the Penguin convents were the refuge of learning during the Middle Ages.

Unending wars between the Penguins and the Porpoises

filled the close of this period. It is extremely difficult to know the truth concerning these wars, not because accounts are wanting, but because there are so many of them. The Porpoise Chronicles contradict the Penguin Chronicles at every point. And, moreover, the Penguins contradict each other as well as the Porpoises. I have discovered two chronicles that are in agreement, but one has copied from the other. A single fact is certain, namely, that massacres, rapes, conflagrations, and plunder succeeded one another without interruption.

Under the unhappy prince Bosco IX. the kingdom was at the very verge of ruin. On the news that the Porpoise fleet, composed of six hundred great ships, was in sight of Alca, the bishop ordered a solemn procession. The cathedral chapter, the elected magistrates, the members of Parliament, and the clerics of the University entered the Cathedral and, taking up St. Orberosia's shrine, led it in procession through the town, followed by the entire people singing hymns. The holy patron of Penguinia was not invoked in vain. Nevertheless, the Porpoises besieged the town both by land and sea, took it by assault, and for three days and three nights killed, plundered, violated, and burned, with all the indifference that habit produces.

Our astonishment cannot be too great at the fact that, during those iron ages, the faith was preserved intact among the Penguins. The splendour of the truth in those times illumined all souls that had not been corrupted by sophisms. This is the explanation of the unity of belief. A constant practice of the Church doubtless contributed also to maintain this happy communion of the faithful—every Penguin who thought differently from the others was immediately burned at the stake.

IV

LETTERS: JOHANNES TALPA

DURING the minority of King Gun, Johannes Talpa, in the monastery of Beargarden, where at the age of fourteen he had made his profession and from which he never departed for a single day throughout his life, composed his celebrated Latin chronicle in twelve books called "De Gestis Penguino-rum."

The monastery of Beargarden lifts its high walls on the summit of an inaccessible peak. One sees around it only the blue tops of mountains, divided by the clouds.

When he began to write his "Gesta Penguinorum," Johannes Talpa was already old. The good monk has taken care to tell us this in his book: "My head has long since lost," he says, "its adornment of fair hair, and my scalp resembles those convex mirrors of metal which the Penguin ladies consult with so much care and zeal. My stature, naturally small, has with years become diminished and bent. My white beard gives warmth to my breast."

With a charming simplicity, Talpa informs us of certain circumstances in his life and some features in his character. "Descended," he tells us, "from a noble family, and destined from childhood for the ecclesiastical state, I was taught grammer and music. I learned to read under the guidance of a master who was called Amicus, and who would have been better named Inimicus. As I did not easily attain to a knowledge of my letters, he beat me violently with rods so that I can say that he printed the alphabet in strokes upon my back."

In another passage Talpa confesses his natural inclination towards pleasure. These are his expressive words: "In my youth the ardour of my senses was such that in the shadow of the woods I experienced a sensation of boiling in a pot rather than of breathing the fresh air. I fled from women, but in vain, for every object recalled them to me."

While he was writing his chronicle, a terrible war, at once foreign and domestic, laid waste the Penguin land. The soldiers of Crucha came to defend the monastery of Beargarden against the Penguin barbarians and established themselves strongly within its walls. In order to render it impregnable they pierced loop-holes through the walls and they took the lead off the church roof to make balls for their slings. At night they lighted huge fires in the courts and cloisters and on them they roasted whole oxen which they spitted upon the ancient pine-trees of the mountain. Sitting around the flames, amid smoke filled with a mingled odour of resin and fat, they broached huge casks of wine and beer. Their songs, their blasphemies, and the noise of their quarrels drowned the sound of the morning bells.

At last the Porpoises, having crossed the defiles, laid siege to the monastery. They were warriors from the North, clad in copper armour. They fastened ladders a hundred and fifty fathoms long to the sides of the cliffs and sometimes in the darkness and storm these broke beneath the weight of men and arms, and bunches of the besiegers were hurled into the ravines and precipices. A prolonged wail would be heard going down into the darkness, and the assault would begin again. The Penguins poured streams of burning wax upon their assailants, which made them blaze like torches. Sixty times the enraged Porpoises attempted to scale the monastery and sixty times they were repulsed.

For six months they had closely invested the monastery, when, on the day of the Epiphany, a shepherd of the valley showed them a hidden path by which they climbed the mountain, penetrated into the vaults of the abbey, ran through the cloisters, the kitchens, the church, the chapter halls, the library, the laundry, the cells, the refectories, and the dormitories, and burned the buildings, killing and violating without distinction of age or sex. The Penguins, awakened unexpectedly, ran to arms, but in the darkness and alarm they struck at one another, whilst the Porpoises with blows of their axes disputed the sacred vessels, the censers, the candlesticks, dalmatics, reliquaries, golden crosses, and precious stones.

The air was filled with an acrid odour of burnt flesh. Groans and death-cries arose in the midst of the flames, and on the edges of the crumbling roofs monks ran in thousands like ants, and fell into the valley. Yet Johannes Talpa kept on writing his Chronicle. The soldiers of Crucha retreated speedily and filled up all the issues from the monastery with pieces of rock so as to shut up the Porpoises in the burning buildings. And to crush the enemy beneath the ruin they employed the trunks of old oaks as battering-rams. The burning timbers fell in with a noise like thunder and the lofty arches of the naves crumbled beneath the shock of these giant trees when moved by six hundred men together. Soon there was left nothing of the rich and extensive abbey but the cell of Johannes Talpa, which, by a marvellous chance, hung from the ruin of a smoking gable. The old chronicler still kept writing.

This admirable intensity of thought may seem excessive in the case of an annalist who applies himself to relate the events of his own time. For, however abstracted and detached we may be from surrounding things, we nevertheless resent their influence. I have consulted the original manuscript of Johannes Talpa in the National Library, where it is preserved (*Monumenta Peng.*, K. L6., 12390 *four*). It is a parchment manuscript of 628 leaves. The writing is extremely confused, the letters instead of being in a straight line, stray in all directions and are mingled together in great disorder, or, more correctly speaking, in absolute confusion. They are so badly formed that for the most part it is impossible not merely to say what they are, but even to distinguish them from the splashes of ink with which they are plentifully interspersed. Those ines-

timable pages bear witness in this way to the troubles amid
which they were written. To read them is difficult. On the other
hand, the monk of Beargarden's style shows no trace of emotion. The tone of the "Gesta Penguinorum" never departs from
simplicity. The narration is rapid and of a conciseness that
sometimes approaches dryness. The reflections are rare and,
as a rule, judicious.

V

THE ARTS: THE PRIMITIVES OF
PENGUIN PAINTING

THE Penguin critics vie with one another in affirming that
Penguin art has from its origin been distinguished by a power,
ful and pleasing originality, and that we may look elsewhere
in vain for the qualities of grace and reason that characterise
its earliest works. But the Porpoises claim that their artists
were undoubtedly the instructors and masters of the Penguins
It is difficult to form an opinion on the matter, because the
Penguins, before they began to admire their primitive paint
ers, destroyed all their works.

We cannot be too sorry for this loss. For my own part I
feel it cruelly, for I venerate the Penguin antiquities and I
adore the primitives. They are delightful. I do not say they
are all alike, for that would be untrue, but they have common
characters that are found in all schools—I mean formulas
from which they never depart—and there is besides something finished in their work, for what they know they know
well. Luckily we can form a notion of the Penguin primitives
from the Italian, Flemish, and Dutch primitives, and from
the French primitives, who are superior to all the rest;
as M. Gruyer tells us they are more logical, logic being a
peculiarly French quality. Even if this is denied it must at
least be admitted that to France belongs the credit of having
kept primitives when the other nations knew them no longer.
The Exhibition of French Primitives at the Pavilion Marsan
in 1904 contained several little panels contemporary with the
later Valois kings and with Henry IV.

I have made many journeys to see the pictures of the

brothers Van Eyck, of Memling, of Roger van der Weyden, of the painter of the death of Mary, of Ambrogio Lorenzetti, and of the old Umbrian masters. It was, however, neither Bruges, nor Cologne, nor Sienna, nor Perugia, that completed my initiation; it was in the little town of Arezzo that I became a conscious adept in primitive painting. That was ten years ago or even longer. At that period of indigence and simplicity, the municipal museums, though usually kept shut, were always opened to foreigners. One evening, an old woman with a candle showed me, for half a lira, the sordid museum of Arezzo, and in it I discovered a painting by Margaritone, a "St. Francis," the pious sadness of which moved me to tears. I was deeply touched, and Margaritone of Arezzo became from that day my dearest primitive.

I picture to myself the Penguin primitives in conformity with the works of that master. It will not therefore be thought superfluous if in this place I consider his works with some attention, if not in detail, at least under their more general and, if I dare say so, most representative aspect.

We possess five or six pictures signed with his hand. His masterpiece, preserved in the National Gallery of London, represents the Virgin seated on a throne and holding the infant Jesus in her arms. What strikes one first when one looks at this figure is the proportion. The body from the neck to the feet is only twice as long as the head, so that it appears extremely short and podgy. This work is not less remarkable for its painting than for its drawing. The great Margaritone had but a limited number of colours in his possession, and he used them in all their purity without ever modifying the tones. From this it follows that his colouring has more vivacity than harmony. The cheeks of the Virgin and those of the Child are of a bright vermilion which the old master, from a naïve preference for clear definitions, has placed on each face in two circumferences as exact as if they had been traced out by a pair of compasses.

A learned critic of the eighteenth century, the Abbé

Lanzi, has treated Margaritone's works with profound disdain. "They are," he says, "merely crude daubs. In those
unfortunate times people could neither draw nor paint." Such
was the common opinion of the connoisseurs of the days of
powdered wigs. But the great Margaritone and his contempo-
raries were soon to be avenged for this cruel contempt. There
was born in the nineteenth century, in the biblical villages
and reformed cottages of pious England, a multitude of little
Samuels and little St. Johns with hair curling like lambs, who,
about 1840 and 1850, became spectacled professors and
founded the cult of the primitives.

That eminent theorist of Pre-Raphaelitism, Sir James
Tuckett, does not shrink from placing the Madonna of the
National Gallery on a level with the masterpieces of Christian
art. "By giving to the Virgin's head," says Sir James Tuckett,
"a third of the total height of the figure, the old master attracts
the spectator's attention and keeps it directed towards the
more sublime parts of the human figure, and in particular the
eyes, which we ordinarily describe as the spiritual organs. In
this picture, colouring and design conspire to produce an ideal
and mystical impression. The vermilion of the cheeks does not
recall the natural appearance of the skin; it rather seems as
if the old master has applied the roses of Paradise to the faces
of the Mother and the Child."

We see, in such a criticism as this, a shining reflection,
so to speak, of the work which it exalts; yet MacSilly, the
seraphic æsthete of Edinburgh, has expressed in a still more
moving and penetrating fashion the impression produced upon
his mind by the sight of this primitive painting. "The Madonna of Margaritone," says the revered MacSilly, "attains
the transcendent end of art. It inspires its beholders with
feelings of innocence and purity; it makes them like little
children. And so true is this, that at the age of sixty-six, after
having had the joy of contemplating it closely for three hours,
I felt myself suddenly transformed into a little child. While
my cab was taking me through Trafalgar Square I kept laugh-

ing and prattling and shaking my spectacle-case as if it were a rattle. And when the maid in my boarding-house had served my meal I kept pouring spoonfuls of soup into my ear with all the artlessness of childhood."

"It is by such results," adds MacSilly, "that the excellence of a work of art is proved."

Margaritone, according to Vasari, died at the age of seventy-seven, "regretting that he had lived to see a new form of art arising and the new artists crowned with fame."

These lines, which I translate literally, have inspired Sir James Tuckett with what are perhaps the finest pages in his work. They form part of his "Breviary for Æsthetes"; all the Pre-Raphaelites know them by heart. I place them here as the most precious ornament of this book. You will agree that nothing more sublime has been written since the days of the Hebrew prophets.

MARGARITONE'S VISION

Margaritone, full of years and labours, went one day to visit the studio of a young painter who had lately settled in the town. He noticed in the studio a freshly painted Madonna, which, although severe and rigid, nevertheless, by a certain exactness in the proportions and a devilish mingling of light and shade, assumed an appearance of relief and life. At this sight the artless and sublime worker of Arezzo perceived with horror what the future of painting would be. With his brow clasped in his hands he exclaimed:

"What things of shame does not this figure show forth! I discern in it the end of that Christian art which paints the soul and inspires the beholder with an ardent desire for heaven. Future painters will not restrain themselves as does this one to portraying on the side of a wall or on a wooden panel the cursed matter of which our bodies are formed; they will celebrate and glorify it. They will clothe their figures with dangerous appearances of flesh, and these figures will seem like real persons. Their bodies will be seen; their forms will appear through their clothing. St. Magdalen will have a bosom. St. Martha a belly, St. Barbara hips, St. Agnes buttocks; St. Sebastian will unveil his youthful beauty, and St. George will display beneath his armour the muscular wealth of a robust virility; apostles, confessors, doctors, and God the Father himself will appear as ordinary beings like you and me; the angels will affect an equivocal, ambiguous, mysterious beauty which will trouble hearts. What desire for heaven will these representations impart? None; but from them you will learn to take pleasure in the forms of terrestrial life. Where will painters stop in their indiscreet inquiries? They will stop no-where. They will go so far as to show men and women naked like the idols of the Romans. There will be a sacred art and a profane art, and the sacred art will not be less profane than the other."

"Get ye behind me, demons," exclaimed the old master. For in prophetic vision he saw the righteous and the saints assuming the appearance of melancholy athletes. He saw Apollos playing the lute on a flowery hill, in the midst of the Muses wearing light tunics. He saw Venuses lying under shady myrtles and the Danaë exposing their charming sides to the golden rain. He saw pictures of Jesus under the pillars of the temple amidst patricians, fair ladies, musicians, pages, negroes, dogs, and parrots. He saw in an inextricable confusion of human limbs, outspread wings, and flying draperies, crowds of tumultuous Nativities, opulent Holy Families, emphatic Crucifixions. He saw St. Catherines, St. Barbaras, St. Agneses humiliating patricians by the sumptuousness of their velvets, their brocades, and their pearls, and by the splendour of their breasts. He saw Auroras scattering roses, and a multitude of naked Dianas and Nymphs surprised on the banks of retired streams. And the great Margaritone died, strangled by so hor-rible a presentiment of the Renaissance and the Bolognese School.

VI

MARBODIUS

WE possess a precious monument of the Penguin literature of the fifteenth century. It is a narrative of a journey to hell undertaken by the monk Marbodius, of the order of St. Benedict, who professed a fervent admiration for the poet Virgil. This narrative, written in fairly good Latin, has been published by M. du Clos des Lunes. It is here translated for the first time. I believe that I am doing a service to my fellow-countrymen in making them acquainted with these pages, though doubtless they are far from forming a unique example of this class of mediæval Latin literature. Among the fictions that may be compared with them we may mention "The Voyage of St. Brendan," "The Vision of Albericus," and "St. Patrick's Purgatory," imaginary descriptions, like Dante Alighieri's "Divine Comedy," of the supposed abode of the dead. The narrative of Marbodius is one of the latest works dealing with this theme, but it is not the least singular.

THE DESCENT OF MARBODIUS INTO HELL

In the fourteen hundred and fifty-third year of the incarnation of the Son of God, a few days before the enemies of the Cross entered the city of Helena and the great Constantine, it was given to me, Brother Marbodius, an unworthy monk, to see and to hear what none had hitherto seen or heard. I have composed a faithful narrative of those things so that their memory may not perish with me, for man's time is short.

On the first day of May in the aforesaid year, at the hour of vespers, I was seated in the Abbey of Corrigan on a stone in

the cloisters and, as my custom was, I read the verses of the
poet whom I love best of all, Virgil, who has sung of the labours
of the field, of shepherds, and of heroes. Evening was hanging
its purple folds from the arches of the cloisters and in a voice
of emotion I was murmuring the verses which describe how
Dido, the Phœnician queen, wanders with her ever-bleeding
wound beneath the myrtles of hell. At that moment Brother
Hilary happened to pass by, followed by Brother Jacinth, the
porter.

Brought up in the barbarous ages before the resurrection
of the Muses, Brother Hilary has not been initiated into the
wisdom of the ancients; nevertheless, the poetry of the Mantuan has, like a subtle torch, shed some gleams of light into
his understanding.

"Brother Marbodius," he asked me, "do those verses that
you utter with swelling breast and sparkling eyes—do they
belong to that great 'Æneid' from which morning or evening
your glances are never withheld?"

I answered that I was reading in Virgil how the son of
Anchises perceived Dido like a moon behind the foliage.*

"Brother Marbodius," he replied, "I am certain that on all
occasions Virgil gives expression to wise maxims and profound
thoughts. But the songs that he modulates on his Syracusan
flute hold such a lofty meaning and such exalted doctrine that
I am continually puzzled by them."

"Take care, father," cried Brother Jacinth, in an agitated
voice. "Virgil was a magician who wrought marvels by the
help of demons. It is thus he pierced through a mountain near
Naples and fashioned a bronze horse that had power to heal
all the diseases of horses. He was a necromancer, and there is
still shown, in a certain town in Italy, the mirror in which he
made the dead appear. And yet a woman deceived this great

---

* The text runs

> . . . qualem primo qui surgere mense
> Aut videt aut vidisse putat per nubila lunam.

Brother Marbodius, by a strange misunderstanding, substitutes an en
tirely different image for the one created by the poet.

sorcerer. A Neapolitan courtesan invited him to hoist himself up to her window in the basket that was used to bring the provisions, and she left him all night suspended between two storeys."

Brother Hilary did not appear to hear these observations.

"Virgil is a prophet," he replied, "and a prophet who leaves far behind him the sibyls with their sacred verses as well as the daughter of King Priam, and that great diviner of future things, Plato of Athens. You will find in the fourth of his Syracusan cantos the birth of our Lord foretold in a language that seems of heaven rather than of earth.* In the time of my early studies, when I read for the first time JAM REDIT ET VIRGO, I felt myself bathed in an infinite delight, but I immediately experienced intense grief at the thought that, for ever deprived of the presence of God, the author of this prophetic verse, the noblest that has come from human lips, was pining among the heathen in eternal darkness. This cruel thought did not leave me. It pursued me even in my studies, my prayers, my meditations, and my ascetic labours. Thinking that Virgil was deprived of the sight of God and that possibly he might even be suffering the fate of the reprobate in hell, I could neither enjoy peace nor rest, and I went so far as to exclaim several times a day with my arms outstretched to heaven:

" 'Reveal to me, O Lord, the lot thou hast assigned to him who sang on earth as the angels sing in heaven!'

"After some years my anguish ceased when I read in an old book that the great Apostle St. Paul, who called the Gentiles into the Church of Christ, went to Naples and sanctified with his tears the tomb of the prince of poets.† This was

---

* Three centuries before the epoch in which our Marbodius lived the words—

> Maro, vates gentilium
> Da Christo testimonium

were sung in the churches on Christmas Day.

> † Ad maronis mausoleum
> Ductus, fudit super eum
> Piae rorem lacrymæ.

some ground for believing that Virgil, like the Emperor Trajan, was admitted to Paradise because even in error he had a presentiment of the truth. We are not compelled to believe it, but I can easily persuade myself that it is true."

Having thus spoken, old Hilary wished me the peace of a holy night and went away with Brother Jacinth.

I resumed the delightful study of my poet. Book in hand, I meditated upon the way in which those whom Love destroys with its cruel malady wander through the secret paths in the depth of the myrtle forest, and, as I meditated, the quivering reflections of the stars came and mingled with those of the leafless eglantines in the waters of the cloister fountain. Suddenly the lights and the perfumes and the stillness of the sky were overwhelmed, a fierce Northwind charged with storm and darkness burst roaring upon me. It lifted me up and carried me like a wisp of straw over fields, cities, rivers, and mountains, and through the midst of thunder-clouds, during a long night composed of a whole series of nights and days. And when, after this prolonged and cruel rage, the hurricane was at last stilled, I found myself far from my native land at the bottom of a valley bordered by cypress trees. Then a woman of wild beauty, trailing long garments behind her, approached me. She placed her left hand on my shoulder, and, pointing her right arm to an oak with thick foliage:

"Look!" said she to me.

Immediately I recognised the Sibyl who guards the sacred wood of Avernus, and I discerned the fair Proserpine's beautiful golden twig amongst the tufted boughs of the tree to which her finger pointed.

"O prophetic Virgin," I exclaimed, "thou hast comprehended my desire and thou hast satisfied it in this way. Thou hast revealed to me the tree that bears the shining twig without which none can enter alive into the dwelling-place of the dead.

> Quem te, inquit, reddidissem,
> Si te vivum invenissem
> Poetarum maxime!

And in truth, eagerly did I long to converse with the shade of Virgil."

Having said this, I snatched the golden branch from its ancient trunk and I advanced without fear into the smoking gulf that leads to the miry banks of the Styx, upon which the shades are tossed about like dead leaves. At sight of the branch dedicated to Proserpine, Charon took me in his bark, which groaned beneath my weight, and I alighted on the shores of the dead, and was greeted by the mute baying of the threefold Cerberus. I pretended to throw the shade of a stone at him, and the vain monster fled into his cave. There, amidst the rushes, wandered the souls of those children whose eyes had but opened and shut to the kindly light of day, and there in a gloomy cavern Minos judges men. I penetrated into the myrtle wood in which the victims of love wander languishing, Phædra, Procris, the sad Eriphyle, Evadne, Pasiphaë, Laodamia, and Cenis, and the Phœnician Dido. Then I went through the dusty plains reserved for famous warriors. Beyond them open two ways. That to the left leads to Tartarus, the abode of the wicked. I took that to the right, which leads to Elysium and to the dwellings of Dis. Having hung the sacred branch at the goddess's door, I reached pleasant fields flooded with purple light. The shades of philosophers and poets hold grave converse there. The Graces and the Muses formed sprightly choirs upon the grass. Old Homer sang, accompanying himself upon his rustic lyre. His eyes were closed, but divine images shone upon his lips. I saw Solon, Democritus, and Pythagoras watching the games of the young men in the meadow, and, through the foliage of an ancient laurel, I perceived also Hesiod, Orpheus, the melancholy Euripides, and the masculine Sappho. I passed and recognised, as they sat on the bank of a fresh rivulet, the poet Horace, Varius, Gallus, and Lycoris. A little apart, leaning against the trunk of a dark holm-oak, Virgil was gazing pensively at the grove. Of lofty stature, though spare, he still preserved that swarthy complexion, that rustic air, that negligent bearing, and unpolished appearance which during his lifetime concealed his genius. I saluted him piously and remained for a long time without speech.

At last when my halting voice could proceed out of my throat:

"O thou, so dear to the Ausonian Muses, thou honour of the Latin name, Virgil," cried I, "it is through thee I have known what beauty is, it is through thee I have known what the tables of the gods and the beds of the goddesses are like. Suffer the praises of the humblest of thy adorers."

"Arise, stranger," answered the divine poet. "I perceive that thou art a living being among the shades, and that thy body treads down the grass in this eternal evening. Thou art not the first man who has descended before his death into these dwellings, although all intercourse between us and the living is difficult. But cease from praise; I do not like eulogies and the confused sounds of glory have always offended my ears. That is why I fled from Rome, where I was known to the idle and curious, and laboured in the solitude of my beloved Parthenope. And then I am not so convinced that the men of thy generation understand my verses that I should be gratified by thy praises. Who art thou?"

"I am called Marbodius of the Kingdom of Alca. I made my profession in the Abbey of Corrigan. I read thy poems by day and I read them by night. It is thee whom I have come to see in Hell; I was impatient to know what thy fate was. On earth the learned often dispute about it. Some hold it probable that, having lived under the power of demons, thou art now burning in inextinguishable flames; others, more cautious, pronounce no opinion, believing that all which is said concerning the dead is uncertain and full of lies; several, though not in truth the ablest, maintain that, because thou didst elevate the tone of the Sicilian Muses and foretell that a new progeny would descend from heaven, thou wert admitted, like the Emperor Trajan, to enjoy eternal blessedness in the Christian heaven."

"Thou seest that such is not the case," answered the shade, smiling.

"I meet thee in truth, O Virgil, among the heroes and sages in those Elysian Fields which thou thyself hast described. Thus, contrary to what several on earth believe, no one has come to seek thee on the part of Him who reigns on high?"

After a rather long silence:

"I will conceal nought from thee. He sent for me; one of His messengers, a simple man, came to say that I was expected, and that, although I had not been initiated into their mysteries, in consideration of my prophetic verses a place had been reserved for me among those of the new sect. But I refused to accept that invitation; I had no desire to change my place. I did so not because I share the admiration of the Greeks for the Elysian fields, or because I taste here those joys which caused Proserpine to lose the remembrance of her mother. I never believed much myself in what I say about these things in the 'Æneid.' I was instructed by philosophers and men of science and I had a correct foreboding of the truth. Life in hell is extremely attenuated; we feel neither pleasure nor pain; we are as if we were not. The dead have no existence here except such as the living lend them. Nevertheless I prefer to remain here."

"But what reason didst thou give, O Virgil, for so strange a refusal?"

"I gave excellent ones. I said to the messenger of the god that I did not deserve the honour he brought me, and that a meaning had been given to my verses which they did not bear. In truth I have not in my fourth Eclogue betrayed the faith of my ancestors. Some ignorant Jews alone have interpreted in favour of a barbarian god a verse which celebrates the return of the golden age predicted by the Sibylline oracles. I excused myself then on the ground that I could not occupy a place which was destined for me in error and to which I recognised that I had no right. Then I alleged my disposition and my tastes, which do not accord with the customs of the new heavens.

" 'I am not unsociable,' said I to this man. 'I have shown in life a complaisant and easy disposition, although the extreme simplicity of my habits caused me to be suspected of avarice. I kept nothing for myself alone. My library was open to all and I have conformed my conduct to that fine saying of Euripides, "all ought to be common among friends." Those praises that seemed obtrusive when I myself received them became agreeable to me when addressed to Varius or to Macer. But at bottom I am rustic and uncultivated. I take pleasure in the society of animals; I was so zealous in observing them and took so much care of them that I was regarded, not altogether wrongly, as a good veterinary surgeon. I am told that the people of thy sect claim an immortal soul for themselves, but refuse one to the animals. That is a piece of non sense that makes me doubt their judgment. Perhaps I love the flocks and the shepherds a little too much. That would not seem right amongst you. There is a maxim to which I en deavour to conform my actions, "Nothing too much." More even than my feeble health my philosophy teaches me to use things with measure. I am sober; a lettuce and some olives with a drop of Falernian wine form all my meals. I have, indeed, to some extent gone with strange women, but I have not delayed over long in taverns to watch the young Syrians dance to the sound of the *crotalum*.* But if I have restrained my desires it was for my own satisfaction and for the sake of good discipline. To fear pleasure and to fly from joy appears to me the worst insult that one can offer to nature. I am assured that during their lives certain of the elect of thy god abstained from food and avoided women through love of asceticism, and voluntarily exposed themselves to useless sufferings. I should be afraid of meeting those criminals whose frenzy horrifies me. A poet must not be asked to attach him-

* This phrase seems to indicate that, if one is to believe Macrobius, the "Copa" is by Virgil.

self too strictly to any scientific or moral doctrine. Moreover, I am a Roman, and the Romans, unlike the Greeks, are unable to pursue profound speculations in a subtle manner. If they adopt a philosophy it is above all in order to derive some practical advantages from it. Siro, who enjoyed a great renown among us, taught me the system of Epicurus and thus freed me from vain terrors and turned me aside from the cruelties to which religion persuades ignorant men. I have embraced the views of Pythagoras concerning the souls of men and animals, both of which are of divine essence; this invites us to look upon ourselves without pride and without shame. I have learnt from the Alexandrines how the earth, at first soft and without form, hardened in proportion as Nereus withdrew himself from it to dig his humid dwellings; I have learned how things were formed insensibly; in what manner the rains, falling from the burdened clouds, nourished the silent forests, and by what progress a few animals at last began to wander over the nameless mountains. I could not accustom myself to your cosmogony either, for it seems to me fitter for a camel-driver on the Syrian sands than for a disciple of Aristarchus and Samos. And what would become of me in the abode of your beatitude if I did not find there my friends, my ancestors, my masters, and my gods, and if it is not given me to see Rhea's noble son, or Venus, mother of Æneas, with her winning smile, or Pan, or the young Dryads, or the Sylvans, or old Silenus, with his face stained by Ægle's purple mulberries.' These are the reasons which I begged that simple man to plead before the successor of Jupiter."

"And since then, O great shade, thou hast received no other message?"

"I have received none."

"To console themselves for thy absence, O Virgil, they have three poets, Commodianus, Prudentius, and Fortunatus, who were all three born in those dark days when neither prosody nor grammar were known. But tell me, O Mantuan, hast thou

never received other intelligence of the God whose company
thou didst so deliberately refuse?"

"Never that I remember."

"Hast thou not told me that I am not the first who
descended alive into these abodes and presented himself before thee?"

"Thou dost remind me of it. A century and a half ago,
or so it seems to me (it is difficult to reckon days and years
amid the shades), my profound peace was intruded upon
by a strange visitor. As I was wandering beneath the gloomy
foliage that borders the Styx, I saw rising before me a human
form more opaque and darker than that of the inhabitants
of these shores. I recognised a living person. He was of high
stature, thin, with an aquiline nose, sharp chin, and hollow
cheeks. His dark eyes shot forth fire; a red hood girt with a
crown of laurels bound his lean brows. His bones pierced
through the tight brown cloak that descended to his heels.
He saluted me with deference, tempered by a sort of fierce
pride, and addressed me in a speech more obscure and incor-
rect than that of those Gauls with whom the divine Julius
filled both his legions and the Curia. At last I understood that
he had been born near Fiesole, in an ancient Etruscan colony
that Sulla had founded on the banks of the Arno, and which
had prospered; that he had obtained municipal honours, but
that he had thrown himself vehemently into the sanguinary
quarrels which arose between the senate, the knights, and the
people, that he had been defeated and banished, and now he
wandered in exile throughout the world. He described Italy to
me as distracted by more wars and discords than in the time
of my youth, and as sighing anew for a second Augustus. I
pitied his misfortunes, remembering what I myself had formerly endured.

"An audacious spirit unceasingly disquieted him, and his
mind harboured great thoughts, but alas! his rudeness and
ignorance displayed the triumph of barbarism. He knew
neither poetry, nor science, nor even the tongue of the Greeks,

and he was ignorant, too, of the ancient traditions concerning the origin of the world and the nature of the gods. He gravely repeated fables which in my time would have brought smiles to the little children who were not yet old enough to pay for admission at the baths. The vulgar easily believe in monsters. The Etruscans especially peopled hell with demons, hideous as a sick man's dreams. That they have not abandoned their childish imaginings after so many centuries is explained by the continuation and progress of ignorance and misery, but that one of their magistrates whose mind is raised above the common level should share these popular illusions and should be frightened by the hideous demons that the inhabitants of that country painted on the walls of their tombs in the time of Porsena—that is something which might sadden even a sage. My Etruscan visitor repeated verses to me which he had composed in a new dialect, called by him the vulgar tongue, the sense of which I could not understand. My ears were more surprised than charmed as I heard him repeat the same sound three or four times at regular intervals in his efforts to mark the rhythm. That artifice did not seem ingenious to me; but it is not for the dead to judge of novelties.

"But I do not reproach this colonist of Sulla, born in an unhappy time, for making inharmonious verses or for being, if it be possible, as bad a poet as Bavius or Maevius. I have grievances against him which touch me more closely. The thing is monstrous and scarcely credible, but when this man returned to earth he disseminated the most odious lies about me. He affirmed in several passages of his barbarous poems that I had served him as a guide in the modern Tartarus, a place I know nothing of. He insolently proclaimed that I had spoken of the gods of Rome as false and lying gods, and that I held as the true God the present successor of Jupiter. Friend, when thou art restored to the kindly light of day and beholdest again thy native land, contradict those abominable falsehoods. Say to thy people that the singer of the pious Æneas has never worshipped the god of the Jews.

I am assured that his power is declining and that his approaching fall is manifested by undoubted indications. This news would give me some pleasure if one could rejoice in these abodes, where we feel neither fears nor desires."

He spoke, and with a gesture of farewell he went away. I beheld his shade gliding over the asphodels without bending their stalks. I saw that it became fainter and vaguer as it receded farther from me, and it vanished before it reached the wood of evergreen laurels. Then I understood the meaning of the words, "The dead have no life, but that which the living lend them," and I walked slowly through the pale meadow to the gate of horn.

I affirm that all in this writing is true.*

* There is in Marbodius's narrative a passage very worthy of notice, viz., that in which the monk of Corrigan describes Dante Alighieri such as we picture him to ourselves to-day. The miniatures in a very old manuscript of the "Divine Comedy," the "Codex Venetianus," represent the poet as a little fat man clad in a short tunic, the skirts of which fall above his knees. As for Virgil, he still wears the philosophical beard, in the wood-engravings of the sixteenth century.

One would not have thought either that Marbodius, or even Virgil, could have known the Etruscan tombs of Chiusi and Corneto, where, in fact, there are horrible and burlesque devils closely resembling those of Orcagna. Nevertheless, the authenticity of the "Descent of Marbodius into Hell" is indisputable. M. du Clos des Lunes has firmly established it. To doubt it would be to doubt palæography itself.

VII

SIGNS IN THE MOON

At that time, whilst Penguinia was still plunged in ignorance and barbarism, Giles Bird-catcher, a Franciscan
monk, known by his writings under the name Ægidius Aucupis, devoted himself with indefatigable zeal to the study of
letters and the sciences. He gave his nights to mathematics
and music, which he called the two adorable sisters, the
harmonious daughters of Number and Imagination. He was
versed in medicine and astrology. He was suspected of practis-
ing magic, and it seemed true that he wrought metamorphoses
and discovered hidden things.

The monks of his convent, finding in his cell Greek books
which they could not read, imagined them to be conjuring-
books, and denounced their too learned brother as a wizard.
Ægidius Aucupis fled, and reached the island of Ireland,
where he lived for thirty studious years. He went from monastery to monastery, searching for and copying the Greek and
Latin manuscripts which they contained. He also studied
physics and alchemy. He acquired a universal knowledge and
discovered notable secrets concerning animals, plants, and
stones. He was found one day in the company of a very
beautiful woman who sang to her own accompaniment on
the lute, and who was afterwards discovered to be a machine
which he had himself constructed.

He often crossed the Irish Sea to go into the land of
Wales and to visit the libraries of the monasteries there.
During one of these crossings, as he remained during the
night on the bridge of the ship, he saw beneath the waters
two sturgeons swimming side by side. He had very good hear-

ing and he knew the languages of the fishes. Now he heard one of the sturgeons say to the other:

"The man in the moon, whom we have often seen carrying fagots on his shoulders, has fallen into the sea."

And the other sturgeon said in its turn:

"And in the silver disk there will be seen the image of two lovers kissing each other on the mouth."

Some years later, having returned to his native country, Ægidius Aucupis found that ancient learning had been restored. Manners had softened. Men no longer pursued the nymphs of the fountains, of the woods, and of the mountains with their insults. They placed images of the Muses and of the modest Graces in their gardens, and they rendered her former honours to the Goddess with ambrosial lips, the joy of men and gods. They were becoming reconciled to nature. They trampled vain terrors beneath their feet and raised their eyes to heaven without fearing, as they formerly did, to read signs of anger and threats of damnation in the skies.

At this spectacle Ægidius Aucupis remembered what the two sturgeons of the sea of Erin had foretold.

BOOK IV

MODERN TIMES: TRINCO

I

MOTHER ROUQUIN

Ægidius Aucupis, the Erasmus of the Penguins, was not mistaken; his age was an age of free inquiry. But that great man mistook the elegances of the humanists for softness of manners, and he did not foresee the effects that the awaking of intelligence would have amongst the Penguins. It brought about the religious Reformation; Catholics massacred Protestants and Protestants massacred Catholics. Such were the first results of liberty of thought. The Catholics prevailed in Penguinia. But the spirit of inquiry had penetrated among them without their knowing it. They joined reason to faith, and claimed that religion had been divested of the superstitious practices that dishonoured it, just as in later days the booths that the cobblers, hucksters, and dealers in old clothes had built against the walls of the cathedrals were cleared away. The word, legend, which at first indicated what the faithful ought to read, soon suggested the idea of pious fables and childish tales.

The saints had to suffer from this state of mind. An obscure canon called Princeteau, a very austere and crabbed man, designated so great a number of them as not worthy of having their days observed, that he was surnamed the exposer of the saints. He did not think, for instance, that if St. Margaret's prayer were applied as a poultice to a woman in travail that the pains of childbirth would be softened.

Even the venerable patron saint of Penguinia did not escape his rigid criticism. This is what he says of her in his "Antiquities of Alca":

"Nothing is more uncertain than the history, or even the

existence, of St. Orberosia. An ancient anonymous annalist. a monk of Dombes, relates that a woman called Orberosia was possessed by the devil in a cavern where, even down to his own days, the little boys and girls of the village used to play at a sort of game representing the devil and the fair Orberosia. He adds that this woman became the concubine of a horrible dragon, who ravaged the country. Such a statement is hardly credible, but the history of Orberosia, as it has since been related, seems hardly more worthy of belief. The life of that saint by the Abbot Simplicissimus is three hundred years later than the pretended events which it relates and that author shows himself excessively credulous and devoid of all critical faculty."

Suspicion attacked even the supernatural origin of the Penguins. The historian Ovidius Capito went so far as to deny the miracle of their transformation. He thus begins his "Annals of Penguinia":

"A dense obscurity envelops this history, and it would be no exaggeration to say that it is a tissue of puerile fables and popular tales. The Penguins claim that they are descended from birds who were baptized by St. Maël and whom God changed into men at the intercession of that glorious apostle. They hold that, situated at first in the frozen ocean, their island, floating like Delos, was brought to anchor in these heaven-favoured seas, of which it is to-day the queen. I conclude that this myth is a reminiscence of the ancient migrations of the Penguins."

In the following century, which was that of the philosophers, scepticism became still more acute. No further evidence of it is needed than the following celebrated passage from the "Moral Essay":

"Arriving we know not from whence (for indeed their origins are not very clear), and successively invaded and conquered by four or five peoples from the north, south, east, and west, miscegenated, inter-bred, amalgamated, and commingled, the Penguins boast of the purity of their race, and with justice, for they have become a pure race. This mixture of all mankind, red, black, yellow, and white, round-headed and long-headed, has formed in the course of ages a fairly homogeneous human family, and one which is recognisable by certain features due to a community of life and customs.

"This idea that they belong to the best race in the world, and that they are its finest family, inspires them with noble pride, indomitable courage, and a hatred for the human race.

"The life of a people is but a succession of miseries, crimes, and follies. This is true of the Penguin nation, as of all other nations. Save for this exception its history is admirable from beginning to end."

The two classic ages of the Penguins are too well-known for me to lay stress upon them. But what has not been sufficiently noticed is the way in which the rationalist theologians such as Canon Princeteau called into existence the unbelievers of the succeeding age. The former employed their reason to destroy what did not seem to them essential to their religion; they only left untouched the most rigid article of faith. Their intellectual successors, being taught by them how to make use of science and reason, employed them against whatever beliefs remained. Thus rational theology engendered natural philosophy.

That is why (if I may turn from the Penguins of former days to the Sovereign Pontiff, who to-day governs the universal Church) we cannot admire too greatly the wisdom of Pope Pius X. in condemning the study of exegesis as contrary to revealed truth, fatal to sound theological doctrine, and deadly to the faith. Those clerics who maintain the rights of science in opposition to him are pernicious doctors and pestilent teachers, and the faithful who approve of them are lacking in either mental or moral ballast.

At the end of the age of philosophers, the ancient kingdom of Penguinia was utterly destroyed, the king put to death, the privileges of the nobles abolished, and a Republic proclaimed in the midst of public misfortunes and while a terrible war was raging. The assembly which then governed Penguinia ordered all the metal articles contained in the churches to be melted down. The patriots even desecrated the tombs of the kings. It is said that when the tomb of Draco the Great was opened, that king presented an appearance as black as ebony and so majestic that those who profaned his corpse fled in terror. According to other accounts, these churlish men insulted him by putting a pipe in his mouth ˅nd derisively offering him a glass of wine.

On the seventeenth day of the month of Mayflowers, the shrine of St. Orberosia, which had for five hundred years been exposed to the veneration of the faithful in the Church of St. Maël, was transported into the town-hall and submitted to the examination of a jury of experts appointed by the municipality. It was made of gilded copper in shape like the nave of a church, entirely covered with enamels and decorated with precious stones, which latter were perceived to be false. The chapter in its foresight had removed the rubies, sapphires, emeralds, and great balls of rock-crystal, and had substituted pieces of glass in their place. It contained only a little dust and a piece of old linen, which were thrown into a great fire that had been lighted on the Place de Grève to burn the relics of the saints. The people danced around it singing patriotic songs.

From the threshold of their booth, which leant against the town-hall, a man called Rouquin and his wife were watching this group of madmen. Rouquin clipped dogs and gelded cats; he also frequented the inns. His wife was a ragpicker and a bawd, but she had plenty of shrewdness.

"You see, Rouquin," said she to her man, "they are committing a sacrilege. They will repent of it."

"You know nothing about it, wife," answered Rouquin; "they have become philosophers, and when one is once a philosopher he is a philosopher for ever."

"I tell you, Rouquin, that sooner or later they will regret

what they are doing to-day. They ill-treat the saints because
they have not helped them enough, but for all that the quails
won't fall ready cooked into their mouths. They will soon
find themselves as badly off as before, and when they have
put out their tongues for enough they will become pious
again. Sooner than people think the day will come when
Penguinia will again begin to honour her blessed patron.
Rouquin, it would be a good thing, in readiness for that day,
if we kept a handful of ashes and some rags and bones in an
old pot in our lodgings. We will say that they are the relics
of St. Orberosia and that we have saved them from the flames
at the peril of our lives. I am greatly mistaken if we don't
get honour and profit out of them. That good action might
be worth a place from the Curé to sell tapers and hire chairs
in the chapel of St. Orberosia."

On that same day Mother Rouquin took home with her
a little ashes and some bones, and put them in an old jam-
pot in her cupboard.

II

TRINCO

THE sovereign Nation had taken possession of the lands of the nobility and clergy to sell them at a low price to the middle classes and the peasants. The middle classes and the peasants thought that the revolution was a good thing for acquiring lands and a bad one for retaining them.

The legislators of the Republic made terrible laws for the defence of property, and decreed death to anyone who should propose a division of wealth. But that did not avail the Republic. The peasants who had become proprietors bethought themselves that though it had made them rich, the Republic had nevertheless caused a disturbance to wealth, and they desired a system more respectful of private property and more capable of assuring the permanence of the new institutions.

They had not long to wait. The Republic, like Agrippina, bore her destroyer in her bosom.

Having great wars to carry on, it created military forces, and these were destined both to save it and to destroy it. Its legislators thought they could restrain their generals by the fear of punishment, but if they sometimes cut off the heads of unlucky soldiers they could not do the same to the fortunate soldiers who obtained over it the advantages of having saved its existence.

In the enthusiasm of victory the renovated Penguins delivered themselves up to a dragon, more terrible than that of their fables, who, like a stork amongst frogs, devoured them for fourteen years with his insatiable beak.

Half a century after the reign of the new dragon a young

Maharajah of Malay, called Djambi, desirous, like the Scythian Anacharsis, of instructing himself by travel, visited Penguinia and wrote an interesting account of his travels. I transcribe the first page of his account:

ACCOUNT OF THE TRAVELS OF YOUNG DJAMBI IN PENGUINIA

After a voyage of ninety days I landed at the vast and deserted port of the Penguins and travelled over untilled fields to their ruined capital. Surrounded by ramparts and full of barracks and arsenals it had a martial though desolate appearance. Feeble and crippled men wandered proudly through the streets, wearing old uniforms and carrying rusty weapons.

"What do you want?" I was rudely asked at the gate of the city by a soldier whose moustaches pointed to the skies.

"Sir," I answered, "I come as an inquirer to visit this island."

"It is not an island," replied the soldier.

"What!" I exclaimed, "Penguin Island is not an island?"

"No, sir, it is an insula. It was formerly called an island, but for a century it has been decreed that it shall bear the name of insula. It is the only insula in the whole universe. Have you a passport?"

"Here it is."

"Go and get it signed at the Ministry of Foreign Affairs."

A lame guide who conducted me came to a pause in a vast square.

"The insula," said he, "has given birth, as you know, to Trinco, the greatest genius of the universe, whose statue you see before you. That obelisk standing to your right commemorates Trinco's birth; the column that rises to your left has Trinco crowned with a diadem upon its summit. You see here the triumphal arch dedicated to the glory of Trinco and his family."

"What extraordinary feat has Trinco performed?" I asked.

"War."

"That is nothing extraordinary. We Malayans make war constantly."

"That may be, but Trinco is the greatest warrior of all countries and all times. There never existed a greater conqueror than he. As you anchored in our port you saw to the east a volcanic island called Ampelophoria, shaped like a cone, and of small size, but renowned for its wines. And to the west a larger island which raises to the sky a long range of sharp teeth; for this reason it is called the Dog's Jaws. It is rich in copper mines. We possessed both before Trinco's reign and they were the boundaries of our empire. Trinco extended the Penguin dominion over the Archipelago of the Turquoises and the Green Continent, subdued the gloomy Porpoises, and planted his flag amid the icebergs of the Pole and on the burning sands of the African deserts. He raised troops in all the countries he conquered, and when his armies marched past in the wake of our own light infantry, our island grenadiers, our hussars, our dragoons, our artillery, and our engineers there were to be seen yellow soldiers looking in their blue armour like crayfish standing on their tails; red men with parrots' plumes, tatooed with solar and Phallic emblems, and with quivers of poisoned arrows resounding on their backs; naked blacks armed only with their teeth and nails; pygmies riding on cranes; gorillas carrying trunks of trees and led by an old ape who wore upon his hairy breast the cross of the Legion of Honour. And all those troops, led to Trinco's banner by the most ardent patriotism, flew on from victory to victory, and in thirty years of war Trinco conquered half the known world."

"What!" cried I, "you possess half of the world."

"Trinco conquered it for us, and Trinco lost it to us. As great in his defeats as in his victories he surrendered all that he had conquered. He even allowed those two islands we possessed before his time, Ampelophoria and the Dog's Jaws, to be taken from us. He left Penguinia impoverished and depopulated. The flower of the insula perished in his wars. At the time of his fall there were left in our country none but the hunchbacks and cripples from whom we are descended. But he gave us glory."

"He made you pay dearly for it!"

"Glory never costs too much," replied my guide.

III

THE JOURNEY OF DOCTOR OBNUBILE

AFTER a succession of amazing vicissitudes, the memory of which is in great part lost by the wrongs of time and the bad style of historians, the Penguins established the government of the Penguins by themselves. They elected a diet or assembly, and invested it with the privilege of naming the Head of the State. The latter, chosen from among the simple Penguins, wore no formidable monster's crest upon his head and exercised no absolute authority over the people. He was himself subject to the laws of the nation. He was not given the title of king, and no ordinal number followed his name. He bore such names as Paturle, Janvion, Truffaldin, Coquenhot, and Bredouille. These magistrates did not make war. They were not suited for that.

The new state received the name of Public Thing or Republic. Its partisans were called republicanists or republicans. They were also named Thingmongers and sometimes Scamps, but this latter name was taken in ill part.

The Penguin democracy did not itself govern. It obeyed a financial oligarchy which formed opinion by means of the newspapers, and held in its hands the representatives, the ministers, and the president. It controlled the finances of the republic, and directed the foreign affairs of the country as if it were possessed of sovereign power.

Empires and kingdoms in those days kept up enormous fleets. Penguinia, compelled to do as they did, sank under the pressure of her armaments. Everybody deplored or pretended to deplore so grievous a necessity. However, the rich, and those engaged in business or affairs, submitted to it with a good heart through a spirit of patriotism, and because they counted on the soldiers and sailors to defend their goods at home and to acquire markets and territories abroad. The great manufacturers encouraged the making of cannons and ships through a zeal for the national defence and in order to obtain orders. Among the citizens of middle rank and of the liberal professions some resigned themselves to this state of affairs without complaining, believing that it would last for ever; others waited impatiently for its end and thought they might be able to lead the powers to a simultaneous disarmament.

The illustrious Professor Obnubile belonged to this latter class.

"War," said he, "is a barbarity to which the progress of civilization will put an end. The great democracies are pacific and will soon impose their will upon the aristocrats."

Professor Obnubile, who had for sixty years led a solitary and retired life in his laboratory, whither external noises did not penetrate, resolved to observe the spirit of the peoples for himself. He began his studies with the greatest of all democracies and set sail for New Atlantis.

After a voyage of fifteen days his steamer entered, during the night, the harbour of Titanport, where thousands of ships were anchored. An iron bridge thrown across the water and shining with lights, stretched between two piers so far apart that Professor Obnubile imagined he was sailing on the seas of Saturn and that he saw the marvellous ring which girds the planet of the Old Man. And this immense conduit bore upon it more than a quarter of the wealth of the world. The learned Penguin, having disembarked, was waited on by automatons in a hotel forty-eight stories high. Then he took the great railway that led to Gigantopolis, the capital of New Atlantis. In the train there were restaurants, gaming-rooms, athletic arenas, telegraphic, commercial, and financial offices, a Protestant Church, and the printing-office of a great newspaper, which latter the doctor was unable to read, as he did not know the language of the New Atlantans. The train passed along the banks of great rivers, through manufacturing cities which concealed the sky with the smoke from their chimneys, towns black in the day, towns red at night, full of noise by day and full of noise also by night.

"Here," thought the doctor, "is a people far too much engaged in industry and trade to make war. I am already certain that the New Atlantans pursue a policy of peace. For it is an axiom admitted by all economists that peace without and peace within are necessary for the progress of commerce and industry."

As he surveyed Gigantopolis, he was confirmed in this opinion. People went through the streets so swiftly propelled by hurry that they knocked down all who were in their way. Obnubile was thrown down several times, but soon succeeded in learning how to demean himself better; after an hour's walking he himself knocked down an Atlantan.

Having reached a great square he saw the portico of a palace in the classic style, whose Corinthian columns reared their capitals of arborescent acanthus seventy metres above the stylobate.

As he stood with his head thrown back admiring the building, a man of modest appearance approached him and said in Penguin:

"I see by your dress that you are from Penguinia. I know your language; I am a sworn interpreter. This is the Parliament palace. At the present moment the representatives of the States are in deliberation. Would you like to be present at the sitting?"

The doctor was brought into the hall and cast his looks upon the crowd of legislators who were sitting on cane chairs with their feet upon their desks.

The President arose and, in the midst of general inattention, muttered rather than spoke the following formulas which the interpreter immediately translated to the doctor.

"The war for the opening of the Mongol markets being

ended to the satisfaction of the States, I propose that the accounts be laid before the finance committee. . . ."

"Is there any opposition? . . ."

"The proposal is carried."

"The war for the opening of the markets of Third-Zealand being ended to the satisfaction of the States, I propose that the accounts be laid before the finance committee. . . ."

"Is there any opposition? . . ."

"The proposal is carried."

"Have I heard aright?" asked Professor Obnubile. "What? you an industrial people and engaged in all these wars!"

"Certainly," answered the interpreter, "these are industrial wars. Peoples who have neither commerce nor industry are not obliged to make war, but a business people is forced to adopt a policy of conquest. The number of wars necessarily increases with our productive activity. As soon as one of our industries fails to find a market for its products a war is necessary to open new outlets. It is in this way we have had a coal war, a copper war, and a cotton war. In Third-Zealand we have killed two-thirds of the inhabitants in order to compel the remainder to buy our umbrellas and braces."

At that moment a fat man who was sitting in the middle of the assembly ascended the tribune.

"I claim," said he, "a war against the Emerald Republic, which insolently contends with our pigs for the hegemony of hams and sauces in all the markets of the universe."

"Who is that legislator?" asked Doctor Obnubile.

"He is a pig merchant."

"Is there any opposition?" said the President. "I put the proposition to the vote."

The war against the Emerald Republic was voted with uplifted hands by a very large majority.

"What?" said Obnubile to the interpreter; "you have voted a war with that rapidity and that indifference!"

"Oh! it is an unimportant war which will hardly cost eight million dollars."

"And men . . ."

"The men are included in the eight million dollars."

Then Doctor Obnubile bent his head in bitter reflection.

"Since wealth and civilization admit of as many causes of wars as poverty and barbarism, since the folly and wickedness of men are incurable, there remains but one good action to be done. The wise man will collect enough dynamite to blow up this planet. When its fragments fly through space an imperceptible amelioration will be accomplished in the universe and a satisfaction will be given to the universal conscience. Moreover, this universal conscience does not exist."

BOOK V

MODERN TIMES: CHATILLON

THE REVEREND FATHERS AGARIC
AND CORNEMUSE

EVERY system of government produces people who are dissatisfied. The Republic or Public Thing produced them at
first from among the nobles who had been despoiled of their
ancient privileges. These looked with regret and hope to
Prince Crucho, the last of the Draconides, a prince adorned
both with the grace of youth and the melancholy of exile. It
also produced them from among the smaller traders, who,
owing to profound economic causes, no longer gained a liveli-
hood. They believed that this was the fault of the republic
which they had at first adored and from which each day they
were now becoming more detached. The financiers, both
Christians and Jews, became by their insolence and their
cupidity the scourge of the country, which they plundered
and degraded, as well as the scandal of a government which
they never troubled either to destroy or preserve, so confident
were they that they could operate without hindrance under all
governments. Nevertheless, their sympathies inclined to absolute power as the best protection against the socialists, their
puny but ardent adversaries. And just as they imitated the
habits of the aristocrats, so they imitated their political and
religious sentiments. Their women, in particular, loved the
Prince and had dreams of appearing one day at his Court.

However, the Republic retained some partisans and defenders. If it was not in a position to believe in the fidelity of its
own officials it could at least still count on the devotion of the
manual labourers, although it had never relieved their misery.
These came forth in crowds from their quarries and their fac-

tories to defend it, and marched in long processions, gloomy,
emaciated, and sinister. They would have died for it because
it had given them hope.

Now, under the Presidency of Theodore Formose, there
lived in a peaceable suburb of Alca a monk called Agaric, who
kept a school and assisted in arranging marriages. In his school
he taught fencing and riding to the sons of old families, illustrious by their birth, but now as destitute of wealth as of
privilege. And as soon as they were old enough he married
them to the daughters of the opulent and despised caste of
financiers.

Tall, thin, and dark, Agaric used to walk in deep thought,
with his breviary in his hand and his brow loaded with care,
through the corridors of the school and the alleys of the garden. His care was not limited to inculcating in his pupils
abstruse doctrines and mechanical precepts and to endowing
them afterwards with legitimate and rich wives. He entertained political designs and pursued the realisation of a gigantic plan. His thought of thoughts and labour of labours was
to overthrow the Republic. He was not moved to this by any
personal interest. He believed that a democratic state was
opposed to the holy society to which body and soul he belonged. And all the other monks, his brethren, thought the
same. The Republic was perpetually at strife with the congregation of monks and the assembly of the faithful. True, to plot
the death of the new government was a difficult and perilous
enterprise. Still, Agaric was in a position to carry on a formidable conspiracy. At that epoch, when the clergy guided the
superior classes of the Penguins, this monk exercised a tremendous influence over the aristocracy of Alca.

All the young men whom he had brought up waited only
for a favourable moment to march against the popular power.
The sons of the ancient families did not practise the arts or
engage in business. They were almost all soldiers and served
the Republic. They served it, but they did not love it; they
regretted the dragon's crest. And the fair Jewesses shared in

these regrets in order that they might be taken for Christians.

One July as he was walking in a suburban street which ended in some dusty fields, Agaric heard groans coming from a moss-grown well that had been abandoned by the gardeners. And almost immediately he was told by a cobbler of the neighbourhood that a ragged man who had shouted out "Hurrah for the Republic!" had been thrown into the well by some cavalry officers who were passing, and had sunk up to his ears in the mud. Agaric was quite ready to see a general significance in this particular fact. He inferred a great fermentation in the whole aristocratic and military caste, and concluded that it was the moment to act.

The next day he went to the end of the Wood of Conils to visit the good Father Cornemuse. He found the monk in his laboratory pouring a golden-coloured liquor into a still. He was a short, fat little man, with vermilion-tinted cheeks and elaborately polished bald head. His eyes had ruby-coloured pupils like a guinea-pig's. He graciously saluted his visitor and offered him a glass of the St. Orberosian liqueur, which he manufactured, and from the sale of which he gained immense wealth.

Agaric made a gesture of refusal. Then, standing on his long feet and pressing his melancholy hat against his stomach, he remained silent.

"Take a seat," said Cornemuse to him.

Agaric sat down on a rickety stool, but continued mute.

Then the monk of Conils inquired:

"Tell me some news of your young pupils. Have the dear children sound views?"

"I am very satisfied with them," answered the teacher. "It is everything to be nurtured in sound principles. It is necessary to have sound views before having any views at all, for afterwards it is too late. . . . Yes, I have great grounds for comfort. But we live in a sad age."

"Alas!" sighed Cornemuse.

"We are passing through evil days. . . ."

"Times of trial."

"Yet, Cornemuse, the mind of the public is not so entirely corrupted as it seems."

"Perhaps you are right."

"The people are tired of a government that ruins them and does nothing for them. Every day fresh scandals spring up. The Republic is sunk in shame. It is ruined."

"May God grant it!"

"Cornemuse, what do you think of Prince Crucho?"

"He is an amiable young man and, I dare say, a worthy scion of an august stock. I pity him for having to endure the pains of exile at so early an age. Spring has no flowers for the exile, and autumn no fruits. Prince Crucho has sound views; he respects the clergy; he practises our religion; besides, he consumes a good deal of my little products."

"Cornemuse, in many homes, both rich and poor, his return is hoped for. Believe me, he will come back."

"May I live to throw my mantle beneath his feet!" sighed Cornemuse.

Seeing that he held these sentiments, Agaric depicted to him the state of people's minds such as he himself imagined them. He showed him the nobles and the rich exasperated against the popular government; the army refusing to endure fresh insults; the officials willing to betray their chiefs; the people discontented, riot ready to burst forth, and the enemies of the monks, the agents of the constituted authority, thrown into the wells of Alca. He concluded that it was the moment to strike a great blow.

"We can," he cried, "save the Penguin people, we can deliver it from its tyrants, deliver it from itself, restore the Dragon's crest, re-establish the ancient State, the good State, for the honour of the faith and the exaltation of the Church. We can do this if we will. We possess great wealth and we exert secret influences; by our evangelistic and outspoken journals we communicate with all the ecclesiastics in towns and county alike, and we inspire them with our own eager enthusi-

asm and our own burning faith. They will kindle their peni-
tents and their congregations. I can dispose of the chiefs of
the army; I have an understanding with the men of the
people. Unknown to them I sway the minds of umbrella sellers,
publicans, shopmen, gutter merchants, newspaper boys,
women of the streets, and police agents. We have more people
on our side than we need. What are we waiting for? Let us
act!"

"What do you think of doing?" asked Cornemuse.

"Of forming a vast conspiracy and overthrowing the Republic, of re-establishing Crucho on the throne of the
Draconides."

Cornemuse moistened his lips with his tongue several times.
Then he said with unction:

"Certainly the restoration of the Draconides is desirable;
it is eminently desirable; and for my part, I desire it with all
my heart. As for the Republic, you know what I think of it.
... But would it not be better to abandon it to its fate and
let it die of the vices of its own constitution? Doubtless, Agaric,
what you propose is noble and generous. It would be a fine
thing to save this great and unhappy country, to re-establish
it in its ancient splendour. But reflect on it, we are Christians
before we are Penguins. And we must take heed not to compromise religion in political enterprises."

Agaric replied eagerly:

"Fear nothing. We shall hold all the threads of the plot,
but we ourselves shall remain in the background. We shall
not be seen."

"Like flies in milk," murmured the monk of Conils.

And turning his keen ruby-coloured eyes towards his brother
monk:

"Take care. Perhaps the Republic is stronger than it seems.
Possibly, too, by dragging it out of the nerveless inertia in
which it now rests we may only consolidate its forces. Its
malice is great; if we attack it, it will defend itself. It makes
bad laws which hardly affect us; if it is frightened it will make

terrible ones against us. Let us not lightly engage in an adventure in which we may get fleeced. You think the opportunity a
good one. I don't, and I am going to tell you why. The present
government is not yet known by everybody, that is to say,
it is known by nobody. It proclaims that it is the Public Thing,
the common thing. The populace believes it and remains democratic and Republican. But patience! This same people will
one day demand that the public thing be the people's thing.
I need not tell you how insolent, unregulated, and contrary
to Scriptural polity such claims seem to me. But the people will
make them, and enforce them, and then there will be an end
of the present government. The moment cannot now be far
distant; and it is then that we ought to act in the interests of
our august body. Let us wait. What hurries us? Our existence
is not in peril. It has not been rendered absolutely intolerable
to us. The Republic fails in respect and submission to us; it
does not give the priests the honours it owes them. But it lets
us live. And such is the excellence of our position that with us
to live is to prosper. The Republic is hostile to us, but women
revere us. President Formose does not assist at the celebration
of our mysteries, but I have seen his wife and daughters at
my feet. They buy my phials by the gross. I have no better
clients even among the aristocracy. Let us say what there is
to be said for it. There is no country in the world as good for
priests and monks as Penguinia. In what other country would
you find our virgin wax, our virile incense, our rosaries, our
scapulars, our holy water, and our St. Orberosian liqueur sold
in such great quantities? What other people would, like the
Penguins, give a hundred golden crowns for a wave of our
hands, a sound from our mouths, a movement of our lips? For
my part, I gain a thousand times more, in this pleasant, faithful, and docile Penguinia, by extracting the essence from a
bundle of thyme, than I could make by tiring my lungs with
preaching the remission of sins in the most populous States
of Europe and America. Honestly, would Penguinia be better

off if a police officer came to take me away from here and put me on a steamboat bound for the Islands of Night?"

Having thus spoken, the monk of Conils got up and led his guest into a huge shed where hundreds of orphans clothed in blue were packing bottles, nailing up cases, and gumming tickets. The ear was deafened by the noise of hammers mingled with the dull rumbling of bales being placed upon the rails.

"It is from here that consignments are forwarded," said Cornemuse. "I have obtained from the government a railway through the Wood and a station at my door. Every three days I fill a truck with my own products. You see that the Republic has not killed all beliefs."

Agaric made a last effort to engage the wise distiller in his enterprise. He pointed him to a prompt, certain, dazzling success.

"Don't you wish to share in it?" he added. "Don't you wish to bring back your king from exile?"

"Exile is pleasant to men of good will," answered the monk of Conils. "If you are guided by me, my dear Brother Agaric, you will give up your project for the present. For my own part I have no illusions. Whether or not I belong to your party, if you lose, I shall have to pay like you."

Father Agaric took leave of his friend and went back satisfied to his school. "Cornemuse," thought he, "not being able to prevent the plot, would like to make it succeed and he will give money." Agaric was not deceived. Such, indeed, was the solidarity among priests and monks that the acts of a single one bound them all. That was at once both their strength and their weakness.

II

PRINCE CRUCHO

AGARIC resolved to proceed without delay to Prince Crucho, who honoured him with his familiarity. In the dusk of the evening he went out of his school by the side door, disguised as a cattle merchant and took passage on board the *St. Maël*.

The next day he landed in Porpoisia, for it was at Chitterlings Castle on this hospitable soil that Crucho ate the bitter bread of exile.

Agaric met the prince on the road driving in a motor-car with two young ladies at the rate of a hundred miles an hour. When the monk saw him he shook his red umbrella and the prince stopped his car.

"Is it you, Agaric? Get in! There are already three of us, but we can make room for you. You can take one of these young ladies on your knee."

The pious Agaric got in.

"What news, worthy father?" asked the young prince.

"Great news," answered Agaric. "Can I speak?"

"You can. I have nothing secret from these two ladies."

"Sire, Penguinia claims you. You will not be deaf to her call."

Agaric described the state of feeling and outlined a vast plot.

"On my first signal," said he, "all your partisans will rise at once. With cross in hand and habits girded up, your venerable clergy will lead the armed crowd into Formose's palace. We shall carry terror and death among your enemies. For a reward of our efforts we only ask of you, Sire, that you will not render them useless. We entreat you to come and seat yourself on the throne that we shall prepare."

The prince returned a simple answer:

"I shall enter Alca on a green horse."

Agaric declared that he accepted this manly response. Although contrary to his custom, he had a lady on his knee, he adjured the young prince, with a sublime loftiness of soul, to be faithful to his royal duties.

"Sire," he cried with tears in his eyes, "you will live to remember the day on which you have been restored from exile, given back to your people, re-established on the throne of your ancestors by the hands of your monks, and crowned by them with the august crest of the Dragon. King Crucho, may you equal the glory of your ancestor Draco the Great!"

The young prince threw himself with emotion on his restorer and attempted to embrace him, but he was prevented from reaching him by the girth of the two ladies, so tightly packed were they all in that historic carriage.

"Worthy father," said he, "I would like all Penguinia to witness this embrace."

"It would be a cheering spectacle," said Agaric.

In the mean time the motor-car rushed like a tornado through hamlets and villages, crushing hens, geese, turkeys, ducks, guinea-fowls, cats, dogs, pigs, children, labourers, and women beneath its insatiable tyres. And the pious Agaric turned over his great designs in his mind. His voice, coming from behind one of the ladies, expressed this thought:

"We must have money, a great deal of money."

"That is your business," answered the prince.

But already the park gates were opening to the formidable motor-car.

The dinner was sumptuous. They toasted the Dragon's crest. Everybody knows that a closed goblet is a sign of sovereignty; so Prince Crucho and Princess Gudrune, his wife, drank out of goblets that were covered over like ciboriums. The prince had his filled several times with the wines of Penguinia, both white and red.

Crucho had received a truly princely education, and he

excelled in motoring, but was not ignorant of history either.
He was said to be well versed in the antiquities and famous
deeds of his family; and, indeed, he gave a notable proof of
his knowledge in this respect. As they were speaking of the
various remarkable peculiarities that had been noticed in
famous women,

"It is perfectly true," said he, "that Queen Crucha, whose
name I bear, had the mark of a little monkey's head upon
her body."

During the evening Agaric had a decisive interview with
three of the prince's oldest councillors. It was decided to ask
for funds from Crucho's father-in-law, as he was anxious to
have a king for son-in-law, from several Jewish ladies, who
were impatient to become ennobled, and, finally, from the
Prince Regent of the Porpoises, who had promised his aid to
the Draconides, thinking that by Crucho's restoration he
would weaken the Penguins, the hereditary enemies of his
people. The three old councillors divided among themselves
the three chief offices of the Court, those of Chamberlain,
Seneschal, and High Steward, and authorised the monk to
distribute the other places to the prince's best advantage.

"Devotion has to be rewarded," said the three old councillors.

"And treachery also," said Agaric.

"It is but too true," replied one of them, the Marquis of
Sevenwounds, who had experience of revolutions.

There was dancing, and after the ball Princess Gudrune tore
up her green robe to make cockades. With her own hands she
sewed a piece of it on the monk's breast, upon which he shed
tears of sensibility and gratitude.

M. de Plume, the prince's equerry, set out the same evening
to look for a green horse.

III

THE CABAL

AFTER his return to the capital of Penguinia, the Reverend Father Agaric disclosed his projects to Prince Adélestan des Boscénos, of whose Draconian sentiments he was well aware.

The prince belonged to the highest nobility. The Torticol des Boscénos went back to Brian the Good, and under the Draconides had held the highest offices in the kingdom. In 1179, Philip Torticol, High Admiral of Penguinia, a brave, faithful, and generous, but vindictive man, delivered over the port of La Cirque and the Penguin fleet to the enemies of the kingdom, because he suspected that Queen Crucha, whose lover he was, had been unfaithful to him and loved a stable-boy. It was that great queen who gave to the Boscénos the silver warming-pan which they bear in their arms. As for their motto, it only goes back to the sixteenth century. The story of its origin is as follows: One gala night, as he mingled with the crowd of courtiers who were watching the fire-works in the king's garden, Duke John des Boscénos approached the Duchess of Skull and put his hand under the petticoat of that lady, who made no complaint at the gesture. The king, happening to pass, surprised them and contented himself with saying, "And thus I find you." These four words became the motto of the Boscénos.

Prince Adélestan had not degenerated from his ancestors. He preserved an unalterable fidelity for the race of the Draconides and desired nothing so much as the restoration of Prince Crucho, an event which was in his eyes to be the fore-runner of the restoration of his own fortune. He therefore readily entered into the Reverend Father Agaric's plans. He joined himself at once to the monk's projects, and hastened to put him into communication with the most loyal Royalists of his acquaintance, Count Cléna, M. de La Trumelle, Viscount Olive, and M. Bigourd. They met together one night in the Duke of Ampoule's country house, six miles eastward of Alca, to consider ways and means.

M. de La Trumelle was in favour of legal action.

"We ought to keep within the law," said he in substance. "We are for order. It is by an untiring propaganda that we shall best pursue the realisation of our hopes. We must change the feeling of the country. Our cause will conquer because it is just."

The Prince des Boscénos expressed a contrary opinion. He thought that, in order to triumph, just causes need force quite as much and even more than unjust causes require it.

"In the present situation," said he tranquilly, "three methods of action present themselves: to hire the butcher boys, to corrupt the ministers, and to kidnap President Formose."

"It would be a mistake to kidnap Formose," objected M. de La Trumelle. "The President is on our side."

The attitude and sentiments of the President of the Republic are explained by the fact that one Dracophil proposed to seize Formose while another Dracophil regarded him as a friend. Formose showed himself favourable to the Royalists, whose habits he admired and imitated. If he smiled at the mention of the Dragon's crest it was at the thought of putting it on his own head. He was envious of sovereign power, not because he felt himself capable of exercising it, but because he loved to appear so. According to the expression of a Penguin chronicler, "he was a goose."

Prince des Boscénos maintained his proposal to march against Formose's palace and the House of Parliament.

Count Cléna was even still more energetic.

"Let us begin," said he, "by slaughtering, disembowelling, and braining the Republicans and all partisans of the government. Afterwards we shall see what more need be done."

M. de La Trumelle was a moderate, and moderates are always moderately opposed to violence. He recognised that Count Cléna's policy was inspired by a noble feeling and that it was high-minded, but he timidly objected that perhaps it was not conformable to principle, and that it presented certain dangers. At last he consented to discuss it.

"I propose," added he, "to draw up an appeal to the people. Let us show who we are. For my own part I can assure you that I shall not hide my flag in my pocket."

M. Bigourd began to speak.

"Gentlemen, the Penguins are dissatisfied with the new order because it exists, and it is natural for men to complain of their condition. But at the same time the Penguins are afraid to change their government because new things alarm them. They have not known the Dragon's crest and, although they sometimes say that they regret it, we must not believe them. It is easy to see that they speak in this way either without thought or because they are in an ill-temper. Let us not have any illusions about their feelings towards ourselves. They do not like us. They hate the aristocracy both from a base envy and from a generous love of equality. And these two united feelings are very strong in a people. Public opinion is not against us, because it knows nothing about us. But when it knows what we want it will not follow us. If we let it be seen that we wish to destroy democratic government and restore the Dragon's crest, who will be our partisans? Only the butcher-boys and the little shopkeepers of Alca. And could we even count on them to the end? They are dissatisfied, but at the bottom of their hearts they are Republicans. They are more anxious to sell their cursed wares than to see Crucho again. If we act openly we shall only cause alarm.

"To make people sympathise with us and follow us we must make them believe that we want, not to overthrow the Republic, but, on the contrary, to restore it, to cleanse, to purify, to embellish, to adorn, to beautify, and to ornament it, to render it, in a word, glorious and attractive. Therefore, we ought not to act openly ourselves. It is known that we are not favourable to the present order. We must have recourse to a friend of the Republic, and, if we are to do what is best, to a defender of this government. We have plenty to choose from. It would be well to prefer the most popular and, if I dare say so, the most republican of them. We shall win him over to us by flattery, by presents, and above all by promises. Promises cost less than presents, and are worth more. No one gives as much as he who gives hopes. It is not necessary for the man we choose to be of brilliant intellect. I would even prefer him to be of no great ability. Stupid people show an inimitable grace in roguery. Be guided by me, gentlemen, and overthrow the Republic by the agency of a Republican. Let us be prudent. But prudence does not exclude energy. If you need me you will find me at your disposal."

This speech made a great impression upon those who heard it. The mind of the pious Agaric was particularly impressed. But each of them was anxious to appoint himself to a position of honour and profit. A secret government was organised of which all those present were elected active members. The Duke of Ampoule, who was the great financier of the party, was chosen treasurer and charged with organising funds for the propaganda.

The meeting was on the point of coming to an end when a rough voice was heard singing an old air:

> Boscénos est un gros cochon;
> On en va faire des audouilles
> Des saucisses et du jambon
> Pour le réveillon des pauv' bougres.

It had, for two hundred years, been a well-known song in the slums of Alca. Prince Boscénos did not like to hear it. He went down into the street, and, perceiving that the singer was a workman who was placing some slates on the roof of a church, he politely asked him to sing something else.

"I will sing what I like," answered the man.

"My friend, to please me...."

"I don't want to please you."

Prince Boscénos was as a rule good-tempered, but he was easily angered and a man of great strength.

"Fellow, come down or I will go up to you," cried he, in a terrible voice.

As the workman, astride on his coping, showed no sign of budging, the prince climbed quickly up the staircase of the tower and attacked the singer. He gave him a blow that broke his jaw-bone and sent him rolling into a water-spout. At that moment seven or eight carpenters, who were working on the rafters, heard their companion's cry and looked through the window. Seeing the prince on the coping they climbed along a ladder that was leaning on the slates and reached him just as he was slipping into the tower. They sent him, head foremost, down the one hundred and thirty-seven steps of the spiral staircase.

IV

VISCOUNTESS OLIVE

THE Penguins had the finest army in the world. So had the Porpoises. And it was the same with the other nations of Europe. The smallest amount of thought will prevent any surprise at this. For all armies are the finest in the world. The second finest army, if one could exist, would be in a notoriously inferior position; it would be certain to be beaten. It ought to be disbanded at once. Therefore, all armies are the finest in the world. In France the illustrious Colonel Marchand understood this when, before the passage of the Yalou, being questioned by some journalists about the Russo-Japanese war, he did not hesitate to describe the Russian army as the finest in the world, and also the Japanese. And it should be noticed that even after suffering the most terrible reverses an army does not fall from its position of being the finest in the world. For if nations ascribe their victories to the ability of their generals and the courage of their soldiers, they always attribute their defeats to an inexplicable fatality. On the other hand, navies are classed according to the number of their ships. There is a first, a second, a third, and so on. So that there exists no doubt as to the result of naval wars.

The Penguins had the finest army and the second navy in the world. This navy was commanded by the famous Chatillon, who bore the title of Emiralbahr, and by abbreviation Emiral. It is the same word which, unfortunately in a corrupt form, is used to-day among several European nations to designate the highest grade in the naval service. But as there was but one Emiral among the Penguins, a singular prestige, if I dare say so, was attached to that rank.

The Emiral did not belong to the nobility. A child of the people, he was loved by the people. They were flattered to see a man who sprang from their own ranks holding a position of honour. Chatillon was good-looking and fortune favoured him. He was not over-addicted to thought. No event ever disturbed his serene outlook.

The Reverend Father Agaric, surrendering to M. Bigourd's reasons and recognising that the existing government could only be destroyed by one of its defenders, cast his eyes upon Emiral Chatillon. He asked a large sum of money from his friend, the Reverend Father Cornemuse, which the latter handed him with a sigh. And with this sum he hired six hundred butcher boys of Alca to run behind Chatillon's horse and shout, "Hurrah for the Emiral!" Henceforth Chatillon could not take a single step without being cheered.

Viscountess Olive asked him for a private interview. He received her at the Admiralty * in a room decorated with anchors, shells, and grenades.

She was discreetly dressed in greyish blue. A hat trimmed with roses covered her pretty, fair hair. Behind her veil her eyes shone like sapphires. Although she came of Jewish origin there was no more fashionable woman in the whole nobility. She was tall and well shaped; her form was that of the year, her figure that of the season.

"Emiral," said she, in a delightful voice, "I cannot conceal my emotion from you. . . . It is very natural . . . before a hero."

"You are too kind. But tell me, Viscountess, what brings me the honour of your visit."

"For a long time I have been anxious to see you, to speak to you. . . . So I very willingly undertook to convey a message to you."

"Please take a seat."

"How still it is here."

"Yes, it is quiet enough."

"You can hear the birds singing."

* Or better, *Emiralty*.

"Sit down, then, dear lady."

And he drew up an arm-chair for her.

She took a seat with her back to the light.

"Emiral, I came to bring you a very important message, a message . . ."

"Explain."

"Emiral, have you ever seen Prince Crucho?"

"Never."

She sighed.

"It is a great pity. He would be so delighted to see you! He esteems and appreciates you. He has your portrait on his desk beside his mother's. What a pity it is he is not better known! He is a charming prince and so grateful for what is done for him! He will be a great king. For he will be king without doubt. He will come back and sooner than people think. . . . What I have to tell you, the message with which I am entrusted, refers precisely to . . ."

The Emiral stood up.

"Not a word more, dear lady. I have the esteem, the confidence of the Republic. I will not betray it. And why should I betray it? I am loaded with honours and dignities."

"Allow me to tell you, my dear Emiral, that your honours and dignities are far from equalling what you deserve. If your services were properly rewarded, you would be Emiralissimo and Generalissimo, Commander-in-chief of the troops both on land and sea. The Republic is very ungrateful to you."

"All governments are more or less ungrateful."

"Yes, but the Republicans are jealous of you. That class of person is always afraid of his superiors. They cannot endure the Services. Everything that has to do with the navy and the army is odious to them. They are afraid of you."

"That is possible."

"They are wretches; they are ruining the country. Don't you wish to save Penguinia?"

"In what way?"

"By sweeping away all the rascals of the Republic, all the Republicans."

"What a proposal to make to me, dear lady!"

"It is what will certainly be done, if not by you, then by some one else. The Generalissimo, to mention him alone, is ready to throw all the ministers, deputies, and senators into the sea, and to recall Prince Crucho."

"Oh, the rascal, the scoundrel," exclaimed the Emiral.

"Do to him what he would do to you. The prince will know how to recognise your services. He will give you the Constable's sword and a magnificent grant. I am commissioned, in the mean time, to hand you a pledge of his royal friendship."

As she said these words she drew a green cockade from her bosom.

"What is that?" asked the Emiral.

"It is his colours which Crucho sends you."

"Be good enough to take them back."

"So that they may be offered to the Generalissimo who will accept them! ... No, Emiral, let me place them on your glorious breast."

Chatillon gently repelled the lady. But for some minutes he thought her extremely pretty, and he felt this impression still more when two bare arms and the rosy palms of two delicate hands touched him lightly. He yielded almost immediately. Olive was slow in fastening the ribbon. Then when it was done she made a low courtesy and saluted Chatillon with the title of Constable.

"I have been ambitious like my comrades," answered the sailor, "I don't hide it, and perhaps I am so still; but upon my word of honour, when I look at you, the only desire I feel is for a cottage and a heart."

She turned upon him the charming sapphire glances that flashed from under her eyelids.

"That is to be had also ... what are you doing, Emiral?"

"I am looking for the heart."

When she left the Admiralty, the Viscountess went immediately to the Reverend Father Agaric to give an account of her visit.

"You must go to him again, dear lady," said that austere monk.

V

THE PRINCE DES BOSCÉNOS

MORNING and evening the newspapers that had been bought by the Dracophils proclaimed Chatillon's praises and hurled shame and opprobrium upon the Ministers of the Republic Chatillon's portrait was sold through the streets of Alca Those young descendants of Remus who carry plaster figures on their heads, offered busts of Chatillon for sale upon the bridges.

Every evening Chatillon rode upon his white horse round the Queen's Meadow, a place frequented by the people of fashion. The Dracophils posted along the Emiral's route a crowd of needy Penguins who kept shouting: "It is Chatillon we want." The middle classes of Alca conceived a profound admiration for the Emiral. Shopwomen murmured: "He is good-looking." Women of fashion slackened the speed of their motor-cars and kissed hands to him as they passed, amidst the hurrahs of an enthusiastic populace.

One day, as he went into a tobacco shop, two Penguins who were putting letters in the box recognised Chatillon and cried at the top of their voices: "Hurrah for the Emiral! Down with the Republicans." All those who were passing stopped in front of the shop. Chatillon lighted his cigar before the eyes of a dense crowd of frenzied citizens who waved their hats and cheered. The crowd kept increasing, and the whole town, singing and marching behind its hero, went back with him to the Admiralty.

The Emiral had an old comrade in arms, Under-Emiral Vulcanmould, who had served with great distinction, a man as true as gold and as loyal as his sword. Vulcanmould plumed

153

himself on his thoroughgoing independence and he went among the partisans of Crucho and the Ministers of the Republic telling both parties what he thought of them. M. Bigourd maliciously declared that he told each party what the other party thought of it. In truth he had on several occasions been guilty of regrettable indiscretions, which were overlooked as being the freedoms of a soldier who knew nothing of intrigue. Every morning he went to see Chatillon, whom he treated with the cordial roughness of a brother in arms.

"Well, old buffer, so you are popular," said he to him. "Your phiz is sold on the heads of pipes and on liqueur bottles and every drunkard in Alca spits out your name as he rolls in the gutter. . . . Chatillon, the hero of the Penguins! Chatillon, defender of the Penguin glory! . . . Who would have said it? Who would have thought it?"

And he laughed with his harsh laugh. Then changing his tone:

"But, joking aside, are you not a bit surprised at what is happening to you?"

"No, indeed," answered Chatillon.

And out went the honest Vulcanmould, banging the door behind him.

In the mean time Chatillon had taken a little flat at number 18 Johannes-Talpa Street, so that he might receive Viscountess Olive. They met there every day. He was desperately in love with her. During his martial and neptunian life he had loved crowds of women, red, black, yellow, and white, and some of them had been very beautiful. But before he met the Viscountess he did not know what a woman really was. When the Viscountess Olive called him her darling, her dear darling, he felt in heaven and it seemed to him that the stars shone in her hair.

She would come a little late, and, as she put her bag on the table, she would ask pensively:

"Let me sit on your knee."

And then she would talk of subjects suggested by the pious

Agaric, interrupting the conversation with sighs and kisses. She would ask him to dismiss such and such an officer, to give a command to another, to send the squadron here or there. And at the right moment she would exclaim:

"How young you are, my dear!"

And he did whatever she wished, for he was simple, he was anxious to wear the Constable's sword, and to receive a large grant; he did not dislike playing a double part, he had a vague idea of saving Penguinia, and he was in love.

This delightful woman induced him to remove the troops that were at La Cirque, the port where Crucho was to land. By this means it was made certain that there would be no obstacle to prevent the prince from entering Penguinia.

The pious Agaric organised public meetings so as to keep up the agitation. The Dracophils held one or two every day in some of the thirty-six districts of Alca, and preferably in the poorer quarters. They desired to win over the poor, for they are the most numerous. On the fourth of May a particularly fine meeting was held in an old cattle-market, situated in the centre of a populous suburb filled with housewives sitting on the doorsteps and children playing in the gutters. There were present about two thousand people, in the opinion of the Republicans, and six thousand according to the reckoning of the Dracophils. In the audience was to be seen the flower of Penguin society, including Prince and Princess des Boscénos, Count Cléna, M. de La Trumelle, M. Bigourd, and several rich Jewish ladies.

The Generalissimo of the national army had come in uniform. He was cheered.

The committee had been carefully formed. A man of the people, a workman, but a man of sound principles, M. Rauchin, the secretary of the yellow syndicate, was asked to preside, supported by Count Cléna and M. Michaud, a butcher.

The government which Penguinia had freely given itself was called by such names as cesspool and drain in several eloquent speeches. But President Formose was spared and no mention was made of Crucho or the priests.

The meeting was not unanimous. A defender of the modern State and of the Republic, a manual labourer, stood up.

"Gentlemen," said M. Rauchin, the chairman, "we have told you that this meeting would not be unanimous. We are not like our opponents, we are honest men. I allow our opponents to speak. Heaven knows what you are going to hear. Gentlemen, I beg of you to restrain as long as you can the expression of your contempt, your disgust, and your indignation."

"Gentlemen," said the opponent. . . .

Immediately he was knocked down, trampled beneath the feet of the indignant crowd, and his unrecognisable remains thrown out of the hall.

The tumult was still resounding when Count Cléna ascended the tribune. Cheers took the place of groans and when silence was restored the orator uttered these words:

"Comrades, we are going to see whether you have blood in your veins. What we have got to do is to slaughter, disembowel, and brain all the Republicans."

This speech let loose such a thunder of applause that the old shed rocked with it, and a cloud of acrid and thick dust fell from its filthy walls and worm-eaten beams and enveloped the audience.

A resolution was carried vilifying the government and acclaiming Chatillon. And the audience departed singing the hymn of the liberator: "It is Chatillon we want."

The only way out of the old market was through a muddy alley shut in by omnibus stables and coal sheds. There was no moon and a cold drizzle was coming down. The police, who were assembled in great numbers, blocked the alley and compelled the Dracophils to disperse in little groups. These were the instructions they had received from their chief, who was anxious to check the enthusiasm of the excited crowd.

The Dracophils who were detained in the alley kept mark-

ing time and singing, "It is Chatillon we want." Soon, becoming impatient of the delay, the cause of which they did not
know, they began to push those in front of them. This movement, propagated along the alley, threw those in front against
the broad chests of the police. The latter had no hatred for the
Dracophils. In the bottom of their hearts they liked Chatillon.
But it is natural to resist aggression and strong men are inclined to make use of their strength. For these reasons the
police kicked the Dracophils with their hob-nailed boots. As
a result there were sudden rushes backwards and forwards.
Threats and cries mingled with the songs.

"Murder! Murder! ... It is Chatillon we want! Murder!
Murder!"

And in the gloomy alley the more prudent kept saying,
"Don't push." Among these latter, in the darkness, his lofty
figure rising above the moving crowd, his broad shoulders and
robust body noticeable among the trampled limps and crushed
sides of the rest, stood the Prince des Boscénos, calm, immov-
able and placid. Serenely and indulgently he waited. In the
mean time, as the exit was opened at regular intervals between
the ranks of the police, the pressure of elbows against the
chests of those around the prince diminished and people began
to breathe again.

"You see we shall soon be able to go out," said that kindly
giant, with a pleasant smile. "Time and patience . . ."

He took a cigar from his case, raised it to his lips and struck
a match. Suddenly, in the light of the match, he saw Princess
Anne, his wife, clasped in Count Cléna's arms. At this sight he
rushed towards them, striking them both and those around
with his cane. He was disarmed, though not without difficulty,
but he could not be separated from his opponent. And whilst
the fainting princess was lifted from arm to arm to her carriage
over the excited and curious crowd, the two men still fought
furiously. Prince des Boscénos lost his hat, his eye-glass, his
cigar, his necktie, and his portfolio full of private letters and
political correspondence; he even lost the miraculous medals

that he had received from the good Father Cornemuse. But he gave his opponent so terrible a kick in the stomach that the unfortunate Count was knocked through an iron grating and went, head foremost, through a glass door and into a coal shed.

Attracted by the struggle and the cries of those around, the police rushed towards the prince, who furiously resisted them. He stretched three of them gasping at his feet and put seven others to flight, with, respectively, a broken jaw, a split lip, a nose pouring blood, a fractured skull, a torn ear, a dislocated collar-bone, and broken ribs. He fell, however, and was dragged bleeding and disfigured, with his clothes in rags, to the nearest police-station, where, jumping about and bellowing, he spent the night.

Until daybreak groups of demonstrators went about the town singing, "It is Chatillon we want," and breaking the windows of the houses in which the Ministers of the Republic lived.

VI

THE EMIRAL'S FALL

THAT night marked the culmination of the Dracophil move‹ ment. The Royalists had no longer any doubt of its triumph. Their chiefs sent congratulations to Prince Crucho by wire‹ less telegraphy. Their ladies embroidered scarves and slippers for him. M. de Plume had found the green horse.

The pious Agaric shared the common hope. But he still worked to win partisans for the Pretender. They ought, he said, to lay their foundations upon the bed-rock.

With this design he had an interview with three Trade Union workmen.

In these times the artisans no longer lived, as in the days of the Draconides, under the government of corporations. They were free, but they had no assured pay. After having remained isolated from each other for a long time, without help and without support, they had formed themselves into unions. The coffers of the unions were empty, as it was not the habit of the unionists to pay their subscriptions. There were unions numbering thirty thousand members, others with a thousand, five hundred, two hundred, and so forth. Several numbered two or three members only, or even a few less. But as the lists of adherents were not published, it was not easy to distinguish the great unions from the small ones.

After some dark and indirect steps the pious Agaric was put into communication in a room in the Moulin de la Galette, with comrades Dagobert, Tronc, and Balafille, the secretaries of three unions of which the first numbered fourteen members, the second twenty-four, and the third only one. Agaric showed extreme cleverness at this interview.

"Gentlemen," said he, "you and I have not, in most respects, the same political and social views, but there are points in which we may come to an understanding. We have a common enemy. The government exploits you and despises us. Help us to overthrow it; we will supply you with the means so far as we are able, and you can in addition count on our gratitude."

"Fork out the tin," said Dagobert.

The Reverend Father placed on the table a bag which the distiller of Conils had given him with tears in his eyes.

"Done!" said the three companions.

Thus was the solemn compact sealed.

As soon as the monk had departed, carrying with him the joy of having won over the masses to his cause, Dagobert, Tronc, and Balafille whistled to their wives, Amelia, Queenie, and Matilda, who were waiting in the street for the signal, and all six holding each other's hands, danced around the bag, singing:

> J'ai du bon pognon,
> Tu n'l'auras pas Chatillon!
> Hou! Hou! la calotte!

And they ordered a salad-bowl of warm wine.

In the evening all six went through the street from stall to stall singing their new song. The song became popular, for the detectives reported that every day showed an increase of the number of workpeople who sang through the slums:

> J'ai du bon pognon;
> Tu n'l'auras pas Chatillon!
> Hou! Hou! la calotte!

The Dracophil agitation made no progress in the provinces. The pious Agaric sought to find the cause of this, but was unable to discover it until old Cornemuse revealed it to him.

"I have proofs," sighed the monk of Conils, "that the Duke of Ampoule, the treasurer of the Dracophils, has bought property in Porpoisia with the funds that he received for the propaganda."

The party wanted money. Prince des Boscénos had lost his

portfolio in a brawl and he was reduced to painful expedients which were repugnant to his impetuous character. The Viscountess Olive was expensive. Cornemuse advised that the monthly allowance of that lady should be diminished.

"She is very useful to us," objected the pious Agaric.

"Undoubtedly," answered Cornemuse, "but she does us an injury by ruining us."

A schism divided the Dracophils. Misunderstandings reigned in their councils. Some wished that in accordance with the policy of M. Bigourd and the pious Agaric, they should carry on the design of reforming the Republic. Others, wearied by their long constraint, had resolved to proclaim the Dragon's crest and swore to conquer beneath that sign.

The latter urged the advantage of a clear situation and the impossibility of making a pretence much longer, and in truth, the public began to see whither the agitation was tending and that the Emiral's partisans wanted to destroy the very foundations of the Republic.

A report was spread that the prince was to land at La Cirque and make his entry into Alca on a green horse.

These rumours excited the fanatical monks, delighted the poor nobles, satisfied the rich Jewish ladies, and put hope in the hearts of the small traders. But very few of them were inclined to purchase these benefits at the price of a social catastrophe and the overthrow of the public credit; and there were fewer still who would have risked their money, their peace, their liberty, or a single hour from their pleasures in the business. On the other hand, the workmen held themselves ready, as ever, to give a day's work to the Republic, and a strong resistance was being formed in the suburbs.

"The people are with us," the pious Agaric used to say.

However, men, women, and children, when leaving their factories, used to shout with one voice:

> A bas Chatillon!
> Hou! Hou! la calotte!

As for the government, it showed the weakness, indecision, flabbiness, and heedlessness common to all governments, and from which none has ever departed without falling into arbitrariness and violence. In three words it knew nothing, wanted nothing, and could do nothing. Formose, shut in his presidential palace, remained blind, dumb, deaf, huge, invisible, wrapped up in his pride as in an eider-down.

Count Olive advised the Dracophils to make a last appeal for funds and to attempt a great stroke while Alca was still in a ferment.

An executive committee, which he himself had chosen, decided to kidnap the members of the Chamber of Deputies, and considered ways and means.

The affair was fixed for the twenty-eighth of July. On that day the sun rose radiantly over the city. In front of the legislative palace women passed to market with their baskets; hawkers cried their peaches, pears, and grapes; cab horses with their noses in their bags munched their hay. Nobody expected anything, not because the secret had been kept but because it met with nothing but unbelievers. Nobody believed in a revolution, and from this fact we may conclude that nobody desired one. About two o'clock the deputies began to pass, few and unnoticed, through the side-door of the palace. At three o'clock a few groups of badly dressed men had formed. At half past three black masses coming from the adjacent streets spread over Revolution Square. This vast expanse was soon covered by an ocean of soft hats, and the crowd of demonstrators, continually increased by sight-seers, having crossed the bridge, struck its dark wave against the walls of the legislative enclosure. Cries, murmurs, and songs went up to the impassive sky. "It is Chatillon we want!" "Down with the Deputies!" "Down with the Republicans!" "Death to the Republicans!" The devoted band of Dracophils, led by Prince des Boscénos, struck up the august canticle:

Vive Crucho,
Vaillant et sage,
Plein de courage
Dès le berceau!

Behind the wall silence alone replied.

This silence and the absence of guards encouraged and at the same time frightened the crowd. Suddenly a formidable voice cried out:

"Attack!"

And Prince des Boscénos was seen raising his gigantic form to the top of the wall, which was covered with barbs and iron spikes. Behind him rushed his companions, and the people followed. Some hammered against the wall to make holes in it; others endeavoured to tear down the spikes and to pull out the barbs. These defences had given way in places and some of the invaders had stripped the wall and were sitting astride on the top. Prince des Boscénos was waving an immense green flag. Suddenly the crowd wavered and from it came a long cry of terror. The police and the Republican carabineers issuing out of all the entrances of the palace formed themselves into a column beneath the wall and in a moment it was cleared of its besiegers. After a long moment of suspense the noise of arms was heard, and the police charged the crowd with fixed bayonets. An instant afterwards and on the deserted square strewn with hats and walking-sticks there reigned a sinister silence. Twice again the Dracophils attempted to form, twice they were repulsed. The rising was conquered. But Prince des Boscénos, standing on the wall of the hostile palace, his flag in his hand, still repelled the attack of a whole brigade. He knocked down all who approached him. At last he, too, was thrown down, and fell on an iron spike, to which he remained hooked, still clasping the standard of the Draconides.

On the following day the Ministers of the Republic and the Members of Parliament determined to take energetic measures. In vain this time, did President Formose attempt to evade his responsibilities. The government discussed the question of depriving Chatillon of his rank and dignities and of indicting him before the High Court as a conspirator, an enemy of the public good, a traitor, etc.

At this news the Emiral's old companions in arms, who the very evening before had beset him with their adulations, made no effort to conceal their joy. But Chatillon remained popular with the middle classes of Alca and one still heard the hymn of the liberator sounding in the streets, "It is Chatillon we want."

The Ministers were embarrassed. They intended to indict Chatillon before the High Court. But they knew nothing; they remained in that total ignorance reserved for those who govern men. They were incapable of advancing any grave charges against Chatillon. They could supply the prosecution with nothing but the ridiculous lies of their spies. Chatillon's share in the plot and his relations with Prince Crucho remained the secret of the thirty thousand Dracophils. The Ministers and the Deputies had suspicions and even certainties, but they had no proofs. The Public Prosecutor said to the Minister of Justice: "Very little is needed for a political prosecution! but I have nothing at all and that is not enough." The affair made no progress. The enemies of the Republic were triumphant.

On the eighteenth of September the news ran in Alca that Chatillon had taken flight. Everywhere there was surprise and astonishment. People doubted, for they could not understand.

This is what had happened: One day as the brave Under-Emiral Vulcanmould happened, as if by chance, to go into the office of M. Barbotan, the Minister of Foreign Affairs, he remarked with his usual frankness:

"M. Barbotan, your colleagues do not seem to me to be up to much; it is evident that they have never commanded a ship. That fool Chatillon gives them a deuced bad fit of the shivers."

The Minister, in sign of denial, waved his paper-knife in the air above his desk.

"Don't deny it," answered Vulcanmould. "You don't know how to get rid of Chatillon. You do not dare to indict him before the High Court because you are not sure of being able to bring forward a strong enough charge. Bigourd will defend him, and Bigourd is a clever advocate.... You are right, M. Barbotan, you are right. It would be a dangerous trial."

"Ah! my friend," said the Minister, in a careless tone, "if you knew how satisfied we are.... I receive the most reassuring news from my prefects. The good sense of the Penguins will do justice to the intrigues of this mutinous soldier. Can you suppose for a moment that a great people, an intelligent, laborious people, devoted to liberal institutions which ..."

Vulcanmould interrupted with a great sigh:

"Ah! If I had time to do it I would relieve you of your difficulty. I would juggle away my Chatillon like a nutmeg out of a thimble. I would fillip him off to Porpoisia."

The Minister paid close attention.

"It would not take long," continued the sailor. "I would rid you in a trice of the creature.... But just now I have other fish to fry.... I am in a bad hole. I must find a pretty big sum. But, deuce take it, honour before everything."

The Minister and the Under-Emiral looked at each other for a moment in silence. Then Barbotan said with authority:

"Under-Emiral Vulcanmould, get rid of this seditious soldier. You will render a great service to Penguinia, and the Minister of Home Affairs will see that your gambling debts are paid."

The same evening Vulcanmould called on Chatillon and looked at him for some time with an expression of grief and mystery.

"Why do you look like that?" answered the Emiral in an uneasy tone.

Vulcanmould said to him sadly:

"Old brother in arms, all is discovered. For the past half-hour the government knows everything."

At these words Chatillon sank down overwhelmed.

Vulcanmould continued:

"You may be arrested any moment. I advise you to make off."

And drawing out his watch:

"Not a minute to lose."

"Have I time to call on the Viscountess Olive?"

"It would be mad," said Vulcanmould, handing him a passport and a pair of blue spectacles, and telling him to have courage.

"I will," said Chatillon.

"Good-bye! old chum."

"Good-bye and thanks! You have saved my life."

"That is the least I could do."

A quarter of an hour later the brave Emiral had left the city of Alca.

He embarked at night on an old cutter at La Cirque and set sail for Porpoisia. But eight miles from the coast he was captured by a despatch-boat which was sailing without lights and which was under the flag of the Queen of the Black Islands. That Queen had for a long time nourished a fatal passion for Chatillon.

VII

CONCLUSION

Nunc est bibendum. Delivered from its fears and pleased at having escaped from so great a danger, the government resolved to celebrate the anniversary of the Penguin regeneration and the establishment of the Republic by holding a general holiday.

President Formose, the Ministers, and the members of the Chamber and of the Senate were present at the ceremony.

The Generalissimo of the Penguin army was present in uniform. He was cheered.

Preceded by the black flag of misery and the red flag of revolt, deputations of workmen walked in the procession, their aspect one of grim protection.

President, Ministers, Deputies, officials, heads of the magistracy and of the army, each, in their own names and in the name of the sovereign people, renewed the ancient oath to live in freedom or to die. It was an alternative upon which they were resolutely determined. But they preferred to live in freedom. There were games, speeches, and songs.

After the departure of the representatives of the State the crowd of citizens separated slowly and peaceably, shouting out, "Hurrah for the Republic!" "Hurrah for liberty!" "Down with the shaven pates!"

The newspapers mentioned only one regrettable incident that happened on that wonderful day. Prince des Boscénos was quietly smoking a cigar in the Queen's Meadow when the State procession passed by. The prince approached the Minister's carriage and said in a loud voice: "Death to the Republicans!" He was immediately apprehended by the police, to whom he offered a most desperate resistance. He knocked them down in crowds, but he was conquered by numbers, and, bruised, scratched, swollen, and unrecognisable even to the eyes of his wife, he was dragged through the joyous streets into an obscure prison.

The magistrates carried on the case against Chatillon in a peculiar style. Letters were found at the Admiralty which revealed the complicity of the Reverend Father Agaric in the plot. Immediately public opinion was inflamed against the monks, and Parliament voted, one after the other, a dozen laws which restrained, diminished, limited, prescribed, suppressed, determined, and curtailed, their rights, immunities, exemptions, privileges, and benefits, and created many invalidating disqualifications against them.

The Reverend Father Agaric steadfastly endured the rigour of the laws which struck himself personally, as well as the terrible fall of the Emiral of which he was the chief cause. Far from yielding to evil fortune, he regarded it as but a bird of passage. He was planning new political designs more audacious than the first.

When his projects were sufficiently ripe he went one day to the Wood of Conils. A thrush sang in a tree and a little hedgehog crossed the stony path in front of him with awkward steps. Agaric walked with great strides, muttering fragments of sentences to himself.

When he reached the door of the laboratory in which, for so many years, the pious manufacturer had distilled the golden liqueur of St. Orberosia, he found the place deserted and the door shut. Having walked around the building he saw in the backyard the venerable Cornemuse, who, with his habit pinned up, was climbing a ladder that leant against the wall.

"Is that you, my dear friend?" said he to him. "What are you doing there?"

"You can see for yourself," answered the monk of Conils in a feeble voice, turning a sorrowful look upon Agaric. "I am going into my house."

The red pupils of his eyes no longer imitated the triumph and brilliance of the ruby, they flashed mournful and troubled glances. His countenance had lost its happy fulness. His shining head was no longer pleasant to the sight; perspiration and inflamed blotches had altered its inestimable perfection.

"I don't understand," said Agaric.

"It is easy enough to understand. You see the consequences of your plot. Although a multitude of laws are directed against me I have managed to elude the greater number of them. Some, however, have struck me. These vindictive men have closed my laboratories and my shops, and confiscated my bottles, my stills, and my retorts. They have put seals on my doors and now I am compelled to go in through the window. I am barely able to extract in secret from time to time the juice of a few plants and that with an apparatus which the humblest labourer would despise."

"You suffer from the persecution," said Agaric. "It strikes us all."

The monk of Conils passed his hand over his afflicted brow:

"I told you so, Brother Agaric; I told you that your enterprise would turn against ourselves."

"Our defeat is only momentary," replied Agaric eagerly. "It is due to purely accidental causes; it results from mere contingencies. Chatillon was a fool; he has drowned himself in his own ineptitude. Listen to me, Brother Cornemuse. We have not a moment to lose. We must free the Penguin people, we must deliver them from their tyrants, save them from themselves, restore the Dragon's crest, re-establish the ancient State, the good State, for the honour of religion and the exaltation of the Catholic faith. Chatillon was a bad instrument; he broke in our hands. Let us take a better instrument to replace him. I have the man who will destroy this impious democracy. He is a civil official; his name is Gomoru. The Penguins worship him. He has already betrayed his party for a plate of rice. There's the man we want!"

At the beginning of this speech the monk of Conils had climbed into his window and pulled up the ladder.

"I foresee," answered he, with his nose through the sash, "that you will not stop until you have us all expelled from this pleasant, agreeable, and sweet land of Penguinia. Good night; God keep you!"

Agaric, standing before the wall, entreated his dearest brother to listen to him for a moment:

"Understand your own interest better, Cornemuse! Penguinia is ours. What do we need to conquer it? Just one effort more . . . one more little sacrifice of money and . . ."

But without listening further, the monk of Conils drew in his head and closed his window.

BOOK VI

MODERN TIMES

THE AFFAIR OF THE EIGHTY THOUSAND TRUSSES OF HAY

Ζεῦ πάτερ ἀλλὰ σὺ ῥῦσαι ὑπ' ἠέρος υἶας Ἀχαιῶν,
ποίησον δ'αἴθρην, δὸς δ'ὀφθαλμοῖ σιν ἰδέσθαι·
ἐν δὲ φάιει ὄλεσσον ἔπει νύ τοι εὔαδεν οὕτως.*
(Iliad xvii. 645 *et seq.*)

---

* O Father Zeus, only save thou the sons of the Acheans from the darkness, and make clear sky and vouchsafe sight to our eyes, and then, so it be but light, slay us, since such is thy good pleasure.

BOOK V

MODERN LIFE

The Artist of the True Present
Genius of City

I

GENERAL GREATAUK, DUKE OF SKULL

A SHORT time after the flight of the Emiral, a middle-class
Jew called Pyrot, desirous of associating with the aristocracy
and wishing to serve his country, entered the Penguin army.
The Minister of War, who at the time was Greatauk, Duke of
Skull, could not endure him. He blamed him for his zeal, his
hooked nose, his vanity, his fondness for study, his thick lips,
and his exemplary conduct. Every time the author of any
misdeed was looked for, Greatauk used to say:

"It must be Pyrot!"

One morning General Panther, the Chief of the Staff, informed Greatauk of a serious matter. Eighty thousand trusses
of hay intended for the cavalry had disappeared and not a
trace of them was to be found.

Greatauk exclaimed at once:

"It must be Pyrot who has stolen them!"

He remained in thought for some time and said:

"The more I think of it the more I am convinced that Pyrot
has stolen those eighty thousand trusses of hay. And I know
it is by this: he stole them in order that he might sell them to
our bitter enemies the Porpoises. What an infamous piece of
treachery!"

"There is no doubt about it," answered Panther; "it only
remains to prove it."

The same day, as he passed by a cavalry barracks, Prince
des Boscénos heard the troopers as they were sweeping out the
yard, singing:

> Boscénos est un gros cochon;
> On en va faire des andouilles,

173

Des saucisses et du jambon
Pour le réveillon des pauv' bougres.

It seemed to him contrary to all discipline that soldiers
should sing this domestic and revolutionary refrain which on
days of riot had been uttered by the lips of jeering workmen.
On this occasion he deplored the moral degeneration of the
army and thought with a bitter smile that his old comrade
Greatauk, the head of this degenerate army, basely exposed
him to the malice of an unpatriotic government. And he promised himself that he would make an improvement before long.

"That scoundrel Greatauk," said he to himself, "will not
remain long a Minister."

Prince des Boscénos was the most irreconcilable of the opponents of modern democracy, free thought, and the government
which the Penguins had voluntarily given themselves. He had
a vigorous and undisguised hatred for the Jews, and he worked
in public and in private, night and day, for the restoration of
the line of the Draconides. His ardent royalism was still further excited by the thought of his private affairs, which were
in a bad way and were hourly growing worse. He had no hope
of seeing an end to his pecuniary embarrassments until the
heir of Draco the Great entered the city of Alca.

When he returned to his house, the prince took out of his
safe a bundle of old letters consisting of a private correspondence of the most secret nature, which he had obtained from
a treacherous secretary. They proved that his old comrade
Greatauk, the Duke of Skull, had been guilty of jobbery
regarding the military stores and had received a present of
no great value from a manufacturer called Maloury. The very
smallness of this present deprived the Minister who had accepted it of all excuse.

The prince re-read the letters with a bitter satisfaction, put
them carefully back into his safe, and dashed to the Minister
of War. He was a man of resolute character. On being told
that the Minister could see no one he knocked down the ushers,
swept aside the orderlies, trampled under foot the civil and

military clerks, burst through the doors, and entered the room of the astonished Greatauk.

"I will not say much," said he to him, "but I will speak to the point. You are a confounded cad. I have asked you to put a flea in the ear of General Mouchin, the tool of those Republicans, and you would not do it. I have asked you to give a command to General des Clapiers, who works for the Dracophils, and who has obliged me personally, and you would not do it. I have asked you to dismiss General Tandem, the commander of Port Alca, who robbed me of fifty louis at cards, and who had me handcuffed when I was brought before the High Court as Emiral Chatillon's accomplice. You would not do it. I asked you for the hay and bran stores. You would not give them. I asked you to send me on a secret mission to Porpoisia. You refused. And not satisfied with these repeated refusals you have designated me to your Government colleagues as a dangerous person, who ought to be watched, and it is owing to you that I have been shadowed by the police. You old traitor! I ask nothing more from you and I have but one word to say to you: Clear out; you have bothered us too long. Besides, we will force the vile Republic to replace you by one of our own party. You know that I am a man of my word. If in twenty-four hours you have not handed in your resignation I will publish the Maloury *dossier* in the news papers."

But Greatauk calmly and serenely replied:

"Be quiet, you fool. I am just having a Jew transported. I am handing over Pyrot to justice as guilty of having stolen eighty thousand trusses of hay."

Prince Boscénos, whose anger vanished like a dream, smiled.

"Is that true?"

"You will see."

"My congratulations, Greatauk. But as one always needs to take precautions with you I shall immediately publish the good news. People will read this evening about Pyrot's arrest in every newspaper in Alca. . . ."

And he went away muttering:

"That Pyrot! I suspected he would come to a bad end."

A moment later General Panther appeared before Greatauk.

"Sir," said he, "I have just examined the business of the eighty thousand trusses of hay. There is no evidence against Pyrot."

"Let it be found," answered Greatauk. "Justice requires it. Have Pyrot arrested at once."

II

PYROT

ALL Penguinia heard with horror of Pyrot's crime; at the same time there was a sort of satisfaction that this embezzlement combined with treachery and even bordering on sacrilege, had been committed by a Jew. In order to understand this feeling it is necessary to be acquainted with the state of the public opinion regarding the Jews both great and small. As we have had occasion to say in this history, the universally detested and all powerful financial caste was composed of Christians and of Jews. The Jews who formed part of it and on whom the people poured all their hatred were the upperclass Jews. They possessed immense riches and, it was said, held more than a fifth part of the total property of Penguinia. Outside this formidable caste there was a multitude of Jews of a mediocre condition, who were not more loved than the others and who were feared much less. In every ordered State, wealth is a sacred thing: in democracies it is the only sacred thing. Now the Penguin State was democratic. Three or four financial companies exercised a more extensive, and above all, more effective and continuous power, than that of the Ministers of the Republic. The latter were puppets whom the companies ruled in secret, whom they compelled by intimidation or corruption to favour themselves at the expense of the State, and whom they ruined by calumnies in the press if they remained honest. In spite of the secrecy of the Exchequer, enough appeared to make the country indignant, but the middle-class Penguins had, from the greatest to the last of them, been brought up to hold money in great reverence, and as they all had property, either much or little, they were strongly impressed with the solidarity of capital and understood that a small fortune is not safe unless a big one is protected. For these reasons they conceived a religious respect for the Jews' millions, and self-interest being stronger with them than aversion, they were as much afraid as they were of death to touch a single hair of one of the rich Jews whom they detested. Towards the poorer Jews they felt less ceremonious and when they saw any of them down they trampled on them. That is why the entire nation learnt with thorough satisfaction that the traitor was a Jew. They could take vengeance on all Israel in his person without any fear of compromising the public credit.

That Pyrot had stolen the eighty thousand trusses of hay nobody hesitated for a moment to believe. No one doubted because the general ignorance in which everybody was concerning the affair did not allow of doubt, for doubt is a thing that demands motives. People do not doubt without reasons in the same way that people believe without reasons. The thing was not doubted because it was repeated everywhere and, with the public, to repeat is to prove. It was not doubted because people wished to believe Pyrot guilty and one believes what one wishes to believe. Finally, it was not doubted because the faculty of doubt is rare amongst men; very few minds carry in them its germs and these are not developed without cultivation. Doubt is singular, exquisite, philosophic, immoral, transcendent, monstrous, full of malignity, injurious to persons and to property, contrary to the good order of governments, and to the prosperity of empires, fatal to humanity, destructive of the gods, held in horror by heaven and earth. The mass of the Penguins were ignorant of doubt: it believed in Pyrot's guilt and this conviction immediately became one of its chief national beliefs and an essential truth in its patriotic creed.

Pyrot was tried secretly and condemned.

General Panther immediately went to the Minister of War to tell him the result.

"Luckily," said he, "the judges were certain, for they had no proofs."

"Proofs," muttered Greatauk, "proofs, what do they prove? There is only one certain, irrefragable proof—the confession of the guilty person. Has Pyrot confessed?"

"No, General."

"He will confess, he ought to. Panther, we must induce him; tell him it is to his interest. Promise him that, if he confesses, he will obtain favours, a reduction of his sentence, full pardon; promise him that if he confesses his innocence will be admitted, that he will be decorated. Appeal to his good feelings. Let him confess from patriotism, for the flag, for the sake of order, from respect for the hierarchy, at the special command of the Minister of War militarily.... But tell me, Panther, has he not confessed already? There are tacit confessions; silence is a confession."

"But, General, he is not silent; he keeps on squealing like a pig that he is innocent."

"Panther, the confessions of a guilty man sometimes result from the vehemence of his denials. To deny desperately is to confess. Pyrot has confessed; we must have witnesses of his confessions, justice requires them."

There was in Western Penguinia a seaport called La Cirque, formed of three small bays and formerly greatly frequented by ships, but now solitary and deserted. Gloomy lagoons stretched along its low coasts exhaling a pestilent odour, while fever hovered over its sleepy waters. Here, on the borders of the sea, there was built a high square tower, like the old Campanile at Venice, from the side of which, close to the summit, hung an open cage which was fastened by a chain to a transverse beam. In the times of the Draconides the Inquisitors of Alca used to put heretical clergy into this cage. It had been empty for three hundred years, but now Pyrot was imprisoned in it under the guard of sixty warders, who lived in the tower and did not lose sight of him night or day, spying on him for confessions that they might afterwards report to the Minister of War. For Greatauk, careful and prudent, desired confessions and still further confessions. Greatauk, who was looked upon as a fool, was in reality a man of great ability and full of rare foresight.

In the mean time Pyrot, burnt by the sun, eaten by mosquitoes, soaked in the rain, hail and snow, frozen by the cold, tossed about terribly by the wind, beset by the sinister croaking of the ravens that perched upon his cage, kept writing down his innocence on pieces torn off his shirt with a toothpick dipped in blood. These rags were lost in the sea or fell into the hands of the gaolers. Some of them, however, came under the eyes of the public. But Pyrot's protests moved nobody because his confessions had been published.

III

COUNT DE MAUBEC DE LA DENTDULYNX

THE morals of the Jews were not always pure; in most cases they were averse from none of the vices of Christian civilization, but they retained from the Patriarchal age a recognition of family ties and an attachment to the interest of the tribe. Pyrot's brothers, half-brothers, uncles, great-uncles, first, second, and third cousins, nephews and great-nephews, relations by blood and relations by marriage, and all who were related to him to the number of about seven hundred, were at first overwhelmed by the blow that had struck their relative, and they shut themselves up in their houses, covering themselves with ashes and blessing the hand that had chastised them. For forty days they kept a strict fast. Then they bathed themselves and resolved to search, without rest, at the cost of any toil and at the risk of every danger, for the demonstration of an innocence which they did not doubt. And how could they have doubted? Pyrot's innocence had been revealed to them in the same way that his guilt had been revealed to Christian Penguinia; for these things, being hidden, assume a mystic character and take on the authority of religious truths. The seven hundred Pyrotists set to work with as much zeal as prudence, and made the most thorough inquiries in secret. They were everywhere; they were seen nowhere. One would have said that, like the pilot of Ulysses, they wandered freely over the earth. They penetrated into the War Office and approached, under different disguises, the judges, the registrars, and the witnesses of the affair. Then Greatauk's cleverness was seen. The witnesses knew nothing; the judges and registrars knew nothing. Emissaries reached even Pyrot and anxiously questioned him in his cage amid the prolonged moan-ings of the sea and the hoarse croaks of the ravens. It was in vain; the prisoner knew nothing. The seven hundred Pyrotists could not subvert the proofs of the accusation because they could not know what they were, and they could not know what they were because there were none. Pyrot's guilt was indefeasible through its very nullity. And it was with a legiti-mate pride that Greatauk, expressing himself as a true artist, said one day to General Panther: "This case is a masterpiece: it is made out of nothing." The seven hundred Pyrotists despaired of ever clearing up this dark business, when sud-denly they discovered, from a stolen letter, that the eighty thousand trusses of hay had never existed, that a most dis-tinguished nobleman, Count de Maubec, had sold them to the State, that he had received the price but had never delivered them. Indeed seeing that he was descended from the richest land proprietors of ancient Penguinia, the heir of the Maubecs of Dentdulynx, once the possessors of four duchies, sixty counties, and six hundred and twelve marquisates, baronies, and viscounties, he did not possess as much land as he could cover with his hand, and would not have been able to cut a single day's mowing of forage off his own domains. As to his getting a single rush from a land-owner or a merchant, that would have been quite impossible, for everybody except the Ministers of State and the Government officials knew that it would be easier to get blood from a stone than a farthing from a Maubec.

The seven hundred Pyrotists made a minute inquiry concerning the Count Maubec de la Dentdulynx's financial re-sources, and they proved that that nobleman was chiefly sup-ported by a house in which some generous ladies were ready to furnish all comers with the most lavish hospitality. They publicly proclaimed that he was guilty of the theft of the eighty thousand trusses of straw for which an innocent man had been condemned and was now imprisoned in the cage.

Maubec belonged to an illustrious family which was allied

to the Draconides. There is nothing that a democracy esteems more highly than noble birth. Maubec had also served in the Penguin army, and since the Penguins were all soldiers, they loved their army to idolatry. Maubec, on the field of battle, had received the Cross, which is a sign of honour among the Penguins and which they valued even more highly than the embraces of their wives. All Penguinia declared for Maubec, and the voice of the people which began to assume a threatening tone, demanded severe punishments for the seven hundred calumniating Pyrotists.

Maubec was a nobleman; he challenged the seven hundred Pyrotists to combat with either sword, sabre, pistols, carabines, or sticks.

"Vile dogs," he wrote to them in a famous letter, "you have crucified my God and you want my life too; I warn you that I will not be such a duffer as He was and that I will cut off your fourteen hundred ears. Accept my boot on your seven hundred behinds."

The Chief of the Government at the time was a peasant called Robin Mielleux, a man pleasant to the rich and powerful, but hard towards the poor, a man of small courage and ignorant of his own interests. In a public declaration he guaranteed Maubec's innocence and honour, and presented the seven hundred Pyrotists to the criminal courts where they were condemned, as libellers, to imprisonment, to enormous fines, and to all the damages that were claimed by their innocent victim.

It seemed as if Pyrot was destined to remain for ever shut in the cage on which the ravens perched. But all the Penguins being anxious to know and prove that this Jew was guilty, all the proofs brought forward were found not to be good, while some of them were also contradictory. The officers of the Staff showed zeal but lacked prudence. Whilst Greatauk kept an admirable silence, General Panther made inexhaustible speeches and every morning demonstrated in the newspapers that the condemned man was guilty. He would have done better, perhaps, if he had said nothing. The guilt was evident and what is evident cannot be demonstrated. So much reasoning disturbed people's minds; their faith, though still alive, became less serene. The more proofs one gives a crowd the more they ask for.

Nevertheless the danger of proving too much would not have been great if there had not been in Penguinia, as there are, indeed, everywhere, minds framed for free inquiry, capable of studying a difficult question, and inclined to philosophic doubt. They were few; they were not all inclined to speak, and the public was by no means inclined to listen to them. Still, they did not always meet with deaf ears. The great Jews, all the Israelite millionaires of Alca, when spoken to of Pyrot, said: "We do not know the man"; but they thought of saving him. They preserved the prudence to which their wealth inclined them and wished that others would be less timid. Their wish was to be gratified.

IV

COLOMBAN

SOME weeks after the conviction of the seven hundred Pyrotists, a little, gruff, hairy, short-sighted man left his house one morning with a paste-pot, a ladder, and a bundle of posters and went about the streets pasting placards to the walls on which might be read in large letters: *Pyrot is innocent, Maubec is guilty*. He was not a bill-poster; his name was Colomban, and as the author of sixty volumes on Penguin sociology he was numbered among the most laborious and respected writers in Alca. Having given sufficient thought to the matter and no longer doubting Pyrot's innocence, he proclaimed it in the manner which he thought would be most sensational. He met with no hindrance while posting his bills in the quiet streets, but when he came to the populous quarters, every time he mounted his ladder, inquisitive people crowded round him and, dumbfounded with surprise and indignation, threw at him threatening looks which he received with the calm that comes from courage and short-sightedness. Whilst caretakers and tradespeople tore down the bills he had posted, he kept on zealously placarding, carrying his tools and followed by little boys who, with their baskets under their arms or their satchels on their backs, were in no hurry to reach school. To the mute indignation against him, protests and murmurs were now added. But Colomban did not condescend to see or hear anything. As, at the entrance to the Rue St. Orberosia, he was posting one of his squares of paper bearing the words: *Pyrot is innocent, Maubec is guilty,* the riotous crowd showed signs of the most violent anger. They called after him, "Traitor, thief, rascal, scoundrel." A woman opened a window and emptied a vessel full of filth over his head, a cabby sent his hat flying from one end of the street to the other by a blow of his whip amid the cheers of the crowd who now felt themselves avenged. A butcher's boy knocked Colomban with his paste-pot, his brush, and his posters, from the top of his ladder into the gutter, and the proud Penguins then felt the greatness of their country. Colomban stood up, covered with filth, lame, and with his elbow injured, but tranquil and resolute.

"Low brutes," he muttered, shrugging his shoulders.

Then he went down on all-fours in the gutter to look for his glasses which he had lost in his fall. It was then seen that his coat was split from the collar to the tails and that his trousers were in rags. The rancour of the crowd grew stronger.

On the other side of the street stretched the big St. Orberosian Stores. The patriots seized whatever they could lay their hands on from the shop front, and hurled at Colomban oranges, lemons, pots of jam, pieces of chocolate, bottles of liqueurs, boxes of sardines, pots of *foie gras,* hams, fowls, flasks of oil, and bags of haricots. Covered with the débris of the food, bruised, tattered, lame, and blind, he took to flight, followed by the shop-boys, bakers, loafers, citizens, and hooligans whose number increased each moment and who kept shouting: "Duck him! Death to the traitor! Duck him!" This torrent of vulgar humanity swept along the streets and rushed into the Rue St. Maël. The police did their duty. From all the adjacent streets constables proceeded and, holding their scabbards with their left hands, they went at full speed in front of the pursuers. They were on the point of grabbing Colomban in their huge hands when he suddenly escaped them by falling through an open man-hole to the bottom of a sewer.

He spent the night there in the darkness, sitting close by the dirty water amidst the fat and slimy rats. He thought of his task, and his swelling heart filled with courage and pity. And when the dawn threw a pale ray of light into the air-hole he got up and said, speaking to himself:

"I see that the fight will be a stiff one."

Forthwith he composed a memorandum in which he clearly showed that Pyrot could not have stolen from the Ministry of War the eighty thousand trusses of hay which it had never received, for the reason that Maubec had never delivered them, though he had received the money. Colomban caused this statement to be distributed in the streets of Alca. The people refused to read it and tore it up in anger. The shop-keepers shook their fists at the distributors, who made off, chased by angry women armed with brooms. Feeling grew warm and the ferment lasted the whole day. In the evening bands of wild and ragged men went about the streets yelling: "Death to Colomban!" The patriots snatched whole bundles of the memorandum from the newsboys and burned them in the public squares, dancing wildly round these bon-fires with girls whose petticoats were tied up to their waists.

Some of the more enthusiastic among them went and broke the windows of the house in which Colomban had lived in perfect tranquillity during his forty years of work.

Parliament was roused and asked the Chief of the Government what measures he proposed to take in order to repel the odious attacks made by Colomban upon the honour of the National Army and the safety of Penguinia. Robin Mielleux denounced Colomban's impious audacity and proclaimed amid the cheers of the legislators that the man would be summoned before the Courts to answer for his infamous libel.

The Minister of War was called to the tribune and appeared in it transfigured. He had no longer the air, as in former days, of one of the sacred geese of the Penguin citadels. Now, bristling, with outstretched neck and hooked beak, he seemed the symbolical vulture fastened to the livers of his country's enemies.

In the august silence of the assembly he pronounced these words only:

"I swear that Pyrot is a rascal."

This speech of Greatauk was reported all over Penguinia and satisfied the public conscience.

V

THE REVEREND FATHERS AGARIC
AND CORNEMUSE

COLOMBAN bore with meekness and surprise the weight of
the general reprobation. He could not go out without being
stoned, so he did not go out. He remained in his study with
a superb obstinacy, writing new memoranda in favour of the
encaged innocent. In the mean time among the few readers
that he found, some, about a dozen, were struck by his reasons
and began to doubt Pyrot's guilt. They broached the subject
to their friends and endeavoured to spread the light that had
arisen in their minds. One of them was a friend of Robin
Mielleux and confided to him his perplexities, with the result
that he was no longer received by that Minister. Another demanded explanations in an open letter to the Minister of
War. A third published a terrible pamphlet. The latter, whose
name was Kerdanic, was a formidable controversialist. The
public was unmoved. It was said that these defenders of the
traitor had been bribed by the rich Jews; they were stig-
matized by the name of Pyrotists and the patriots swore to
exterminate them. There were only a thousand or twelve
hundred Pyrotists in the whole vast Republic, but it was
believed that they were everywhere. People were afraid of
finding them in the promenades, at meetings, at receptions,
in fashionable drawing-rooms, at the dinner-table, even in the
conjugal couch. One half of the population was suspected by
the other half. The discord set all Alca on fire.

In the mean time Father Agaric, who managed his big school
for young nobles, followed events with anxious attention. The
misfortunes of the Penguin Church had not disheartened him.

He remained faithful to Prince Crucho and preserved the hope of restoring the heir of the Draconides to the Penguin throne. It appeared to him that the events that were happening or about to happen in the country, the state of mind of which they were at once the effect and the cause, and the troubles that necessarily resulted from them might—if they were directed, guided, and led by the profound wisdom of a monk —overthrow the Republic and incline the Penguins to restore Prince Crucho, from whose piety the faithful hoped for so much solace. Wearing his huge black hat, the brims of which looked like the wings of Night, he walked through the Wood of Conils towards the factory where his venerable friend, Father Cornemuse, distilled the hygienic St. Orberosian liqueur. The good monk's industry, so cruelly affected in the time of Emiral Chatillon, was being restored from its ruins. One heard goods trains rumbling through the Wood and one saw in the sheds hundreds of orphans clothed in blue, packing bottles and nailing up cases.

Agaric found the venerable Cornemuse standing before his stoves and surrounded by his retorts. The shining pupils of the old man's eyes had again become as bright as rubies, his skull shone with its former elaborate and careful polish.

Agaric first congratulated the pious distiller on the restored activity of his laboratories and workshops.

"Business is recovering. I thank God for it," answered the old man of Conils. "Alas! it had fallen into a bad state, Brother Agaric. You saw the desolation of this establishment. I need say no more."

Agaric turned away his head.

"The St. Orberosian liqueur," continued Cornemuse, "is making fresh conquests. But none the less my industry remains uncertain and precarious. The laws of ruin and desolation that struck it have not been abrogated, they have only been suspended."

And the monk of Conils lifted his ruby eyes to heaven.

Agaric put his hand on his shoulder.

"What a sight, Cornemuse, does unhappy Penguinia present to us! Everywhere disobedience, independence, liberty! We see the proud, the haughty, the men of revolt rising up. After having braved the Divine laws they now rear themselves against human laws, so true is it that in order to be a good citizen a man must be a good Christian. Colomban is trying to imitate Satan. Numerous criminals are following his fatal example. They want, in their rage, to put aside all checks, to throw off all yokes, to free themselves from the most sacred bonds, to escape from the most salutary restraints. They strike their country to make it obey them. But they will be overcome by the weight of public animadversion, vituperation, indignation, fury, execration, and abomination. That is the abyss to which they have been led by atheism, free thought, and the monstrous claim to judge for themselves and to form their own opinions."

"Doubtless, doubtless," replied Father Cornemuse, shaking his head, "but I confess that the care of distilling these simples has prevented me from following public affairs. I only know that people are talking a great deal about a man called Pyrot. Some maintain that he is guilty, others affirm that he is innocent, but I do not clearly understand the motives that drive both parties to mix themselves up in a business that concerns neither of them."

The pious Agaric asked eagerly:

"You do not doubt Pyrot's guilt?"

"I cannot doubt it, dear Agaric," answered the monk of Conils. "That would be contrary to the laws of my country which we ought to respect as long as they are not opposed to the Divine laws. Pyrot is guilty, for he has been convicted. As to saying more for or against his guilt, that would be to erect my own authority against that of the judges, a thing which I will take good care not to do. Besides, it is useless, for Pyrot has been convicted. If he has not been convicted because he is guilty, he is guilty because he has been convicted; it comes to the same thing. I believe in his guilt as every good

citizen ought to believe in it; and I will believe in it as long
as the established jurisdiction will order me to believe in it,
for it is not for a private person but for a judge to proclaim
the innocence of a convicted person. Human justice is venerable even in the errors inherent in its fallible and limited
nature. These errors are never irreparable; if the judges do
not repair them on earth, God will repair them in Heaven.
Besides I have great confidence in General Greatauk, who,
though he certainly does not look it, seems to me to be an
abler man than all those who are attacking him."

"Dearest Cornemuse," cried the pious Agaric, "the Pyrot
affair, if pushed to the point whither we can lead it by the
help of God and the necessary funds, will produce the greatest
benefits. It will lay bare the vices of this Anti-Christian Republic and will incline the Penguins to restore the throne of
the Draconides and the prerogatives of the Church. But to
do that it is necessary for the people to see the clergy in the
front rank of its defenders. Let us march against the enemies
of the army, against those who insult our heroes, and everybody will follow us."

"Everybody will be too many," murmured the monk of
Conils, shaking his head. "I see that the Penguins want to
quarrel. If we mix ourselves up in their quarrel they will
become reconciled at our expense and we shall have to pay
the cost of the war. That is why, if you are guided by me, dear
Agaric, you will not engage the Church in this adventure."

"You know my energy; you know my prudence. I will
compromise nothing. . . . Dear Cornemuse, I only want from
you the funds necessary for us to begin the campaign."

For a long time Cornemuse refused to bear the expenses
of what he thought was a fatal enterprise. Agaric was in turn
pathetic and terrible. At last, yielding to his prayers and
threats, Cornemuse, with hanging head and swinging arms,
went to the austere cell that concealed his evangelical poverty.
In the whitewashed wall under a branch of blessed box, there
was fixed a safe. He opened it, and with a sigh took out a

bundle of bills which, with hesitating hands, he gave to the pious Agaric.

"Do not doubt it, dear Cornemuse," said the latter, thrusting the papers into the pocket of his overcoat, "this Pyrot affair has been sent us by God for the glory and exaltation of the Church of Penguinia."

"I pray that you may be right!" sighed the monk of Conils.

And, left alone in his laboratory, he gazed, through his exquisite eyes, with an ineffable sadness at his stoves and his retorts.

VI

THE SEVEN HUNDRED PYROTISTS

THE seven hundred Pyrotists inspired the public with an increasing aversion. Every day two or three of them were beaten to death in the streets. One of them was publicly whipped, another thrown into the river, a third tarred and feathered and led through a laughing crowd, a fourth had his nose cut off by a captain of dragoons. They did not dare to show themselves at their clubs, at tennis, or at the races; they put on a disguise when they went to the Stock Exchange. In these circumstances the Prince des Boscénos thought it urgent to curb their audacity and repress their insolence. For this purpose he joined with Count Cléna, M. de La Trumelle, Viscount Olive, and M. Bigourd in founding a great anti Pyrotist association to which citizens in hundreds of thou· sands, soldiers in companies, regiments, brigades, divisions, and army corps, towns, districts, and provinces, all gave their adhesion.

About this time the Minister of War happening to visit one day his Chief of Staff, saw with surprise that the large room where General Panther worked, which was formerly quite bare, had now along each wall from floor to ceiling in sets of deep pigeon-holes, triple and quadruple rows of paper bundles of every form and colour. These sudden and monstrous records had in a few days reached the dimensions of a pile of archives such as it takes centuries to accumulate.

"What is this?" asked the astonished minister.

"Proofs against Pyrot," answered General Panther with patriotic satisfaction. "We had not got them when we con· victed him, but we have plenty of them now."

The door was open, and Greatauk saw coming up the staircase a long file of porters who were unloading heavy bales
of papers in the hall, and he saw the lift slowly rising heavily
loaded with paper packets.

"What are those others?" said he.

"They are fresh proofs against Pyrot that are now reaching
us," said Panther. "I have asked for them in every county
of Penguinia, in every Staff Office and in every Court in
Europe. I have ordered them in every town in America and
in Australia, and in every factory in Africa, and I am expecting
bales of them from Bremen and a ship-load from Melbourne."

And Panther turned towards the Minister of War the tranquil and radiant look of a hero. However, Greatauk, his eye-
glass in his eye, was looking at the formidable pile of papers
with less satisfaction than uneasiness.

"Very good," said he, "very good! but I am afraid that
this Pyrot business may lose its beautiful simplicity. It was
limpid; like a rock-crystal its value lay in its transparency.
You could have searched it in vain with a magnifying-glass
for a straw, a bend, a blot, for the least fault. When it left
my hands it was as pure as the light. Indeed it was the light.
I give you a pearl and you make a mountain out of it. To
tell you the truth I am afraid that by wishing to do too well
you have done less well. Proofs! of course it is good to have
proofs, but perhaps it is better to have none at all. I have
already told you, Panther, there is only one irrefutable proof,
the confession of the guilty person (or if the innocent what
matter!). The Pyrot affair, as I arranged it, left no room
for criticism; there was no spot where it could be touched.
It defied assault. It was invulnerable because it was invisible.
Now it gives an enormous handle for discussion. I advise
you, Panther, to use your paper packets with great reserve.
I should be particularly grateful if you would be more sparing
of your communications to journalists. You speak well, but
you say too much. Tell me, Panther, are there any forged
documents among these?"

"There are some adapted ones."

"That is what I meant. There are some adapted ones. So much the better. As proofs, forged documents, in general, are better than genuine ones, first of all because they have been expressly made to suit the needs of the case, to order and measure, and therefore they are fitting and exact. They are also preferable because they carry the mind into an ideal world and turn it aside from the reality which, alas! in this world is never without some alloy.... Nevertheless, I think I should have preferred, Panther, that we had no proofs at all."

The first act of the Anti-Pyrotist Association was to ask the Government immediately to summon the seven hundred Pyrotists and their accomplices before the High Court of Justice as guilty of high treason. Prince des Boscénos was charged to speak on behalf of the Association and presented himself before the Council which had assembled to hear him. He expressed a hope that the vigilance and firmness of the Government would rise to the height of the occasion. He shook hands with each of the ministers and as he passed General Greatauk he whispered in his ear:

"Behave properly, you ruffian, or I will publish the Maloury *dossier!*"

Some days later by a unanimous vote of both Houses, on a motion proposed by the Government, the Anti-Pyrotist Association was granted a charter recognising it as beneficial to the public interest.

The Association immediately sent a deputation to Chitterlings Castle in Porpoisia, where Crucho was eating the bitter bread of exile, to assure the prince of the love and devotion of the Anti-Pyrotist members.

However, the Pyrotists grew in numbers, and now counted ten thousand. They had their regular cafés on the boulevards. The patriots had theirs also, richer and bigger, and every evening glasses of beer, saucers, match-stands, jugs, chairs, and tables were hurled from one to the other. Mirrors were smashed to bits, and the police ended the struggles by impartially trampling the combatants of both parties under their hob-nailed shoes.

On one of these glorious nights, as Prince des Boscénos was leaving a fashionable café in the company of some patriots, M. de La Trumelle pointed out to him a little, bearded man with glasses, hatless, and having only one sleeve to his coat, who was painfully dragging himself along the rubbish-strewn pavement.

"Look!" said he, "there is Colomban!"

The prince had gentleness as well as strength; he was exceedingly mild; but at the name of Colomban his blood boiled. He rushed at the little spectacled man, and knocked him down with one blow of his fist on the nose.

M. de La Trumelle then perceived that, misled by an undeserved resemblance, he had mistaken for Colomban, M. Bazile, a retired lawyer, the secretary of the Anti-Pyrotist Association, and an ardent and generous patriot. Prince des Boscénos was one of those antique souls who never bend. However, he knew how to recognise his faults.

"M. Bazile," said he, raising his hat, "if I have touched your face with my hand you will excuse me and you will understand me, you will approve of me, nay, you will compliment me, you will congratulate me and felicitate me, when you know the cause of that act. I took you for Colomban."

M. Bazile, wiping his bleeding nostrils with his handkerchief and displaying an elbow laid bare by the absence of his sleeve:

"No, sir," answered he drily, "I shall not felicitate you, I shall not congratulate you, I shall not compliment you, for your action was, at the very least, superfluous; it was, I will even say, supererogatory. Already this evening I have been three times mistaken for Colomban and received a sufficient amount of the treatment he deserves. The patriots have knocked in my ribs and broken my back, and, sir, I was of opinion that that was enough."

Scarcely had he finished this speech than a band of Pyrotists appeared, and misled in their turn by the insidious resemblance, they believed that the patriots were killing Colomban. They fell on Prince des Boscénos and his companions with loaded canes and leather thongs, and left them for dead. Then seizing Bazile they carried him in triumph, and in spite of his protests, along the boulevards, amid cries of: "Hurrah for Colomban! Hurrah for Pyrot!" At last the police, who had been sent after them, attacked and defeated them and dragged them ignominiously to the station, where Bazile, under the name of Colomban, was trampled on by an innumerable quan v tity of thick, hob-nailed shoes.

VII

BIDAULT-COQUILLE AND MANIFLORE, THE SOCIALISTS

Whilst the wind of anger and hatred blew in Alca, Eugène Bidault-Coquille, poorest and happiest of astronomers, installed in an old steam-engine of the time of the Draconides, was observing the heavens through a bad telescope, and photographing the paths of the meteors upon some damaged photographic plates. His genius corrected the errors of his instruments and his love of science triumphed over the worthlessness of his apparatus. With an inextinguishable ardour he observed aerolites, meteors, and fire-balls, and all the glowing ruins and blazing sparks which pass through the terrestrial atmosphere with prodigious speed, and as a reward for his studious vigils he received the indifference of the public, the ingratitude of the State and the blame of the learned societies. Engulfed in the celestial spaces he knew not what occurred upon the surface of the earth. He never read the newspapers, and when he walked through the town his mind was occupied with the November asteroids, and more than once he found himself at the bottom of a pond in one of the public parks or beneath the wheels of a motor omnibus.

Elevated in stature as in thought he respected himself and others. This was shown by his cold politeness as well as by a very thin black frock coat and a tall hat which gave to his person an appearance at once emaciated and sublime. He took his meals in a little restaurant from which all customers less intellectual than himself had fled, and thenceforth his napkin bound by its wooden ring rested alone in the abandoned rack.

In this cook-shop his eyes fell one evening upon Colomban's

memorandum in favour of Pyrot. He read it as he was cracking some bad nuts and suddenly, exalted with astonishment, admiration, horror, and pity, he forgot all about falling meteors and shooting stars and saw nothing but the innocent man hanging in his cage, exposed to the winds of heaven and the ravens perching upon it.

That image did not leave him. For a week he had been obsessed by the innocent convict, when, as he was leaving his cook-shop, he saw a crowd of citizens entering a public-house in which a public meeting was going on. He went in. The meeting was disorderly; they were yelling, abusing one another and knocking one another down in the smoke-laden hall. The Pyrotists and the Anti-Pyrotists spoke in turn and were alternately cheered and hissed at. An obscure and confused enthusiasm moved the audience. With the audacity of a timid and retired man Bidault-Coquille leaped upon the platform and spoke for three-quarters of an hour. He spoke very quickly, without order, but with vehemence, and with all the conviction of a mathematical mystic. He was cheered. When he got down from the platform a big woman of uncertain age, dressed in red, and wearing an immense hat trimmed with heroic feathers, throwing herself into his arms, embraced him, and said to him:

"You are splendid!"

He thought in his simplicity that there was some truth in the statement.

She declared to him that henceforth she would live but for Pyrot's defence and Colomban's glory. He thought her sublime and beautiful. She was Maniflore, a poor old courtesan, now forgotten and discarded, who had suddenly become a vehement politician.

She never left him. They spent glorious hours together in doss-houses and in lodgings beautified by their love, in newspaper offices, in meeting-halls and in lecture-halls. As he was an idealist, he persisted in thinking her beautiful, although she gave him abundant opportunity of seeing that she had preserved no charm of any kind. From her past beauty she only retained a confidence in her capacity for pleasing and a lofty assurance in demanding homage. Still, it must be admitted that this Pyrot affair, so fruitful in prodigies, invested Maniflore with a sort of civic majesty, and transformed her, at public meetings, into an august symbol of justice and truth.

Bidault-Coquille and Maniflore did not kindle the least spark of irony or amusement in a single Anti-Pyrotist, a single defender of Greatauk, or a single supporter of the army. The gods, in their anger, had refused to those men the precious gift of humour. They gravely accused the courtesan and the astronomer of being spies, of treachery, and of plotting against their country. Bidault-Coquille and Maniflore grew visibly greater beneath insult, abuse, and calumny.

For long months Penguinia had been divided into two camps and, though at first sight it may appear strange, hitherto the socialists had taken no part in the contest. Their groups comprised almost all the manual workers in the country, necessarily scattered, confused, broken up, and divided, but formidable. The Pyrot affair threw the group leaders into a singular embarrassment. They did not wish to place themselves either on the side of the financiers or on the side of the army. They regarded the Jews, both great and small, as their uncompromising opponents. Their principles were not at stake, nor were their interests concerned in the affair. Still the greater number felt how difficult it was growing for them to remain aloof from struggles in which all Penguinia was engaged.

Their leaders called a sitting of their federation at the Rue de la Queue-du-diable-St. Maël, to take into consideration the conduct they ought to adopt in the present circumstances and in future eventualities.

Comrade Phœnix was the first to speak.

"A crime," said he, "the most odious and cowardly of crimes, a judicial crime, has been committed. Military judges, coerced or misled by their superior officers, have condemned an innocent man to an infamous and cruel punishment. Let us not say that the victim is not one of our own party, that he belongs to a caste which was, and always will be, our enemy. Our party is the party of social justice; it can look upon no iniquity with indifference.

"It would be a shame for us if we left it to Kerdanic, a radical, to Colomban, a member of the middle classes, and to a few moderate Republicans, alone to proceed against the crimes of the army. If the victim is not one of us, his executioners are our brothers' executioners, and before Greatauk struck down this soldier he shot our comrades who were on strike.

"Comrades, by an intellectual, moral and material effort you must rescue Pyrot from his torment, and in performing this generous act you are not turning aside from the liberating and revolutionary task you have undertaken, for Pyrot has become the symbol of the oppressed and of all the social iniquities that now exist; by destroying one you make all the others tremble."

When Phœnix ended, comrade Sapor spoke in these terms:

"You are advised to abandon your task in order to do something with which you have no concern. Why throw yourselves into a conflict where, on whatever side you turn, you will find none but your natural, uncompromising, even necessary opponents? Are the financiers to be less hated by us than the army? What inept and criminal generosity is it that hurries you to save those seven hundred Pyrotists whom you will always find confronting you in the social war?

"It is proposed that you act the part of the police for your enemies, and that you are to re-establish for them the order which their own crimes have disturbed. Magnanimity pushed to this degree changes its name.

"Comrades, there is a point at which infamy becomes fatal to a society. Penguin society is being strangled by its infamy, and you are requested to save it, to give it air that it can breathe. This is simply turning you into ridicule.

"Leave it to smother itself and let us gaze at its last convulsions with joyful contempt, only regretting that it has so entirely corrupted the soil on which it has been built that we shall find nothing but poisoned mud on which to lay the foundations of a new society."

When Sapor had ended his speech comrade Lapersonne pronounced these few words:

"Phœnix calls us to Pyrot's help for the reason that Pyrot is innocent. It seems to me that that is a very bad reason. If Pyrot is innocent he has behaved like a good soldier and has always conscientiously worked at his trade, which principally consists in shooting the people. That is not a motive to make the people brave all dangers in his defence. When it is demonstrated to me that Pyrot is guilty and that he stole the army hay, I shall be on his side."

Comrade Larrivée afterwards spoke.

"I am not of my friend Phœnix's opinion but I am not with my friend Sapor either. I do not believe that the party is bound to embrace a cause as soon as we are told that that cause is just. That, I am afraid, is a grievous abuse of words and a dangerous equivocation. For social justice is not revolutionary justice. They are both in perpetual antagonism: to serve the one is to oppose the other. As for me, my choice is made. I am for revolutionary justice as against social justice. Still, in the present case I am against abstention. I say that when a lucky chance brings us an affair like this we should be fools not to profit by it.

"How? We are given an opportunity of striking terrible, perhaps fatal, blows against militarism. And am I to fold my arms? I tell you, comrades, I am not a fakir, I have never been a fakir, and if there are fakirs here let them not count on me. To sit in meditation is a policy without results and one which I shall never adopt.

"A party like ours ought to be continually asserting itself. It ought to prove its existence by continual action. We will intervene in the Pyrot affair but we will intervene in it in a revolutionary manner; we will adopt violent action. . . . Per-

haps you think that violence is old-fashioned and super-annu-
ated, to be scrapped along with diligences, hand-presses and
aerial telegraphy. You are mistaken. To-day as yesterday
nothing is obtained except by violence; it is the one efficient
instrument. The only thing necessary is to know how to use
it. You ask what will our action be? I will tell you: it will
be to stir up the governing classes against one another, to put
the army in conflict with the capitalists, the government with
the magistracy, the nobility and clergy with the Jews, and if
possible to drive them all to destroy one another. To do this
would be to carry on an agitation which would weaken government in the same way that fever wears out the sick.

"The Pyrot affair, little as we know how to turn it to advantage, will put forward by ten years the growth of the
Socialist party and the emancipation of the proletariat, by
disarmament, the general strike, and revolution."

The leaders of the party having each expressed a different
opinion, the discussion was continued, not without vivacity.
The orators, as always happens in such a case, reproduced
the arguments they had already brought forward, though with
less order and moderation than before. The dispute was prolonged and none changed his opinion. But these opinions, in
the final analysis, were reduced to two, that of Sapor and
Lapersonne who advised abstention, and that of Phœnix and
Larrivée, who wanted intervention. Even these two contrary
opinions were united in a common hatred of the heads of the
army and of their justice, and in a common belief in Pyrot's
innocence. So that public opinion was hardly mistaken in
regarding all the Socialist leaders as pernicious Anti-Pyrotists.

As for the vast masses in whose name they spoke and whom
they represented as far as speech can express the inexpressible
—as for the proletarians whose thought is difficult to know
and who do not know it themselves, it seemed that the Pyrot
affair did not interest them. It was too literary for them, it
was in too classical a style, and had an upper-middle-class
and high-finance tone about it that did not please them much.

VIII

THE COLOMBAN TRIAL

WHEN the Colomban trial began, the Pyrotists were not many more than thirty thousand, but they were everywhere and might be found even among the priests and millionaires. What injured them most was the sympathy of the rich Jews. On the other hand they derived valuable advantages from their feeble number. In the first place there were among them fewer fools than among their opponents, who were over-burdened with them. Comprising but a feeble minority they co-operated easily, acted with harmony, and had no temptation to divide and thus counteract one another's efforts. Each of them felt the necessity of doing the best possible and was the more careful of his conduct as he found himself more in the public eye. Finally, they had every reason to hope that they would gain fresh adherents, while their opponents, having had everybody with them at the beginning, could only decrease.

Summoned before the judges at a public sitting, Colomban immediately perceived that his judges were not anxious to discover the truth. As soon as he opened his mouth the President ordered him to be silent in the superior interests of the State. For the same reason, which is the supreme reason, the witnesses for the defence were not heard. General Panther, the Chief of the Staff, appeared in the witness-box, in full uniform and decorated with all his orders. He deposed as follows:

"The infamous Colomban states that we have no proofs against Pyrot. He lies; we have them. I have in my archives seven hundred and thirty-two square yards of them which at five hundred pounds each make three hundred and sixty-six thousand pounds weight."

That superior officer afterwards gave, with elegance and ease, a summary of those proofs.

"They are of all colours and all shades," said he in sub-stance, "they are of every form—pot, crown, sovereign, grape, dove-cot, grand eagle, etc. The smallest is less than the hundredth part of a square inch, the largest measures seventy yards long by ninety yards broad."

At this revelation the audience shuddered with horror.

Greatauk came to give evidence in his turn. Simpler, and perhaps greater, he wore a grey tunic and held his hands joined behind his back.

"I leave," said he calmly and in a slightly raised voice, "I leave to M. Colomban the responsibility for an act that has brought our country to the brink of ruin. The Pyrot affair is secret; it ought to remain secret. If it were divulged the cruelest ills, wars, pillages, depredations, fires, massacres, and epidemics would immediately burst upon Penguinia. I should consider myself guilty of high treason if I uttered another word."

Some persons known for their political experience, among others M. Bigourd, considered the evidence of the Minister of War as abler and of greater weight than that of his Chief of Staff.

The evidence of Colonel de Boisjoli made a great impression.

"One evening at the Ministry of War," said that officer, "the attaché of a neighbouring Power told me that while visiting his sovereign's stables he had once admired some soft and fragrant hay, of a pretty green colour, the finest hay he had ever seen! 'Where did it come from?' I asked him. He did not answer, but there seemed to me no doubt about its origin. It was the hay Pyrot had stolen. Those qualities of verdure, softness, and aroma, are those of our national hay. The forage of the neighbouring Power is grey and brittle; it sounds under the fork and smells of dust. One can draw one's own conclusions."

Lieutenant-Colonel Hastaing said in the witness-box, amid hisses, that he did not believe Pyrot guilty. He was immediately seized by the police and thrown into the bottom of a dungeon where, amid vipers, toads, and broken glass, he remained insensible both to promises and threats.

The usher called:

"Count Pierre Maubec de la Dentdulynx."

There was deep silence, and a stately but ill-dressed nobleman, whose moustaches pointed to the skies and whose dark eyes shot forth flashing glances, was seen advancing toward the witness-box.

He approached Colomban and casting upon him a look of ineffable disdain:

"My evidence," said he, "here it is: you excrement!"

At these words the entire hall burst into enthusiastic applause and jumped up, moved by one of those transports that stir men's hearts and rouse them to extraordinary actions. Without another word Count Maubec de la Dentdulynx withdrew.

All those present left the court and formed a procession behind him. Prostrate at his feet, Princess des Boscénos held his legs in a close embrace, but he went on, stern and impassive, beneath a shower of handkerchiefs and flowers. Viscountess Olive, clinging to his neck, could not be removed, and the calm hero bore her along with him, floating on his breast like a light scarf.

When the court resumed its sitting, which it had been compelled to suspend, the President called the experts.

Vermillard, the famous expert in handwriting, gave the results of his researches.

"Having carefully studied," said he, "the papers found in Pyrot's house, in particular his account book and his laundry books, I noticed that, though apparently not out of the common, they formed an impenetrable cryptogram, the key to which, however, I discovered. The traitor's infamy is to be seen in every line. In this system of writing the words 'Three glasses of beer and twenty francs for Adèle,' mean 'I have delivered thirty thousand trusses of hay to a neighbouring Power.' From these documents I have even been able to establish the composition of the hay delivered by this officer. The words waistcoat, drawers, pocket handkerchief, collars, drink, tobacco, cigars, mean clover, meadowgrass, lucern, burnet, oats, rye-grass, vernal-grass, and common cat's tail grass. And these are precisely the constituents of the hay furnished by Count Maubec to the Penguin cavalry. In this way Pyrot mentioned his crimes in a language that he believed would always remain indecipherable. One is confounded by so much astuteness and so great a want of conscience."

Colomban, pronounced guilty without any extenuating circumstances, was condemned to the severest penalty. The judges immediately signed a warrant consigning him to solitary confinement.

In the Place du Palais on the sides of a river whose banks had during the course of twelve centuries seen so great a history, fifty thousand persons were tumultuously awaiting the result of the trial. Here were the heads of the Anti-Pyrotist Association, among whom might be seen Prince des Boscénos, Count Cléna, Viscount Olive, and M. de La Trumelle; here crowded the Reverend Father Agaric and the teachers of St. Maël College with their pupils; here the monk Douillard and General Caraguel, embracing each other, formed a sublime group. The market women and laundry women with spits, shovels, tongs, beetles, and kettles full of water might be seen running across the Pont-Vieux. On the steps in front of the bronze gates were assembled all the defenders of Pyrot in Alca, professors, publicists, workmen, some conservatives, others Radicals or Revolutionaries, and by their negligent dress and fierce aspect could be recognised comrades Phœnix, Larrivée, Lapersonne, Dagobert, and Varambille. Squeezed in his funereal frock-coat and wearing his hat of ceremony,

Bidault-Coquille invoked the sentimental mathematics on behalf of Colomban and Colonel Hastaing. Maniflore shone smiling and resplendent on the topmost step, anxious, like Leæna, to deserve a glorious monument, or to be given, like Epicharis, the praises of history.

The seven hundred Pyrotists disguised as lemonade sellers, gutter-merchants, collectors of odds and ends, or as Anti-Pyrotists, wandered round the vast building.

When Colomban appeared, so great an uproar burst forth that, struck by the commotion of air and water, birds fell from the trees and fishes floated on the surface of the stream.

On all sides there were yells:

"Duck Colomban, duck him, duck him!"

There were some cries of "Justice and truth!" and a voice was even heard shouting:

"Down with the Army!"

This was the signal for a terrible struggle. The combatants fell in thousands, and their bodies formed howling and moving mounds on top of which fresh champions gripped each other by the throats. Women, eager, pale, and dishevelled, with clenched teeth and frantic nails, rushed on the man, in transports that, in the brilliant light of the public square, gave to their faces expressions unsurpassed even in the shade of curtains and in the hollows of pillows. They were going to seize Colomban, to bite him, to strangle, dismember and rend him, when Maniflore, tall and dignified in her red tunic, stood forth, serene and terrible, confronting these furies who recoiled from before her in terror. Colomban seemed to be saved; his partisans succeeded in clearing a passage for him through the Place du Palais and in putting him into a cab stationed at the corner of the Pont-Vieux. The horse was already in full trot when Prince des Boscénos, Count Cléna, and M. de La Trumelle knocked the driver off his seat. Then, making the animal back and pushing the spokes of the wheels, they ran the vehicle on to the parapet of the bridge, whence they overturned it into the river amid the cheers of the delirious crowd. With a resounding splash a jet of water rose upwards, and then nothing but a slight eddy was to be seen on the surface of the stream.

Almost immediately comrades Dagobert and Varambille, with the help of the seven hundred disguised Pyrotists, sent Prince des Boscénos head foremost into a river-laundry in which he was lamentably swallowed up.

Serene night descended over the Place du Palais and shed silence and peace upon the frightful ruins with which it was strewed. In the mean time, Colomban, three hundred yards down the stream, cowering beside a lame old horse on a bridge, was meditating on the ignorance and injustice of crowds.

"The business," said he to himself, "is even more troublesome than I believed. I foresee fresh difficulties."

He got up and approached the unhappy animal.

"What have you, poor friend, done to them?" said he. "It is on my account they have used you so cruelly."

He embraced the unfortunate beast and kissed the white star on his forehead. Then he took him by the bridle and led him, both of them limping, through the sleeping city to his house, where sleep soon allowed them to forget mankind.

IX

FATHER DOUILLARD

In their minute gentleness and at the suggestion of the common father of the faithful, the bishops, canons, vicars, curates, abbots, and friars of Penguinia resolved to hold solemn service in the cathedral of Alca, and to pray that Divine mercy would deign to put an end to the troubles that distracted one of the noblest countries in Christendom, and grant to repentant Penguinia pardon for its crimes against God and against ministers of religion.

The ceremony took place on the fifteenth of June. General Caraguel, surrounded by his staff, occupied the churchwarden's pew. The congregation was numerous and brilliant. According to M. Bigourd's expression it was both crowded and select. In the front rank was to be seen M. de la Bertheoseille, Chamberlain to his Highness Prince Crucho. Near the pulpit, which was to be ascended by the Reverend Father Douillard, of the Order of St. Francis, were gathered, in an attitude of attention with their hands crossed upon their wands of office, the great dignitaries of the Anti-Pyrotist Association, Viscount Olive, M. de La Trumelle, Count Cléna, the Duke d'Ampoule, and Prince des Boscénos. Father Agaric was in the apse with the teachers and pupils of St. Maël College. The right-hand transept and aisle were reserved for officers and soldiers in uniform, since the Lord leaned his head to the right when he died on the Cross. The ladies of the aristocracy, and among them Countess Cléna, Viscountess Olive, and Princess des Boscénos, occupied reserved seats. In the immense building and in the square outside were gathered twenty thousand clergy of all sorts, as well as thirty thousand of the laity.

After the expiatory and propitiatory ceremony the Rever,
end Father Douillard ascended the pulpit. The sermon had at
first been entrusted to the Reverend Father Agaric, but, in
spite of his merits, he was thought unequal to the occasion
in zeal and doctrine, and the eloquent Capuchin friar, who
for six months had gone through the barracks preaching
against the enemies of God and authority, had been chosen
in his place.

The Reverend Father Douillard, taking as his text, "He
hath put down the mighty from their seat," established that
all temporal power has God as its principle and its end, and
that it is ruined and destroyed when it turns aside from the
path that Providence has traced out for it and from the end
to which He has directed it.

Applying these sacred rules to the government of Penguinia,
he drew a terrible picture of the evils that the country's rulers
had been unable either to prevent or to foresee.

"The first author of all these miseries and degradations,
my brethren," said he, "is only too well known to you. He is
a monster whose destiny is providentially proclaimed by his
name, for it is derived from the Greek word, *pyros*, which
means fire. Eternal wisdom warns us by this etymology that a
Jew was to set ablaze the country that had welcomed him."

He depicted the country, persecuted by the persecutors of
the Church, and crying in its agony:

"O woe! O glory! Those who have crucified my God are
crucifying me!"

At these words a prolonged shudder passed through the
assembly.

The powerful orator excited still greater indignation when
he described the proud and crime-stained Colomban, plunged
into the stream, all the waters of which could not cleanse him.
He gathered up all the humiliations and all the perils of the
Penguins in order to reproach the President of the Republic
and his Prime Minister with them.

"That Minister," said he, "having been guilty of degrading

cowardice in not exterminating the seven hundred Pyrotists
with their allies and defenders, as Saul exterminated the Phil-
istines at Gibeah, has rendered himself unworthy of exercising
the power that God delegated to him, and every good citizen
ought henceforth to insult his contemptible government.
Heaven will look favourably on those who despise him. 'He
hath put down the mighty from their seat.' God will depose
these pusillanimous chiefs and will put in their place strong
men who will call upon Him. I tell you, gentlemen, I tell you
officers, non-commissioned officers, and soldiers who listen to
me, I tell you General of the Penguin armies, the hour has
come! If you do not obey God's orders, if in His name you do
not depose those now in authority, if you do not establish a
religious and strong government in Penguinia, God will none
the less destroy what He has condemned, He will none the less
save His people. He will save them, but, if you are wanting,
He will do so by means of a humble artisan or a simple cor-
poral. Hasten! The hour will soon be past."

Excited by this ardent exhortation, the sixty thousand people present rose up trembling and shouting: "To arms! To
arms! Death to the Pyrotists! Hurrah for Crucho!" and all
of them, monks, women, soldiers, noblemen, citizens, and
loafers, who were gathered beneath the superhuman arm uplifted in the pulpit, struck up the hymn, "Let us save Penguinia!" They rushed impetuously from the basilica and
marched along the quays to the Chamber of Deputies.

Left alone in the deserted nave, the wise Cornemuse, lifting
his arms to heaven, murmured in broken accents:

"Agnosco fortunam ecclesiæ penguicanæ! I see but too
well whither this will lead us."

The attack which the crowd made upon the legislative palace was repulsed. Vigorously charged by the police and Alcan
guards, the assailants were already fleeing in disorder, when
the Socialists, running from the slums and led by comrades
Phœnix, Dagobert, Lapersonne, and Varambille, threw themselves upon them and completed their discomfiture. MM. de

La Trumelle and d'Ampoule were taken to the police station. Prince des Boscénos, after a valiant struggle, fell upon the bloody pavement with a fractured skull.

In the enthusiasm of victory, the comrades, mingled with an innumerable crowd of paper-sellers and gutter-merchants, ran through the boulevards all night, carrying Maniflore in triumph, and breaking the mirrors of the cafés and the glasses of the street lamps amid cries of "Down with Crucho! Hurrah for the Social Revolution!" The Anti-Pyrotists in their turn upset the newspaper kiosks and tore down the hoardings.

These were spectacles of which cool reason cannot approve and they were fit causes for grief to the municipal authorities, who desired to preserve the good order of the roads and streets. But what was sadder for a man of heart was the sight of the canting humbugs, who, from fear of blows, kept at an equal distance from the two camps, and who, although they allowed their selfishness and cowardice to be visible, claimed admiration for the generosity of their sentiments and the nobility of their souls. They rubbed their eyes with onions, gaped like whitings, blew violently into their handkerchiefs, and, bringing their voices out of the depth of their stomachs, groaned forth: "O Penguins, cease these fratricidal struggles; cease to rend your mother's bosom!" As if men could live in society without disputes and without quarrels, and as if civil discords were not the necessary conditions of national life and prog-ress. They showed themselves hypocritical cowards by pro-posing a compromise between the just and the unjust, offending the just in his rectitude and the unjust in his courage. One of these creatures, the rich and powerful Machimel, a champion coward, rose upon the town like a colossus of grief; his tears formed poisonous lakes at his feet and his sighs capsized the boats of the fishermen.

During these stormy nights Bidault-Coquille at the top of his old steam-engine, under the serene sky, boasted in his heart, while the shooting stars registered themselves upon his photographic plates. He was fighting for justice. He loved and was loved with a sublime passion. Insult and calumny raised him to the clouds. A caricature of him in company with those of Colomban, Kerdanic, and Colonel Hastaing was to be seen in the newspaper kiosks. The Anti-Pyrotists proclaimed that he had received fifty thousand francs from the big Jewish financiers. The reporters of the militarist sheets held interviews regarding his scientific knowledge with official scholars, who declared he had no knowledge of the stars, disputed his most solid observations, denied his most certain discoveries, and condemned his most ingenious and most fruitful hypotheses. He exulted under these flattering blows of hatred and envy.

He contemplated the black immensity pierced by a multitude of lights, without giving a thought to all the heavy slumbers, cruel insomnias, vain dreams, spoilt pleasures, and infinitely diverse miseries that a great city contains.

"It is in this enormous city," said he to himself, "that the just and the unjust are joining battle."

And substituting a simple and magnificent poetry for the multiple and vulgar reality, he represented to himself the Pyrot affair as a struggle between good and bad angels. He awaited the eternal triumph of the Sons of Light and congratulated himself on being a Child of the Day confounding the Children of Night.

X

MR. JUSTICE CHAUSSEPIED

HITHERTO blinded by fear, incautious and stupid before the bands of Friar Douillard and the partisans of Prince Crucho, the Republicans at last opened their eyes and grasped the real meaning of the Pyrot affair. The deputies who had for two years turned pale at the shouts of the patriotic crowds became, not indeed more courageous, but altered their cowardice and blamed Robin Mielleux for disorders which their own compliance had encouraged, and the instigators of which they had several times slavishly congratulated. They reproached him for having imperilled the Republic by a weakness which was really theirs and a timidity which they themselves had imposed upon him. Some of them began to doubt whether it was not to their interest to believe in Pyrot's innocence rather than in his guilt, and thenceforward they felt a bitter anguish at the thought that the unhappy man might have been wrongly convicted and that in his aerial cage he might be expiating another man's crimes. "I cannot sleep on account of it!" was what several members of Minister Guillaumette's majority used to say. But these were ambitious to replace their chief.

These generous legislators overthrew the cabinet, and the President of the Republic put in Robin Mielleux's place, a patriarchal Republican with a flowing beard, La Trinité by name, who, like most of the Penguins, understood nothing about the affair, but thought that too many monks were mixed up in it.

General Greatauk, before leaving the Ministry of War, gave his final advice to Panther, the Chief of the Staff.

"I go and you remain," said he, as he shook hands with him. "The Pyrot affair is my daughter; I confide her to you, she is worthy of your love and your care; she is beautiful. Do not forget that her beauty loves the shade, is pleased with mystery, and likes to remain veiled. Treat her modesty with gentleness. Too many indiscreet looks have already profaned her charms. . . . Panther, you desired proofs and you obtained them. You have many, perhaps too many, in your possession. I see that there will be many tiresome interventions and much dangerous curiosity. If I were in your place, I would tear up all those documents. Believe me, the best of proofs is none at all. That is the only one which nobody discusses."

Alas! General Panther did not realise the wisdom of this advice. The future was only too thoroughly to justify Great-auk's perspicacity. La Trinité demanded the documents belonging to the Pyrot affair. Péniche, his Minister of War, refused them in the superior interests of the national defence, telling him that the documents under General Panther's care formed the hugest mass of archives in the world. La Trinité studied the case as well as he could, and, without penetrating to the bottom of the matter, suspected it of irregularity. Conformably to his rights and prerogatives he then ordered a fresh trial to be held. Immediately, Péniche, his Minister of War, accused him of insulting the army and betraying the country, and flung his portfolio at his head. He was replaced by a second, who did the same. To him succeeded a third, who imitated these examples, and those after him to the number of seventy acted like their predecessors, until the venerable La Trinité groaned beneath the weight of bellicose portfolios. The seventy-first Minister of War, van Julep, retained office. Not that he was in disagreement with so many and such noble colleagues, but he had been commissioned by them generously to betray his Prime Minister, to cover him with shame and opprobrium. and to convert the new trial to the glory of Greatauk, the satisfaction of the Anti-Pyrotists, the profit of the monks, and the restoration of Prince Crucho.

General van Julep, though endowed with high military virtues, was not intelligent enough to employ the subtle conduct and exquisite methods of Greatauk. He thought, like General Panther, that tangible proofs against Pyrot were necessary, that they could never have too many of them, that they could never have even enough. He expressed these sentiments to his Chief of Staff, who was only too inclined to agree with them.

"Panther," said he, "we are at the moment when we need abundant and superabundant proofs."

"You have said enough, General," answered Panther, "I will complete my piles of documents."

Six months later the proofs against Pyrot filled two storeys of the Ministry of War. The ceiling fell in beneath the weight of the bundles, and the avalanche of falling documents crushed two head clerks, fourteen second clerks, and sixty copying clerks, who were at work upon the ground floor arranging a change in the fashion of the cavalry gaiters. The walls of the huge edifice had to be propped. Passers-by saw with amazement enormous beams and monstrous stanchions which reared themselves obliquely against the noble front of the building now tottering and disjointed, and blocked up the streets, stopped the carriages, and presented to the motor-omnibuses an obstacle against which they dashed with their loads of passengers.

The judges who had condemned Pyrot were not, properly speaking, judges but soldiers. The judges who had condemned Colomban were real judges, but of inferior rank, wearing seedy black clothes like church vergers, unlucky wretches of judges, miserable judgelings. Above them were the superior judges who wore ermine robes over their black gowns. These, renowned for their knowledge and doctrine, formed a court whose terrible name expressed power. It was called the Court of Appeal (Cassation) so as to make it clear that it was the hammer suspended over the judgments and decrees of all other jurisdictions.

One of these superior red judges of the Supreme Court,

called Chaussepied, led a modest and tranquil life in a suburb of Alca. His soul was pure, his heart honest, his spirit just. When he had finished studying his documents he used to play the violin and cultivate hyacinths. Every Sunday he dined with his neighbours the Mesdemoiselles Helbivore. His old age was cheerful and robust and his friends often praised the amenity of his character.

For some months, however, he had been irritable and touchy, and when he opened a newspaper his broad and ruddy face would become covered with dolorous wrinkles and darkened with an angry purple. Pyrot was the cause of it. Justice Chaussepied could not understand how an officer could have committed so black a crime as to hand over eighty thousand trusses of military hay to a neighbouring and hostile Power. And he could still less conceive how a scoundrel should have found official defenders in Penguinia. The thought that there existed in his country a Pyrot, a Colonel Hastaing, a Colomban, a Kerdanic, a Phœnix, spoilt his hyacinths, his violin, his heaven, and his earth, all nature, and even his dinner with the Mesdemoiselles Helbivore!

In the mean time the Pyrot case, having been presented to the Supreme Court by the Keeper of the Seals, it fell to Chaussepied to examine it and discover its defects, in case any existed. Although as upright and honest as a man can be, and trained by long habit to exercise his magistracy without fear or favour, he expected to find in the documents to be submitted to him proofs of certain guilt and of obvious criminality. After lengthened difficulties and repeated refusals on the part of General van Julep, Justice Chaussepied was allowed to examine the documents. Numbered and initialed they ran to the number of fourteen millions six hundred and twenty-six thousand three hundred and twelve. As he studied them the judge was at first surprised, then astonished, then stupefied, amazed, and, if I dare say so, flabbergasted. He found among the documents prospectuses of new fancy shops, newspapers, fashion-plates, paper bags, old business letters, exercise books, brown paper, green paper for rubbing parquet floors, playing cards, diagrams, six thousand copies of the "Key to Dreams," but not a single document in which any mention was made of Pyrot.

XI

CONCLUSION

THE appeal was allowed, and Pyrot was brought down from his cage. But the Anti-Pyrotists did not regard themselves as beaten. The military judges re-tried Pyrot. Greatauk, in this second affair, surpassed himself. He obtained a second conviction; he obtained it by declaring that the proofs communicated to the Supreme Court were worth nothing, and that great care had been taken to keep back the good ones, since they ought to remain secret. In the opinion of connoisseurs he had never shown so much address. On leaving the court, as he passed through the vestibule with a tranquil step, and his hands behind his back, amidst a crowd of sight-seers, a woman dressed in red and with her face covered by a black veil rushed at him, brandishing a kitchen knife.

"Die, scoundrel!" she cried. It was Maniflore. Before those present could understand what was happening, the general seized her by the wrist, and with apparent gentleness, squeezed it so forcibly that the knife fell from her aching hand.

Then he picked it up and handed it to Maniflore.

"Madame," said he with a bow, "you have dropped a house-hold utensil."

He could not prevent the heroine from being taken to the police-station; but he had her immediately released and afterwards he employed all his influence to stop the prosecution.

The second conviction of Pyrot was Greatauk's last victory.

Justice Chaussepied, who had formerly liked soldiers so much, and esteemed their justice so highly, being now enraged with the military judges, squashed their judgments as a monkey cracks nuts. He rehabilitated Pyrot a second time; he would, if necessary, have rehabilitated him five hundred times.

Furious at having been cowards and at having allowed themselves to be deceived and made game of, the Republicans turned against the monks and clergy. The deputies passed laws of expulsion, separation, and spoliation against them. What Father Cornemuse had foreseen took place. That good monk was driven from the Wood of Conils. Treasury officers confiscated his retorts and his stills, and the liquidators divided amongst them his bottles of St. Orberosian liqueur. The pious distiller lost the annual income of three million five hundred thousand francs that his products procured for him. Father Agaric went into exile, abandoning his school into the hands of laymen, who soon allowed it to fall into decay. Separated from its foster-mother, the State, the Church of Penguinia withered like a plucked flower.

The victorious defenders of the innocent man now abused each other and overwhelmed each other reciprocally with insults and calumnies. The vehement Kerdanic hurled himself upon Phœnix as if ready to devour him. The wealthy Jews and the seven hundred Pyrotists turned away with disdain from the socialist comrades whose aid they had humbly implored in the past.

"We know you no longer," said they. "To the devil with you and your social justice. Social justice is the defence of property."

Having been elected a Deputy and chosen to be the leader of the new majority, comrade Larrivée was appointed by the Chamber and public opinion to the Premiership. He showed himself an energetic defender of the military tribunals that had condemned Pyrot. When his former socialist comrades claimed a little more justice and liberty for the employés of the State as well as for manual workers, he opposed their proposals in an eloquent speech.

"Liberty," said he, "is not licence. Between order and disorder my choice is made: revolution is impotence. Progress has no more formidable enemy than violence. Gentlemen, those who, as I am, are anxious for reform, ought to apply themselves before everything else to cure this agitation which enfeebles government just as fever exhausts those who are ill. It is time to reassure honest people."

This speech was received with applause. The government of the Republic remained in subjection to the great financial companies, the army was exclusively devoted to the defence of capital, while the fleet was designed solely to procure fresh orders for the mine-owners. Since the rich refused to pay their just share of the taxes, the poor, as in the past, paid for them.

In the mean time from the height of his old steam-engine, beneath the crowded stars of night, Bidault-Coquille gazed sadly at the sleeping city. Maniflore had left him. Consumed with a desire for fresh devotions and fresh sacrifices, she had gone in company with a young Bulgarian to bear justice and vengeance to Sofia. He did not regret her, having perceived, after the Affair, that she was less beautiful in form and in thought than he had at first imagined. His impressions had been modified in the same direction concerning many other forms and many other thoughts. And what was cruelest of all to him, he regarded himself as not so great, not so splendid, as he had believed.

And he reflected:

"You considered yourself sublime when you had but candour and good-will. Of what were you proud, Bidault-Coquille? Of having been one of the first to know that Pyrot was innocent and Greatauk a scoundrel. But three-fourths of those who defended Greatauk against the attacks of the seven hundred Pyrotists knew that better than you. Of what then did you show yourself so proud? Of having dared to say what you thought? That is civic courage, and, like military courage, it is a mere result of imprudence. You have been imprudent. So far so good, but that is no reason for praising yourself beyond measure. Your imprudence was trifling; it exposed you to trifling perils; you did not risk your head by it. The Penguins have lost that cruel and sanguinary pride which formerly gave a tragic grandeur to their revolutions; it is the fatal result of the weakening of beliefs and characters. Ought one to look upon oneself as a superior spirit for having shown a little more clear-sightedness than the vulgar? I am very much afraid, on the contrary, Bidault-Coquille, that you have given proof of a gross misunderstanding of the conditions of the moral and intellectual development of a people. You imagined that social injustices were threaded together like pearls and that it would be enough to pull off one in order to unfasten the whole necklace. That is a very ingenuous conception. You flattered yourself that at one stroke you were establishing justice in your own country and in the universe. You were a brave man, an honest idealist, though without much experimental philosophy. But go home to your own heart and you will recognise that you had in you a spice of malice and that your ingenuousness was not without cunning. You believed you were performing a fine moral action. You said to yourself: 'Here am I, just and courageous once for all. I can henceforth repose in the public esteem and the praise of historians.' And now that you have lost your illusions, now that you know how hard it is to redress wrongs, and that the task must ever be begun afresh, you are going back to your asteroids. You are right; but go back to them with modesty, Bidault-Coquille!''

BOOK VII

MODERN TIMES

MADAME CÉRÈS

"Only extreme things are tolerable."
Count Robert de Montesquiou.

I

MADAME CLARENCE'S DRAWING-ROOM

MADAME CLARENCE, the widow of an exalted functionary of the Republic, loved to entertain. Every Thursday she collected together some friends of modest condition who took pleasure in conversation. The ladies who went to see her, very different in age and rank, were all without money and had all suffered much. There was a duchess who looked like a fortune-teller and a fortune-teller who looked like a duchess. Madame Clarence was pretty enough to maintain some old *liaisons*, but not to form new ones, and she generally inspired a quiet esteem. She had a very pretty daughter, who, since she had no dower, caused some alarm among the male guests; for the Penguins were as much afraid of portionless girls as they were of the devil himself. Eveline Clarence, noticing their reserve and perceiving its cause, used to hand them their tea with an air of disdain. Moreover, she seldom appeared at the parties and talked only to the ladies or the very young people. Her discreet and retiring presence put no restraint upon the conversation, since those who took part in it thought either that as she was a young girl she would not understand it, or that, being twenty-five years old, she might listen to everything.

One Thursday therefore, in Madame Clarence's drawing-room, the conversation turned upon love. The ladies spoke of it with pride, delicacy, and mystery, the men with discretion and fatuity; everyone took an interest in the conversation, for each one was interested in what he or she said. A great deal of wit flowed; brilliant apostrophes were launched forth and keen repartees were returned. But when Professor Haddock began to speak he overwhelmed everybody.

"It is the same with our ideas on love as with our ideas on everything else," said he "they rest upon anterior habits whose very memory has been effaced. In morals, the limitations that have lost their grounds for existing, the most useless obligations, the cruelest and most injurious restraints, are because of their profound antiquity and the mystery of their origin, the least disputed and the least disputable as well as the most respected, and they are those that cannot be violated without incurring the most severe blame. All morality relative to the relations of the sexes is founded on this principle: that a woman once obtained belongs to the man, that she is his property like his horse or his weapons. And this having ceased to be true, absurdities result from it, such as the marriage or contract of sale of a woman to a man, with clauses restricting the right of ownership introduced as a consequence of the gradual diminution of the claims of the possessor.

"The obligation imposed on a girl that she should bring her virginity to her husband comes from the times when girls were married immediately they were of a marriageable age. It is ridiculous that a girl who marries at twenty-five or thirty should be subject to that obligation. You will, perhaps, say that it is a present with which her husband, if she gets one at last, will be gratified; but every moment we see men wooing married women and showing themselves perfectly satisfied to take them as they find them.

"Still, even in our own day, the duty of girls is determined in religious morality by the old belief that God, the most powerful of warriors, is polygamous, that he has reserved all maidens for himself, and that men can only take those whom he has left. This belief, although traces of it exist in several metaphors of mysticism, is abandoned to-day by most civilised peoples. However, it still dominates the education of girls not only among our believers, but even among our free-thinkers, who, as a rule, think freely for the reason that they do not think at all.

"Discretion means ability to separate and discern. We say

that a girl is discreet when she knows nothing at all. We cultivate her ignorance. In spite of all our care the most discreet know something, for we cannot conceal from them their own nature and their own sensations. But they know badly, they know in a wrong way. That is all we obtain by our careful education...."

"Sir," suddenly said Joseph Boutourlé, the High Treasurer of Alca, "believe me, there are innocent girls, perfectly innocent girls, and it is a great pity. I have known three. They married, and the result was tragical."

"I have noticed," Professor Haddock went on, "that Europeans in general and Penguins in particular occupy themselves, after sport and motoring, with nothing so much as with love. It is giving a great deal of importance to a matter that has very little weight."

"Then, Professor," exclaimed Madame Crémeur in a choking voice, "when a woman has completely surrendered herself to you, you think it is a matter of no importance?"

"No, Madame; it can have its importance," answered Professor Haddock, "but it is necessary to examine if when she surrenders herself to us she offers us a delicious fruit-garden or a plot of thistles and dandelions. And then, do we not misuse words? In love, a woman lends herself rather than gives herself. Look at the pretty Madame Pensée...."

"She is my mother," said a tall, fair young man.

"Sir, I have the greatest respect for her," replied Professor Haddock; "do not be afraid that I intend to say anything in the least offensive about her. But allow me to tell you that, as a rule, the opinions of sons about their mothers are not to be relied on. They do not bear enough in mind that a mother is a mother only because she loved, and that she can still love. That, however, is the case, and it would be deplorable were it otherwise. I have noticed, on the contrary, that daughters do not deceive themselves about their mothers' faculty for loving or about the use they make of it; they are rivals; they have their eyes upon them."

The insupportable Professor spoke a great deal longer, adding indecorum to awkwardness, and impertinence to incivility, accumulating incongruities, despising what is respectable, respecting what is despicable; but no one listened to him further.

During this time in a room that was simple without grace, a room sad for the want of love, a room which, like all young girls' rooms, had something of the cold atmosphere of a place of waiting about it, Eveline Clarence turned over the pages of club annuals and prospectuses of charities in order to obtain from them some acquaintance with society. Being convinced that her mother, shut up in her own intellectual but poor world, could neither bring her out nor push her into prominence, she decided that she herself would seek the best means of winning a husband. At once calm and obstinate, without dreams or illusions, and regarding marriage as but a ticket of admission or a passport, she kept before her mind a clear notion of the hazards, difficulties, and chances of her enterprise. She had the art of pleasing and a coldness of temperament that enabled her to turn it to its fullest advantage. Her weakness lay in the fact that she was dazzled by anything that had an aristocratic air.

When she was alone with her mother she said: "Mamma, we will go to-morrow to Father Douillard's retreat."

II

THE CHARITY OF ST. ORBEROSIA

EVERY Friday evening at nine o'clock the choicest of Alcan society assembled in the aristocratic church of St. Maël for the Reverend Father Douillard's retreat. Prince and Princess des Boscénos, Viscount and Viscountess Olive, M. and Madame Bigourd, Monsieur and Madame de La Trumelle were never absent. The flower of the aristocracy might be seen there, and fair Jewish baronesses also adorned it by their presence, for the Jewish baronesses of Alca were Christians.

This retreat, like all religious retreats, had for its object to procure for those living in the world opportunities for recollection so that they might think of their eternal salvation. It was also intended to draw down upon so many noble and illustrious families the benediction of St. Orberosia, who loves the Penguins. The Reverend Father Douillard strove for the completion of his task with a truly apostolical zeal. He hoped to restore the prerogatives of St. Orberosia as the patron saint of Penguinia and to dedicate to her a monumental church on one of the hills that dominate the city. His efforts had been crowned with great success, and for the accomplishing of this national enterprise he had already united more than a hundred thousand adherents and collected more than twenty millions of francs.

It was in the choir of St. Maël's that St. Orberosia's new shrine, shining with gold, sparkling with precious stones, and surrounded by tapers and flowers, had been erected.

The following account may be read in the "History of the Miracles of the Patron Saint of Alca" by the Abbé Plantain:

"The ancient shrine had been melted down during the Terror and the precious relics of the saint thrown into a fire that had been lit on the Place de Grève; but a poor woman of great piety, named Rouquin, went by night at the peril of her life to gather up the calcined bones and the ashes of the blessed saint. She preserved them in a jam-pot, and when religion was again restored, brought them to the venerable Curé of St. Maël's. The woman ended her days piously as a vendor of tapers and custodian of seats in the saint's chapel."

It is certain that in the time of Father Douillard, although faith was declining, the cult of St. Orberosia, which for three hundred years had fallen under the criticism of Canon Princeteau and the silence of the Doctors of the Church, recovered, and was surrounded with more pomp, more splendour, and more fervour than ever. The theologians did not now subtract a single iota from the legend. They held as certainly established all facts related by Abbot Simplicissimus, and in particular declared, on the testimony of that monk, that the devil, assuming a monk's form, had carried off the saint to a cave and had there striven with her until she overcame him. Neither places nor dates caused them any embarrassment. They paid no heed to exegesis and took good care not to grant as much to science as Canon Princeteau had formerly conceded. They knew too well whither that would lead.

The church shone with lights and flowers. An operatic tenor sang the famous canticle of St. Orberosia:

> Virgin of Paradise
> Come, come in the dusky night
> And on us shed
> Thy beams of light.

Mademoiselle Clarence sat beside her mother and in front of Viscount Cléna. She remained kneeling during a considerable time, for the attitude of prayer is natural to discreet virgins and it shows off their figures.

The Reverend Father Douillard ascended the pulpit. He was a powerful orator and could, at once melt, surprise, and rouse his hearers. Women complained only that he fulminated against vice with excessive harshness and in crude terms that made them blush. But they liked him none the less for it.

He treated in his sermon of the seventh trial of St. Orberosia, who was tempted by the dragon which she went forth to combat. But she did not yield, and she disarmed the monster.

The orator demonstrated without difficulty that we, also, by the aid of St. Orberosia, and strong in the virtue which she inspires, can in our turn overthrow the dragons that dart upon us and are waiting to devour us, the dragon of doubt, the dragon of impiety, the dragon of forgetfulness of religious duties. He proved that the charity of St. Orberosia was a work of social regeneration, and he concluded by an ardent appeal to the faithful "to become instruments of the Divine mercy, eager upholders and supporters of the charity of St. Orberosia, and to furnish it with all the means which it required to take its flight and bear its salutary fruits." *

After the ceremony, the Reverend Father Douillard remained in the sacristy at the disposal of those of the faithful who desired information concerning the charity, or who wished to bring their contributions. Mademoiselle Clarence wished to speak to Father Douillard, so did Viscount Cléna. The crowd was large, and a queue was formed. By chance Viscount Cléna and Mademoiselle Clarence were side by side and possibly they were squeezed a little closely to each other by the crowd. Eveline had noticed this fashionable young man, who was almost as well known as his father in the world of sport. Cléna had noticed her, and, as he thought her pretty, he bowed to her, then apologized and pretended to believe that he had been introduced to the ladies, but could not remember where. They pretended to believe it also.

He presented himself the following week at Madame Clarence's, thinking that her house was a bit fast—a thing

* Cf. J. Ernest Charles in the "Censeur," May-August, 1907, p. 562, col. 2.

not likely to displease him—and when he saw Eveline again he felt he had not been mistaken and that she was an extremely pretty girl.

Viscount Cléna had the finest motor-car in Europe. For three months he drove the Clarences every day over hills and plains, through woods and valleys; they visited famous sites and went over celebrated castles. He said to Eveline all that could be said and did all that could be done to overcome her resistance. She did not conceal from him that she loved him, that she would always love him, and love no one but him. She remained grave and trembling by his side. To his devouring passion she opposed the invincible defence of a virtue conscious of its danger. At the end of three months, after having gone uphill and downhill, turned sharp corners and negotiated level crossings, and experienced innumerable break-downs, he knew her as well as he knew the fly-wheel of his car, but not much better. He employed surprises, adventures, sudden stoppages in the depths of forests and before hotels, but he had advanced no farther. He said to himself that it was absurd; then, taking her again in his car he set off at fifty miles an hour quite prepared to upset her in a ditch or to smash himself and her against a tree.

One day, having come to take her on some excursion, he found her more charming than ever, and more provoking. He darted upon her as a storm falls upon the reeds that border a lake. She bent with adorable weakness beneath the breath of the storm and twenty times was almost carried away by its strength, but twenty times she arose, supple and bowing to the wind. After all these shocks one would have said that a light breeze had barely touched her charming stem; she smiled as if ready to be plucked by a bold hand. Then her unhappy aggressor, desperate, enraged, and three parts mad, fled so as not to kill her, mistook the door, went into the bedroom of Madame Clarence, whom he found putting on her hat in front of a wardrobe, seized her, flung her on the bed, and possessed her before she knew what had happened.

The same day Eveline, who had been making inquiries, learned that Viscount Cléna had nothing but debts, lived on money given him by an elderly lady, and promoted the sale of the latest models of a motor-car manufacturer. They separated with common accord and Eveline began again disdainfully to serve tea to her mother's guests.

III

HIPPOLYTE CÉRÈS

In Madame Clarence's drawing-room the conversation turned upon love, and many charming things were said about it.

"Love is a sacrifice," sighed Madame Crémeur.

"I agree with you," replied M. Boutourlé with animation.

But Professor Haddock soon displayed his fastidious insolence.

"It seems to me," said he, "that the Penguin ladies have made a great fuss since, through St. Maël's agency, they became viviparous. But there is nothing to be particularly proud of in that, for it is a state they share in common with cows and pigs, and even with orange and lemon trees, for the seeds of these plants germinate in the pericarp."

"The self-importance which the Penguin ladies give themselves does not go so far back as that," answered M. Boutourlé. "It dates from the day when the holy apostle gave them clothes. But this self-importance was long kept in restraint, and displayed itself fully only with increased luxury of dress and in a small section of society. For go only two leagues from Alca into the country at harvest time, and you will see whether women are over-precise or self-important."

On that day M. Hippolyte Cérès paid his first call. He was a deputy of Alca, and one of the youngest members of the House. His father was said to have kept a dram shop, but he himself was a lawyer of robust physique, a good though prolix speaker, with a self-important air and a reputation for ability.

"M. Cérès," said the mistress of the house, "your constituency is one of the finest in Alca."

"And there are fresh improvements made in it every day, Madame."

"Unfortunately, it is impossible to take a stroll through it any longer," said M. Boutourlé.

"Why?" asked M. Cérès.

"On account of the motors, of course."

"Do not give them a bad name," answered the Deputy. "They are our great national industry."

"I know. The Penguins of to-day make me think of the ancient Egyptians. According to Clement of Alexandria, Taine tells us—though he misquotes the text—the Egyptians worshipped the crocodiles that devoured them. The Penguins to-day worship the motors that crush them. Without a doubt the future belongs to the metal beast. We are no more likely to go back to cabs than we are to go back to the diligence. And the long martyrdom of the horse will come to an end. The motor, which the frenzied cupidity of manufacturers hurls like a Juggernaut's car upon the bewildered people and of which the idle and fashionable make a foolish though fatal elegance, will soon begin to perform its true function, and putting its strength at the service of the entire people, will behave like a docile, toiling monster. But in order that the motor may cease to be injurious and become beneficent we must build roads suited to its speed, roads which it cannot tear up with its ferocious tyres, and from which it will send no clouds of poisonous dust into human lungs. We ought not to allow slower vehicles or mere animals to go upon those roads, and we should establish garages upon them and footbridges over them, and so create order and harmony among the means of communication of the future. That is the wish of every good citizen."

Madame Clarence led the conversation back to the improvements in M. Cérès' constituency. M. Cérès showed his enthusiasm for demolitions, tunnellings, constructions, reconstructions and all other fruitful operations.

"We build to-day in an admirable style," said he; "every

where majestic avenues are being reared. Was ever anything as fine as our arcaded bridges and our domed hotels!"

"You are forgetting that big palace surmounted by an immense melon-shaped dome," grumbled M. Daniset, an old art amateur, in a voice of restrained rage. "I am amazed at the degree of ugliness which a modern city can attain. Alca is becoming Americanised. Everywhere we are destroying all that is free, unexpected, measured, restrained, human, or traditional among the things that are left us. Everywhere we are destroying that charming object, a piece of an old wall that bears up the branches of a tree. Everywhere we are suppressing some fragment of light and air, some fragment of nature, some fragment of the associations that still remain with us, some fragment of our fathers, some fragment of ourselves. And we are putting up frightful, enormous, infamous houses, surmounted in Viennese style by ridiculous domes, or fashioned after the models of the 'new art' without mouldings, or having profiles with sinister corbels and burlesque pinnacles, and such monsters as these shamelessly peer over the surrounding buildings. We see bulbous protuberances stuck on the fronts of buildings and we are told they are 'new art' motives. I have seen the 'new art' in other countries, but it is not so ugly as with us; it has fancy and it has simplicity. It is only in our own country that by a sad privilege we may behold the newest and most diverse styles of architectural ugliness. What an enviable privilege!"

"Are you not afraid," asked M. Cérès severely, "are you not afraid that these bitter criticisms tend to keep out of our capital the foreigners who flow into it from all parts of the world and who leave millions behind them?"

"You may set your mind at rest about that," answered M. Daniset. "Foreigners do not come to admire our buildings; they come to see our courtesans, our dressmakers, and our dancing saloons."

"We have one bad habit," sighed M. Cérès, "it is that we calumniate ourselves."

Madame Clarence as an accomplished hostess thought it was time to return to the subject of love and asked M. Jumel his opinion of M. Léon Blum's recent book in which the author complained. . . .

". . . That an irrational custom," went on Professor Haddock, "prevents respectable young ladies from making love, a thing they would enjoy doing, whilst mercenary girls do it too much and without getting any enjoyment out of it. It is indeed deplorable. But M. Léon Blum need not fret too much. If the evil exists, as he says it does, in our middle-class society, I can assure him that everywhere else he would see a consoling spectacle. Among the people, the mass of the people through town and country, girls do not deny themselves that pleasure."

"It is depravity!" said Madame Crémeur.

And she praised the innocence of young girls in terms full of modesty and grace. It was charming to hear her.

Professor Haddock's views on the same subject were, on the contrary, painful to listen to.

"Respectable young girls," said he, "are guarded and watched over. Besides, men do not, as a rule, pursue them much, either through probity, or from a fear of grave responsibilities, or because the seduction of a young girl would not be to their credit. Even then we do not know what really takes place, for the reason that what is hidden is not seen. This is a condition necessary to the existence of all society. The scruples of respectable young girls could be more easily overcome than those of married women if the same pressure were brought to bear on them, and for this there are two reasons: they have more illusions, and their curiosity has not been satisfied. Women, for the most part, have been so disappointed by their husbands that they have not courage enough to begin again with somebody else. I myself have been met by this obstacle several times in my attempts at seduction."

At the moment when Professor Haddock ended his unpleasant remarks, Mademoiselle Eveline Clarence entered the drawing-room and listlessly handed about tea with that expression of boredom which gave an oriental charm to her beauty.

"For my part," said Hippolyte Cérès, looking at her, "I declare myself the young ladies' champion."

"He must be a fool," thought the girl.

Hippolyte Cérès, who had never set foot outside of his political world of electors and elected, thought Madame Clarence's drawing-room most select, its mistress exquisite, and her daughter amazingly beautiful. His visits became frequent and he paid court to both of them. Madame Clarence, who now liked attention, thought him agreeable. Eveline showed no friendliness towards him, and treated him with a hauteur and disdain that he took for aristocratic behaviour and fashionable manners, and he thought all the more of her on that account.

This busy man taxed his ingenuity to please them, and he sometimes succeeded. He got them cards for fashionable functions and boxes at the Opera. He furnished Mademoiselle Clarence with several opportunities of appearing to great advantage and in particular at a garden party which, although given by a Minister, was regarded as really fashionable, and gained its first success in society circles for the Republic.

At that party Eveline had been much noticed and had attracted the special attention of a young diplomat called Roger Lambilly who, imagining that she belonged to a rather fast set, invited her to his bachelor's flat. She thought him handsome and believed him rich, and she accepted. A little moved, almost disquieted, she very nearly became the victim of her daring, and only avoided defeat by an offensive measure audaciously carried out. This was the most foolish escapade in her unmarried life.

Being now on friendly terms with Ministers and with the President, Eveline continued to wear her aristocratic and pious affectations, and these won for her the sympathy of the chief personages in the anti-clerical and democratic Republic. M. Hippolyte Cérès, seeing that she was succeeding and doing him credit, liked her still more. He even went so far as to fall madly in love with her.

Henceforth, in spite of everything, she began to observe him with interest, being curious to see if his passion would increase. He appeared to her without elegance or grace, and not well bred, but active, clear-sighted, full of resource, and not too great a bore. She still made fun of him, but he had now won her interest.

One day she wished to test him. It was during the elections when members of Parliament were, as the phrase runs, requesting a renewal of their mandates. He had an opponent, who, though not dangerous at first and not much of an orator, was rich and was reported to be gaining votes every day. Hippolyte Cérès, banishing both dull security and foolish alarm from his mind, redoubled his care. His chief method of action was by public meetings at which he spoke vehemently against the rival candidate. His committee held huge meetings on Saturday evenings and at three o'clock on Sunday afternoons. One Sunday, as he called on the Clarences, he found Eveline alone in the drawing-room. He had been chatting for about twenty or twenty-five minutes, when, taking out his watch, he saw that it was a quarter to three. The young girl showed herself amiable, engaging, attractive, and full of promises. Cérès was fascinated, but he stood up to go.

"Stay a little longer," said she in a pressing and agreeable voice which made him promptly sit down again.

She was full of interest, of abandon, curiosity, and weakness. He blushed, turned pale, and again got up.

Then, in order to keep him still longer, she looked at him out of two grey and melting eyes, and though her bosom was heaving, she did not say another word. He fell at her feet in distraction, but once more looking at his watch, he jumped up with a terrible oath.

"D——! a quarter to four! I must be off."

And immediately he rushed down the stairs.

From that time onwards she had a certain amount of esteem for him.

IV

A POLITICIAN'S MARRIAGE

SHE was not quite in love with him, but she wished him to be in love with her. She was, moreover, very reserved with him, and that not solely from any want of inclination to be otherwise, since in affairs of love some things are due to indifference, to inattention, to a woman's instinct, to traditional custom and feeling, to a desire to try one's power, and to satisfaction at seeing its results. The reason of her prudence was that she knew him to be very much infatuated and capable of taking advantage of any familiarities she allowed as well as of reproaching her coarsely afterwards if she discontinued them.

As he was a professed anti-clerical and free-thinker, she thought it a good plan to affect an appearance of piety in his presence and to be seen with huge prayer-books bound in red morocco, such as Queen Marie Leczinska's or the Dauphiness Marie Josephine's "The Last Two Weeks of Lent." She lost no opportunity either, of showing him the subscriptions that she collected for the endowment of the national cult of St. Orberosia. Eveline did not act in this way because she wished to tease him. Nor did it spring from a young girl's archness, or a spirit of constraint, or even from snobbishness, though there was more than a suspicion of this latter in her behaviour. It was but her way of asserting herself, of stamping herself with a definite character, of increasing her value. To rouse the Deputy's courage she wrapped herself up in religion, just as Brunhild surrounded herself with flames so as to attract Sigurd. Her audacity was successful. He thought her still more beautiful thus. Clericalism was in his eyes a sign of good form.

Cérès was re-elected by an enormous majority and returned to a House which showed itself more inclined to the Left, more advanced, and, as it seemed, more eager for reform than its predecessor. Perceiving at once that so much zeal was but intended to hide a fear of change, and a sincere desire to do nothing, he determined to adopt a policy that would satisfy these aspirations. At the beginning of the session he made a great speech, cleverly thought out and well arranged, dealing with the idea that all reform ought to be put off for a long time. He showed himself heated, even fervid; holding the principle that an orator should recommend moderation with extreme vehemence. He was applauded by the entire assembly. The Clarences listened to him from the President's box and Eveline trembled in spite of herself at the solemn sound of the applause. On the same bench the fair Madame Pensée shivered at the intonations of his virile voice.

As soon as he descended from the tribune, Cérès, even while the audience were still clapping, went without a moment's delay to salute the Clarences in their box. Eveline saw in him the beauty of success, and as he leaned towards the ladies, wiping his neck with his handkerchief and receiving their congratulations with an air of modesty though not without a tinge of self-conceit, the young girl glanced towards Madame Pensée and saw her, palpitating and breathless, drinking in the hero's applause with her head thrown backwards. It seemed as if she were on the point of fainting. Eveline immediately smiled tenderly on M. Cérès.

The Alcan deputy's speech had a great vogue. In political "spheres" it was regarded as extremely able. "We have at last heard an honest pronouncement," said the chief Moderate journal. "It is a regular programme!" they said in the House. It was agreed that he was a man of immense talent.

Hippolyte Cérès had now established himself as leader of the radicals, socialists, and anti-clericals, and they appointed him President of their group, which was then the most considerable in the House. He thus found himself marked out for office in the next ministerial combination.

After a long hesitation Eveline Clarence accepted the idea of marrying M. Hippolyte Cérès. The great man was a little common for her taste. Nothing had yet proved that he would one day reach the point where politics bring in large sums of money. But she was entering her twenty-seventh year and knew enough of life to see that she must not be too fastidious or show herself too difficult to please.

Hippolyte Cérès was celebrated; Hippolyte Cérès was happy. He was no longer recognisable; the elegance of his clothes and deportment had increased tremendously. He wore an undue number of white gloves. Now that he was too much of a society man, Eveline began to doubt if it was not worse than being too little of one. Madame Clarence regarded the engagement with favour. She was reassured concerning her daughter's future and pleased to have flowers given her every Thursday for her drawing-room.

The celebration of the marriage raised some difficulties. Eveline was pious and wished to receive the benediction of the Church. Hippolyte Cérès, tolerant but a free-thinker, wanted only a civil marriage. There were many discussions and even some violent scenes upon the subject. The last took place in the young girl's room at the moment when the invitations were being written. Eveline declared that if she did not go to church she would not believe herself married. She spoke of breaking off the engagement, and of going abroad with her mother, or of retiring into a convent. Then she became tender, weak, suppliant. She sighed, and everything in her virginal chamber sighed in chorus, the holy-water font, the palm-branch above her white bed, the books of devotion on their little shelves, and the blue and white statuette of St. Orberosia chaining the dragon of Cappadocia, that stood upon the marble mantelpiece. Hippolyte Cérès was moved, softened, melted.

Beautiful in her grief, her eyes shining with tears, her wrists girt by a rosary of lapis lazuli and, so to speak, chained by her faith, she suddenly flung herself at Hippolyte's feet, and dishevelled, almost dying, she embraced his knees.

He nearly yielded.

"A religious marriage," he muttered, "a marriage in church, I could make my constituents stand that, but my committee would not swallow the matter so easily.... Still I'll explain it to them ... toleration, social necessities.... They all send their daughters to Sunday School.... But as for office, my dear, I am afraid we are going to drown all hope of that in your holy water."

At these words she stood up grave, generous, resigned, conquered also in her turn.

"My dear, I insist no longer."

"Then we won't have a religious marriage. It will be better, much better not."

"Very well, but be guided by me. I am going to try and arrange everything both to your satisfaction and mine."

She sought the Reverend Father Douillard and explained the situation. He showed himself even more accommodating and yielding than she had hoped.

"Your husband is an intelligent man, a man of order and reason; he will come over to us. You will sanctify him. It is not in vain that God has granted him the blessing of a Christian wife. The Church needs no pomp and ceremonial display for her benedictions. Now that she is persecuted, the shadow of the crypts and the recesses of the catacombs are in better accord with her festivals. Mademoiselle, when you have performed the civil formalities come here to my private chapel in walking costume with M. Cérès. I will marry you, and I will observe the most absolute discretion. I will obtain the necessary dispensations from the Archbishop as well as all facilities regarding the banns, confession-tickets, etc."

Hippolyte, although he thought the combination a little

dangerous, agreed to it, a good deal flattered at bottom.
"I will go in a short coat," he said.

He went in a frock coat with white gloves and varnished shoes, and he genuflected.

"Politeness demands. . . ."

V

THE VISIRE CABINET

THE Cérès household was established with modest decency in a pretty flat situated in a new building. Cérès loved his wife in a calm and tranquil fashion. He was often kept late from home by the Commission on the Budget and he worked more than three nights a week at a report on the postal finances of which he hoped to make a masterpiece. Eveline thought she could twist him round her finger, and this did not displease him. The bad side of their situation was that they had not much money; in truth they had very little. The servants of the Republic do not grow rich in her service as easily as people think. Since the sovereign is no longer there to distribute favours, each of them takes what he can, and his depredations, limited by the depredations of all the others, are reduced to modest proportions. Hence that austerity of morals that is noticed in democratic leaders. They can only grow rich during periods of great business activity and then they find themselves exposed to the envy of their less favoured colleagues. Hippolyte Cérès had for a long time foreseen such a period. He was one of those who had made preparations for its arrival. Whilst waiting for it he endured his poverty with dignity, and Eveline shared that poverty without suffering as much as one might have thought. She was in close intimacy with the Reverend Father Douillard and frequented the chapel of St. Orberosia, where she met with serious society and people in a position to render her useful services. She knew how to choose among them and gave her confidence to none but those who deserved it. She had gained experience since her motor excursions with Viscount Cléna, and above all she had now acquired the value of a married woman.

The deputy was at first uneasy about these pious practices, which were ridiculed by the demagogic newspapers, but he was soon reassured, for he saw all around him democratic leaders joyfully becoming reconciled to the aristocracy and the Church.

They found that they had reached one of those periods (which often recur) when advance had been carried a little too far. Hippolyte Cérès gave a moderate support to this view. His policy was not a policy of persecution but a policy of tolerance. He had laid its foundations in his splendid speech on the preparations for reform. The Prime Minister was looked upon as too advanced. He proposed schemes which were admitted to be dangerous to capital, and the great financial companies were opposed to him. Of course it followed that the newspapers of all views supported the companies. Seeing the danger increasing, the Cabinet abandoned its schemes, its programme, and its opinions, but it was too late. A new administration was already ready. An insidious question by Paul Visire which was immediately made the subject of a resolution, and a fine speech by Hippolyte Cérès, overthrew the Cabinet.

The President of the Republic entrusted the formation of a new Cabinet to this same Paul Visire, who, though still very young, had been a Minister twice. He was a charming man, spending much of his time in the green-rooms of theatres, very artistic, a great society man, of amazing ability and industry. Paul Visire formed a temporary ministry intended to reassure public feeling which had taken alarm, and Hippolyte Cérès was invited to hold office in it.

The new ministry, belonging to all the groups in the majority, represented the most diverse and contrary opinions, but they were all moderate and convinced conservatives.* The

* As this ministry exercised considerable influence upon the destinies of the country and of the world, we think it well to give its composition: Minister of the Interior and Prime Minister, Paul Visire; Minister of Justice, Pierre Bouc; Foreign Affairs, Victor Crombile; Finance. Terrasson; Education, Labillette; Commerce, Posts and Telegraphs,

Minister of Foreign Affairs was retained from the former cabinet. He was a little dark man called Crombile, who worked fourteen hours a day with the conviction that he dealt with tremendous questions. He refused to see even his own diplomatic agents, and was terribly uneasy, though he did not disturb anybody else, for the want of foresight of peoples is infinite and that of governments is just as great.

The office of Public Works was given to a Socialist, Fortuné Lapersonne. It was then a political custom and one of the most solemn, most severe, most rigorous, and if I may dare say so, the most terrible and cruel of all political customs, to include a member of the Socialist party in each ministry intended to oppose Socialism, so that the enemies of wealth and property should suffer the shame of being attacked by one of their own party, and so that they could not unite against these forces without turning to some one who might possibly attack themselves in the future. Nothing but a profound ignorance of the human heart would permit the belief that it was difficult to find a Socialist to occupy these functions. Citizen Fortuné Lapersonne entered the Visire cabinet of his own free will and without any constraint; and he found those who approved of his action even among his former friends, so great was the fascination that power exercised over the Penguins!

General Débonnaire went to the War Office. He was looked upon as one of the ablest generals in the army, but he was ruled by a woman, the Baroness Bildermann, who, though she had reached the age of intrigue, was still beautiful. She was in the pay of a neighbouring and hostile Power.

The new Minister of Marine, the worthy Admiral Vivier des Murènes, was generally regarded as an excellent seaman. He displayed a piety that would have seemed excessive in an anti-clerical minister, if the Republic had not recognised that religion was of great maritime utility. Acting on the instruc-

Hippolyte Cérès; Agriculture, Aulac; Public Works, Lapersonne; War, General Débonnaire; Admiralty, Admiral Vivier des Murènes.

tion of his spiritual director, the Reverend Father Douillard, the worthy Admiral had dedicated his fleet to St. Orberosia and directed canticles in honour of the Alcan Virgin to be composed by Christian bards. These replaced the national hymn in the music played by the navy.

Prime Minister Visire declared himself to be distinctly anticlerical but ready to respect all creeds; he asserted that he was a sober-minded reformer. Paul Visire and his colleagues desired reforms, and it was in order not to compromise reform that they proposed none; for they were true politicians and knew that reforms are compromised the moment they are proposed. The government was well received, respectable people were reassured, and the funds rose.

The administration announced that four new ironclads would be put into commission, that prosecutions would be undertaken against the Socialists, and it formally declared its intention to have nothing to do with any inquisitorial income-tax. The choice of Terrasson as Minister of Finance was warmly approved by the press. Terrasson, an old minister famous for his financial operations, gave warrant to all the hopes of the financiers and shadowed forth a period of great business activity. Soon those three udders of modern nations, monopolies, bill discounting, and fraudulent speculation, were swollen with the milk of wealth. Already whispers were heard of distant enterprises, and of planting colonies, and the boldest put forward in the newspapers the project of a military and financial protectorate over Nigritia.

Without having yet shown what he was capable of, Hippolyte Cérès was considered a man of weight. Business people thought highly of him. He was congratulated on all sides for having broken with the extreme sections, the dangerous men, and for having realised the responsibilities of government.

Madame Cérès shone alone amid the Ministers' wives. Crombile withered away in bachelordom. Paul Visire had married money in the person of Mademoiselle Blampignon, an accomplished, estimable, and simple lady who was always

ill, and whose feeble health compelled her to stay with her
mother in the depths of a remote province. The other Ministers' wives were not born to charm the sight, and people
smiled when they read that Madame Labillette had appeared
at the Presidency Ball wearing a headdress of birds of paradise. Madame Vivier des Murènes, a woman of good family,
was stout rather than tall, had a face like a beef-steak and
the voice of a newspaper-seller. Madame Débonnaire, tall,
dry, and florid, was devoted to young officers. She ruined herself by her escapades and crimes and only regained consideration by dint of ugliness and insolence.

Madame Cérès was the charm of the Ministry and its title
to consideration. Young, beautiful, and irreproachable, she
charmed alike society and the masses by her combination of
elegant costumes and pleasant smiles.

Her receptions were thronged by the great Jewish financiers.
She gave the most fashionable garden parties in the Republic.
The newspapers described her dresses and the milliners did
not ask her to pay for them. She went to Mass; she protected
the chapel of St. Orberosia from the ill-will of the people; and
she aroused in aristocratic hearts the hope of a fresh Con-
cordat.

With her golden hair, grey eyes, and supple and slight
though rounded figure, she was indeed pretty. She enjoyed
an excellent reputation and she was so adroit, and calm, so
much mistress of herself, that she would have preserved
it intact even if she had been discovered in the very act of
ruining it.

The session ended with a victory for the cabinet which,
amid the almost unanimous applause of the House, defeated a
proposal for an inquisitorial tax, and with a triumph for
Madame Cérès who gave parties in honour of three kings
who were at the moment passing through Alca.

VI

THE SOFA OF THE FAVOURITE

THE Prime Minister invited Monsieur and Madame Cérès to spend a couple of weeks of the holidays in a little villa that he had taken in the mountains, and in which he lived alone. The deplorable health of Madame Paul Visire did not allow her to accompany her husband, and she remained with her relatives in one of the southern provinces.

The villa had belonged to the mistress of one of the last Kings of Alca: the drawing-room retained its old furniture, and in it was still to be found the Sofa of the Favourite. The country was charming; a pretty blue stream, the Aiselle, flowed at the foot of the hill that dominated the villa. Hippolyte Cérès loved fishing; when engaged at this monotonous occupation he often formed his best Parliamentary combinations, and his happiest oratorical inspirations. Trout swarmed in the Aiselle; he fished it from morning till evening in a boat that the Prime Minister readily placed at his disposal.

In the mean time, Eveline and Paul Visire sometimes took a turn together in the garden, or had a little chat in the drawing-room. Eveline, although she recognised the attraction that Visire had for women, had hitherto displayed towards him only an intermittent and superficial coquetry, without any deep intentions or settled design. He was a connoisseur and saw that she was pretty. The House and the Opera had deprived him of all leisure, but, in a little villa, the grey eyes and rounded figure of Eveline took on a value in his eyes. One day as Hippolyte Cérès was fishing in the Aiselle, he made her sit beside him on the Sofa of the Favourite. Long rays of gold struck Eveline like arrows from a hidden Cupid through the chinks of the curtains which protected her from the heat and glare of a brilliant day. Beneath her white muslin dress her rounded yet slender form was outlined in its grace and youth. Her skin was cool and fresh, and had the fragrance of freshly mown hay. Paul Visire behaved as the occasion warranted, and for her part, she was opposed neither to the games of chance or of society. She believed it would be nothing or a trifle; she was mistaken.

"There was," says the famous German ballad, "on the sunny side of the town square, beside a wall whereon the creeper grew, a pretty little letter-box, as blue as the cornflowers, smiling and tranquil.

"All day long there came to it, in their heavy shoes, small shop-keepers, rich farmers, citizens, the tax-collector and the policeman, and they put into it their business letters, their invoices, their summonses, their notices to pay taxes, the judges' returns, and orders for the recruits to assemble. It remained smiling and tranquil.

"With joy, or in anxiety, there advanced towards it work- men and farm servants, maids and nursemaids, accountants, clerks, and women carrying their little children in their arms; they put into it notifications of births, marriages, and deaths, letters between engaged couples, between husbands and wives, from mothers to their sons, and from sons to their mothers. It remained smiling and tranquil.

"At twilight, young lads and young girls slipped furtively to it, and put in love-letters, some moistened with tears that blotted the ink, others with a little circle to show the place to kiss, all of them very long. It remained smiling and tranquil.

"Rich merchants came themselves through excess of care- fulness at the hour of daybreak, and put into it registered letters, and letters with five red seals, full of bank notes or cheques on the great financial establishments of the Empire. It remained smiling and tranquil.

"But one day, Gaspar, whom it had never seen, and whom it did not know from Adam, came to put in a letter, of which nothing is known but that it was folded like a little hat. Immediately the pretty letter-box fell into a swoon. Henceforth it remains no long in its place; it runs through streets, fields, and woods, girdled with ivy, and crowned with roses. It keeps running up hill and down dale; the country policeman surprises it sometimes, amidst the corn, in Gaspar's arms kissing him upon the mouth."

Paul Visire had recovered all his customary nonchalance. Eveline remained stretched on the Divan of the Favourite in an attitude of delicious astonishment.

The Reverend Father Douillard, an excellent moral theologian, and a man who in the decadence of the Church has preserved his principles, was very right to teach, in conformity with the doctrine of the Fathers, that while a woman commits a great sin by giving herself for money, she commits a much greater one by giving herself for nothing. For, in the first case she acts to support her life, and that is sometimes not merely excusable but pardonable, and even worthy of the Divine Grace, for God forbids suicide, and is unwilling that his creatures should destroy themselves. Besides, in giving herself in order to live, she remains humble, and derives no pleasure from it, a thing which diminishes the sin. But a woman who gives herself for nothing sins with pleasure and exults in her fault. The pride and delight with which she burdens her crime increase its load of moral guilt.

Madame Hippolyte Cérès' example shows the profundity of these moral truths. She perceived that she had senses. A second was enough to bring about this discovery, to change her soul, to alter her whole life. To have learned to know herself was at first a delight. The γνῶθί σεαυτὸν of the ancient philosophy is not a precept the moral fulfilment of which procures any pleasure, since one enjoys little satisfaction from knowing one's soul. It is not the same with the flesh, for in it sources of pleasure may be revealed to us. Eveline immediately felt an obligation to her revealer equal to the benefit she had received, and she imagined that he who had discovered these heavenly depths was the sole possessor of the key to them. Was this an error, and might she not be able to find others who also had the golden key? It is difficult to decide; and Professor Haddock, when the facts were divulged (which happened without much delay as we shall see), treated the matter from an experimental point of view, in a scientific review, and concluded that the chances Madame C—— would have of finding the exact equivalent of M. V—— were in the proportion of 305 to 975008. This is as much as to say that she would never find it. Doubtless her instinct told her the same, for she attached herself distractedly to him.

I have related these facts with all the circumstances which seemed to me worthy of attracting the attention of meditative and philosophic minds. The Sofa of the Favourite is worthy of the majesty of history; on it were decided the destinies of a great people; nay, on it was accomplished an act whose renown was to extend over the neighbouring nations both friendly and hostile, and even over all humanity. Too often events of this nature escape the superficial minds and shallow spirits who inconsiderately assume the task of writing history. Thus the secret springs of events remain hidden from us. The fall of Empires and the transmission of dominions astonish us and remain incomprehensible to us, because we have not discovered the imperceptible point, or touched the secret spring which when put in movement has destroyed and overthrown everything. The author of this great history knows better than anyone else his faults and his weaknesses, but he can do himself this justice—that he has always kept the moderation, the seriousness, the austerity, which an account of affairs of State demands, and that he has never departed from the gravity which is suitable to a recital of human actions.

VII

THE FIRST CONSEQUENCES

WHEN Eveline confided to Paul Visire that she had never experienced anything similar, he did not believe her. He had had a good deal to do with women and knew that they readily say these things to men in order to make them more in love with them. Thus his experience, as sometimes happens, made him disregard the truth. Incredulous, but gratified all the same, he soon felt love and something more for her. This state at first seemed favourable to his intellectual faculties. Visire delivered in the chief town of his constituency a speech full of grace, brilliant and happy, which was considered to be a masterpiece.

The re-opening of Parliament was serene. A few isolated jealousies, a few timid ambitions raised their heads in the House, and that was all. A smile from the Prime Minister was enough to dissipate these shadows. She and he saw each other twice a day, and wrote to each other in the interval. He was accustomed to intimate relationships, was adroit, and knew how to dissimulate; but Eveline displayed a foolish imprudence: she made herself conspicuous with him in drawing-rooms, at the theatre, in the House, and at the Embassies; she wore her love upon her face, upon her whole person, in her moist glances, in the languishing smile of her lips, in the heaving of her breast, in all her heightened, agitated, and distracted beauty. Soon the entire country knew of their intimacy. Foreign Courts were informed of it. The President of the Republic and Eveline's husband alone remained in ignorance. The President became acquainted with it in the country, through a misplaced police report which found its way, it is not known how, into his portmanteau.

Hippolyte Cérès, without being either very subtle, or very perspicacious, noticed that there was something different in his home. Eveline, who quite lately had interested herself in his affairs, and shown, if not tenderness, at least affection, towards him, displayed henceforth nothing but indifference and repulsion. She had always had periods of absence, and made prolonged visits to the Charity of St. Orberosia; now, she went out in the morning, remained out all day, and sat down to dinner at nine o'clock in the evening with the face of a somnambulist. Her husband thought it absurd; however, he might perhaps have never known the reason for this; a profound ignorance of women, a crass confidence in his own merit, and in his own fortune, might perhaps have always hidden the truth from him, if the two lovers had not, so to speak, compelled him to discover it.

When Paul Visire went to Eveline's house and found her alone, they used to say, as they embraced each other: "Not here! not here!" and immediately they affected an extreme reserve. That was their invariable rule. Now, one day, Paul Visire went to the house of his colleague Cérès, with whom he had an engagement. It was Eveline who received him, the Minister of Commerce being delayed by a commission.

"Not here!" said the lovers, smiling.

They said it, mouth to mouth, embracing, and clasping each other. They were still saying it, when Hippolyte Cérès entered the drawing-room.

Paul Visire did not lose his presence of mind. He declared to Madame Cérès that he would give up his attempt to take the dust out of her eye. By this attitude he did not deceive the husband, but he was able to leave the room with some dignity.

Hippolyte Cérès was thunderstruck. Eveline's conduct appeared incomprehensible to him; he asked her what reasons she had for it.

"Why? why?" he kept repeating continually, "why?"

She denied everything, not to convince him, for he had seen them, but from expediency and good taste, and to avoid painful explanations. Hippolyte Cérès suffered all the tortures of jealousy. He admitted it to himself, he kept saying inwardly, "I am a strong man; I am clad in armour; but the wound is underneath, it is in my heart," and turning towards his wife, who looked beautiful in her guilt, he would say:

"It ought not to have been with him."

He was right—Eveline ought not to have loved in government circles.

He suffered so much that he took up his revolver, exclaiming: "I will go and kill him!" But he remembered that a Minister of Commerce cannot kill his own Prime Minister, and he put his revolver back into his drawer.

The weeks passed without calming his sufferings. Each morning he buckled his strong man's armour over his wound and sought in work and fame the peace that fled from him. Every Sunday he inaugurated busts, statues, fountains, artesian wells, hospitals, dispensaries, railways, canals, public markets, drainage systems, triumphal arches, and slaughter houses, and delivered moving speeches on each of these occasions. His fervid activity devoured whole piles of documents; he changed the colours of the postage stamps fourteen times in one week. Nevertheless, he gave vent to outbursts of grief and rage that drove him insane; for whole days his reason abandoned him. If he had been in the employment of a private administration this would have been noticed immediately, but it is much more difficult to discover insanity or frenzy in the conduct of affairs of State. At that moment the government employés were forming themselves into associations and federations amid a ferment that was giving alarm both to the Parliament and to public feeling. The postmen were especially prominent in their enthusiasm for trade unions.

Hippolyte Cérès informed them in a circular that their action was strictly legal. The following day he sent out a second circular forbidding all associations of government employés as illegal. He dismissed one hundred and eighty postmen, reinstated them, reprimanded them, and awarded them gratuities. At Cabinet councils he was always on the point of bursting forth. The presence of the Head of the State scarcely restrained him within the limits of the decencies, and as he did not dare to attack his rival he consoled himself by heaping invectives upon General Débonnaire, the respected Minister of War. The General did not hear them, for he was deaf and occupied himself in composing verses for the Baroness Bildermann. Hippolyte Cérès offered an indistinct opposition to everything the Prime Minister proposed. In a word, he was a madman. One faculty alone escaped the ruin of his intellect: he retained his Parliamentary sense, his consciousness of the temper of majorities, his thorough knowledge of groups, and his certainty of the direction in which affairs were moving.

VIII

FURTHER CONSEQUENCES

The session ended calmly, and the Ministry saw no dangerous signs upon the benches where the majority sat. It was visible, however, from certain articles in the Moderate journals, that the demands of the Jewish and Christian financiers were increasing daily, that the patriotism of the banks required a civilizing expedition to Nigritia, and that the steel trusts, eager in the defence of our coasts and colonies, were crying out for armoured cruisers and still more armoured cruisers. Rumours of war began to be heard. Such rumours sprang up every year as regularly as the trade winds; serious people paid no heed to them and the government usually let them die away from their own weakness unless they grew stronger and spread. For in that case the country would be alarmed. The financiers only wanted colonial wars and the people did not want any wars at all. It loved to see its government proud and even insolent, but at the least suspicion that a European war was brewing, its violent emotion would quickly have reached the House. Paul Visire was not uneasy. The European situation was in his view completely reassuring. He was only irritated by the maniacal silence of his Minister of Foreign Affairs. That gnome went to the Cabinet meetings with a portfolio bigger than himself stuffed full of papers, said nothing, refused to answer all questions, even those asked him by the respected President of the Republic, and, exhausted by his obstinate labours, took a few moments' sleep in his arm-chair in which nothing but the top of his little black head was to be seen above the green tablecloth.

In the mean time Hippolyte Cérès became a strong man

again. In company with his colleague Lapersonne he formed numerous intimacies with ladies of the theatre. They were both to be seen at night entering fashionable restaurants in the company of ladies whom they over-topped by their lofty stature and their new hats, and they were soon reckoned amongst the most sympathetic frequenters of the boulevards. Fortuné Lapersonne had his own wound beneath his armour. His wife, a young milliner whom he carried off from a marquis, had gone to live with a chauffeur. He loved her still, and could not console himself for her loss, so that very often in the private room of a restaurant, in the midst of a group of girls who laughed and ate crayfish, the two ministers exchanged a look full of their common sorrow and wiped away an unbidden tear.

Hippolyte Cérès, although wounded to the heart, did not allow himself to be beaten. He swore that he would be avenged.

Madame Paul Visire, whose deplorable health forced her to live with her relatives in a distant province, received an anonymous letter specifying that M. Paul Visire, who had not a half-penny when he married her, was spending her dowry on a married woman, E—— C——, that he gave this woman thirty-thousand-franc motor-cars, and pearl necklaces costing twenty-five thousand francs, and that he was going straight to dishonour and ruin. Madame Paul Visire read the letter, fell into hysterics, and handed it to her father.

"I am going to box your husband's ears," said M. Blampignon; "he is a blackguard who will land you in the workhouse unless we look out. He may be Prime Minister, but he won't frighten me."

When he stepped off the train M. Blampignon presented himself at the Ministry of the Interior, and was immediately received. He entered the Prime Minister's room in a fury.

"I have something to say to you, sir!" And he waved the anonymous letter.

Paul Visire welcomed him smiling.

"You are welcome, my dear father. I was going to write to you. . . . Yes, to tell you of your nomination to the rank of officer of the Legion of Honour. I signed the patent this morning."

M. Blampignon thanked his son-in-law warmly and threw the anonymous letter into the fire.

He returned to his provincial house and found his daughter fretting and agitated.

"Well! I saw your husband. He is a delightful fellow. But then, you don't understand how to deal with him."

About this time Hippolyte Cérès learned through a little scandalous newspaper (it is always through the newspapers that ministers are informed of the affairs of State) that the Prime Minister dined every evening with Mademoiselle Lysiane of the Folies Dramatiques, whose charm seemed to have made a great impression on him. Thenceforth Cérès took a gloomy joy in watching his wife. She came in every evening to dine or dress with an air of agreeable fatigue and the serenity that comes from enjoyment.

Thinking that she knew nothing, he sent her anonymous communications. She read them at the table before him and remained still listless and smiling.

He then persuaded himself that she gave no heed to these vague reports, and that in order to disturb her it would be necessary to enable her to verify her lover's infidelity and treason for herself. There were at the Ministry a number of trustworthy agents charged with secret inquiries regarding the national defence. They were then employed in watching the spies of a neighbouring and hostile Power who had suc-ceeded in entering the Postal and Telegraphic service. M. Cérès ordered them to suspend their work for the present and to inquire where, when, and how the Minister of the Interior saw Mademoiselle Lysiane. The agents performed their missions faithfully and told the minister that they had several times seen the Prime Minister with a woman, but that she was not Mademoiselle Lysiane. Hippolyte Cérès asked them nothing further. He was right; the loves of Paul Visire and Lysiane were but an alibi invented by Paul Visire himself, with Eveline's approval, for his fame was rather inconvenient to her, and she sighed for secrecy and mystery.

They were not shadowed by the agents of the Ministry of Commerce alone. They were also followed by those of the Prefect of Police, and even by those of the Minister of the Interior, who disputed with each other the honour of protecting their chief. Then there were the emissaries of several royalist, imperialist, and clerical organisations, those of eight or ten blackmailers, several amateur detectives, a multitude of reporters, and a crowd of photographers, who all made their appearance wherever these two took refuge in their perambulating love affairs, at big hotels, small hotels, town houses, country houses, private apartments, villas, museums, palaces, hovels. They kept watch in the streets, from neighbouring houses, trees, walls, stair-cases, landings, roofs, adjoining rooms, and even chimneys. The Minister and his friend saw with alarm all round their bed-room, gimlets boring through doors and shutters, and drills making holes in the walls. A photograph of Madame Cérès in night attire buttoning her boots was the utmost that had been obtained.

Paul Visire grew impatient and irritable, and often lost his good humour and agreeableness. He came to the cabinet meetings in a rage and he, too, poured invectives upon General Débonnaire—a brave man under fire but a lax disciplinarian —and launched his sarcasms against the venerable admiral Vivier des Murènes whose ships went to the bottom without any apparent reason.

Fortuné Lapersonne listened open-eyed, and grumbled scoffingly between his teeth:

"He is not satisfied with robbing Hippolyte Cérès of his wife, but he must go and rob him of his catchwords too."

These storms were made known by the indiscretion of some Ministers and by the complaints of the two old warriors, who declared their intention of flinging their portfolios at the beggar's head, but who did nothing of the sort. These outbursts, far from injuring the lucky Prime Minister, had an excellent effect on Parliament and public opinion, who looked on them as signs of a keen solicitude for the welfare of the national army and navy. The Prime Minister was recipient of general approbation.

To the congratulations of the various groups and of notable personages, he replied with simple firmness: "Those are my principles!" and he had seven or eight Socialists put in prison.

The session ended, and Paul Visire, very exhausted, went to take the waters. Hippolyte Cérès refused to leave his Ministry, where the trade union of telephone girls was in tumultuous agitation. He opposed it with an unheard of violence, for he had now become a woman-hater. On Sundays he went into the suburbs to fish along with his colleague Lapersonne, wearing the tall hat that never left him since he had become a Minister. And both of them, forgetting the fish, complained of the inconstancy of women and mingled their griefs.

Hippolyte still loved Eveline and he still suffered. However, hope had slipped into his heart. She was now separated from her lover, and, thinking to win her back, he directed all his efforts to that end. He put forth all his skill, showed himself sincere, adaptable, affectionate, devoted, even discreet; his heart taught him the delicacies of feeling. He said charming and touching things to the faithless one, and, to soften her, he told her all that he had suffered.

Crossing the band of his trousers upon his stomach.

"See," said he, "how thin I have got."

He promised her everything he thought could gratify a woman, country parties, hats, jewels.

Sometimes he thought she would take pity on him. She no longer displayed an insolently happy countenance. Being separated from Paul, her sadness had an air of gentleness. But the moment he made a gesture to recover her she turned away fiercely and gloomily, girt with her fault as if with a golden girdle.

He did not give up, making himself humble, suppliant, lamentable.

One day he went to Lapersonne and said to him with tears in his eyes:

"Will you speak to her?"

Lapersonne excused himself, thinking that his intervention would be useless, but he gave some advice to his friend.

"Make her think that you don't care about her, that you love another, and she will come back to you."

Hippolyte, adopting this method, inserted in the newspapers that he was always to be found in the company of Mademoiselle Guinaud of the Opera. He came home late or did not come home at all, assumed in Eveline's presence an appearance of inward joy impossible to restrain, took out of his pocket, at dinner, a letter on scented paper which he pretended to read with delight, and his lips seemed as in a dream to kiss invisible lips. Nothing happened. Eveline did not even notice the change. Insensible to all around her, she only came out of her lethargy to ask for some louis from her husband, and if he did not give them she threw him a look of contempt, ready to upbraid him with the shame which she poured upon him in the sight of the whole world. Since she had loved she spent a great deal on dress. She needed money, and she had only her husband to secure it for her; she was so far faithful to him.

He lost patience, became furious, and threatened her with his revolver. He said one day before her to Madame Clarence:

"I congratulate you, Madame; you have brought up your daughter to be a wanton hussy."

"Take me away, Mamma," exclaimed Eveline. "I will get a divorce!"

He loved her more ardently than ever. In his jealous rage, suspecting her, not without probability, of sending and receiving letters, he swore that he would intercept them, re-established a censorship over the post, threw private correspondence into confusion, delayed stock-exchange quotations, prevented assignations, brought out bankruptcies, thwarted passions, and caused suicides. The independent press gave utterance to the complaints of the public and indignantly supported them. To justify these arbitrary measures, the ministerial journals spoke darkly of plots and public dangers, and promoted a belief in a monarchical conspiracy. The less well-informed sheets gave more precise information, told of the seizure of fifty thousand guns, and the landing of Prince Crucho. Feeling grew throughout the country, and the republican organs called for the immediate meeting of Parliament. Paul Visire returned to Paris, summoned his colleagues, held an important Cabinet Council, and proclaimed through his agencies that a plot had been actually formed against the national representation, but that the Prime Minister held the threads of it in his hand, and that a judicial inquiry was about to be opened.

He immediately ordered the arrest of thirty Socialists, and whilst the entire country was acclaiming him as its saviour, baffling the watchfulness of his six hundred detectives, he secretly took Eveline to a little house near the Northern railway station, where they remained until night. After their departure, the maid of their hotel, as she was putting their room in order, saw seven little crosses traced by a hairpin on the wall at the head of the bed.

That is all that Hippolyte Cérès obtained as a reward of his efforts.

IX

THE FINAL CONSEQUENCES

JEALOUSY is a virtue of democracies which preserves them from tyrants. Deputies began to envy the Prime Minister his golden key. For a year his domination over the beauteous Madame Cérès had been known to the whole universe. The provinces, whither news and fashions only arrive after a complete revolution of the earth round the sun, were at last informed of the illegitimate loves of the Cabinet. The provinces preserve an austere morality; women are more virtuous there than they are in the capital.

Various reasons have been alleged for this: Education, example, simplicity of life. Professor Haddock asserts that this virtue of provincial ladies is solely due to the fact that the heels of their shoes are low. "A woman," said he, in a learned article in the "Anthropological Review," "a woman attracts a civilised man in proportion as her feet make an angle with the ground. If this angle is as much as thirty-five degrees, the attraction becomes acute. For the position of the feet upon the ground determines the whole carriage of the body, and it results that provincial women, since they wear low heels, are not very attractive, and preserve their virtue with ease." These conclusions were not generally accepted. It was objected that under the influence of English and American fashions, low heels had been introduced generally without producing the results attributed to them by the learned Professor; moreover, it was said that the difference he pretended to establish between the morals of the metropolis and those of the provinces is perhaps illusory, and that if it exists, it is apparently due to the fact that great cities offer more advantages and facilities for love than small towns provide. However that may be, the provinces began to murmur against the Prime Minister, and to raise a scandal. This was not yet a danger, but there was a possibility that it might become one.

For the moment the peril was nowhere and yet everywhere. The majority remained solid; but the leaders became stiff and exacting. Perhaps Hippolyte Cérès would never have intentionally sacrificed his interests to his vengeance. But thinking that he could henceforth, without compromising his own fortune, secretly damage that of Paul Visire, he devoted himself to the skilful and careful preparation of difficulties and perils for the Head of the Government. Though far from equalling his rival in talent, knowledge, and authority, he greatly surpassed him in his skill as a lobbyist. The most acute parliamentarians attributed the recent misfortunes of the majority to his refusal to vote. At committees, by a calculated imprudence, he favoured motions which he knew the Prime Minister could not accept. One day his intentional awkwardness provoked a sudden and violent conflict between the Minister of the Interior, and his departmental Treasurer. Then Cérès became frightened and went no further. It would have been dangerous for him to overthrow the ministry too soon. His ingenious hatred found an issue by circuitous paths. Paul Visire had a poor cousin of easy morals who bore his name. Cérès, remembering this lady, Céline Visire, brought her into prominence, arranged that she should become intimate with several foreigners, and procured her engagements in the music-halls. One summer night, on a stage in the Champs Elysées before a tumultuous crowd, she performed risky dances to the sounds of wild music which was audible in the gardens where the President of the Republic was entertaining Royalty. The name of Visire, associated with these scandals, covered the walls of the town, filled the newspapers, was repeated in the cafés and at balls, and blazed forth in letters of fire upon the boulevards.

Nobody regarded the Prime Minister as responsible for the

scandal of his relatives, but a bad idea of his family came into existence, and the influence of the statesman was diminished.

Almost immediately he was made to feel this in a pretty sharp fashion. One day in the House, on a simple question, Labillette, the Minister of Religion and Public Worship, who was suffering from an attack of liver, and beginning to be exasperated by the intentions and intrigues of the clergy, threatened to close the Chapel of St. Orberosia, and spoke without respect of the National Virgin. The entire Right rose up in indignation; the Left appeared to give but a half-hearted support to the rash Minister. The leaders of the majority did not care to attack a popular cult which brought thirty millions a year into the country. The most moderate of the supporters of the Right, M. Bigourd, made the question the subject of a resolution and endangered the Cabinet. Luckily, Fortuné Lapersonne, the Minister of Public Works, always conscious of the obligations of power, was able in the Prime Minister's absence to repair the awkwardness and indecorum of his colleague, the Minister of Public Worship. He ascended the tribune and bore witness to the respect in which the Government held the heavenly Patron of the country, the consoler of so many ills which science admitted its powerlessness to relieve.

When Paul Visire, snatched at last from Eveline's arms, appeared in the House, the administration was saved; but the Prime Minister saw himself compelled to grant important concessions to the upper classes. He proposed in Parliament that six armoured cruisers should be laid down, and thus won the sympathies of the Steel Trust; he gave new assurances that the income tax would not be imposed, and he had eighteen Socialists arrested.

He was soon to find himself opposed by more formidable obstacles. The Chancellor of the neighbouring Empire in an ingenious and profound speech upon the foreign relations of his sovereign, made a sly allusion to the intrigues that inspired the policy of a great country. This reference, which was received with smiles by the Imperial Parliament, was certain

to irritate a punctilious republic. It aroused the national sus-
ceptibility, which directed its wrath against its amorous Minister. The Deputies seized upon a frivolous pretext to show
their dissatisfaction. A ridiculous incident, the fact that the
wife of a sub-prefect had danced at the Moulin Rouge, forced
the Minister to face a vote of censure, and he was within a few
votes of being defeated. According to general opinion, Paul
Visire had never been so weak, so vacillating, or so spiritless,
as on that occasion.

He understood that he could only keep himself in office by
a great political stroke, and he decided on the expedition to
Nigritia. This measure was demanded by the great financial
and industrial corporations and was one which would bring
concessions of immense forests to the capitalists, a loan of
eight millions to the banking companies, as well as promotions
and decorations to the naval and military officers. A pretext
presented itself; some insult needed to be avenged, or some
debt to be collected. Six battleships, fourteen cruisers, and
eighteen transports sailed up the mouth of the river Hippo-
potamus. Six hundred canoes vainly opposed the landing of
the troops. Admiral Vivier des Murènes' cannons produced an
appalling effect upon the blacks, who replied to them with
flights of arrows, but in spite of their fanatical courage they
were entirely defeated. Popular enthusiasm was kindled by the
newspapers which the financiers subsidised, and burst into a
blaze. Some Socialists alone protested against this barbarous,
doubtful, and dangerous enterprise. They were at once arrested.

At that moment when the Minister, supported by wealth,
and now beloved by the poor, seemed unconquerable, the
light of hate showed Hippolyte Cérès alone the danger, and
looking with a gloomy joy at his rival, he muttered between
his teeth, "He is wrecked, the brigand!"

Whilst the country intoxicated itself with glory, the neighbouring Empire protested against the occupation of Nigritia
by a European power, and these protests following one an-

other at shorter and shorter intervals became more and more vehement. The newspapers of the interested Republic concealed all causes for uneasiness; but Hippolyte Cérès heard the growing menace, and determined at last to risk everything, even the fate of the Ministry, in order to ruin his enemy. He got men whom he could trust to write and insert articles in several of the official journals, which, seeming to express Paul Visire's precise views, attributed warlike intentions to the Head of the Government.

These articles roused a terrible echo abroad, and they alarmed the public opinion of a nation which, while fond of soldiers, was not fond of war. Questioned in the House on the foreign policy of his government, Paul Visire made a reassuring statement, and promised to maintain a peace compatible with the dignity of a great nation. His Minister of Foreign Affairs, Crombile, read a declaration which was absolutely unintelligible, for the reason that it was couched in diplomatic language. The Minister obtained a large majority.

But the rumours of war did not cease, and in order to avoid a new and dangerous motion, the Prime Minister distributed eighty thousand acres of forest in Nigritia among the Deputies, and had fourteen Socialists arrested. Hippolyte Cérès went gloomily about the lobbies, confiding to the Deputies of his group that he was endeavouring to induce the Cabinet to adopt a pacific policy, and that he still hoped to succeed. Day by day the sinister rumours grew in volume, and penetrating amongst the public, spread uneasiness and disquiet. Paul Visire himself began to take alarm. What disturbed him most were the silence and absence of the Minister of Foreign Affairs. Crombile no longer came to the meetings of the Cabinet. Rising at five o'clock in the morning, he worked eighteen hours at his desk, and at last fell exhausted into his waste-paper basket, from whence the registrars removed him, together with the papers which they were going to sell to the military attachés of the neighbouring Empire.

General Débonnaire believed that a campaign was imminent, and prepared for it. Far from fearing war, he prayed for it, and confided his generous hopes to Baroness Bildermann, who informed the neighbouring nation, which, acting on her information, proceeded to a rapid mobilization.

The Minister of Finance unintentionally precipitated events. At the moment, he was speculating for a fall, and in order to bring about a panic on the Stock Exchange, he spread the rumour that war was now inevitable. The neighbouring Empire, deceived by this action, and expecting to see its territory invaded, mobilized its troops in all haste. The terrified Chamber overthrew the Visire ministry by an enormous majority (814 votes to 7, with 28 abstentions). It was too late. The very day of this fall the neighbouring and hostile nation recalled its ambassador and flung eight millions of men into Madame Cérès' country. War became universal, and the whole world was drowned in a torrent of blood.

THE ZENITH OF PENGUIN CIVILIZATION

HALF a century after the events we have just related, Madame Cérès died surrounded with respect and veneration, in the eighty-ninth year of her age. She had long been the widow of a statesman whose name she bore with dignity. Her modest and quiet funeral was followed by the orphans of the parish and the sisters of the Sacred Compassion.

The deceased left all her property to the Charity of St. Orberosia.

"Alas!" sighed M. Monnoyer, a canon of St. Maël, as he received the pious legacy, "it was high time for a generous benefactor to come to the relief of our necessities. Rich and poor, learned and ignorant, are turning away from us. And when we try to lead back these misguided souls, neither threats nor promises, neither gentleness nor violence, nor anything else is now successful. The Penguin clergy pine in desolation; our country priests, reduced to following the humblest of trades, are shoeless, and compelled to live upon such scraps as they can pick up. In our ruined churches the rain of heaven falls upon the faithful, and during the holy offices they can hear the noise of stones falling from the arches. The tower of the cathedral is tottering and will soon fall. St. Orberosia is forgotten by the Penguins, her devotion abandoned, and her sanctuary deserted. On her shrine, bereft of its gold and precious stones, the spider silently weaves her web."

Hearing these lamentations, Pierre Mille, who at the age of ninety-eight years had lost nothing of his intellectual and moral power, asked the canon if he did not think that St. Orberosia would one day rise out of this wrongful oblivion.

"I hardly dare to hope so," sighed M. Monnoyer.

"It is a pity!" answered Pierre Mille. "Orberosia is a charming figure and her legend is a beautiful one. I discovered the other day by the merest chance, one of her most delightful miracles, the miracle of Jean Violle. Would you like to hear it, M. Monnoyer?"

"I should be very pleased, M. Mille."

"Here it is, then, just as I found it in a fifteenth-century manuscript:

"Cécile, the wife of Nicolas Gaubert, a jeweller on the Pont-au-Change, after having led an honest and chaste life for many years, and being now past her prime, became infatuated with Jean Violle, the Countess de Maubec's page, who lived at the Hôtel du Paon on the Place de Grève. He was not yet eighteen years old, and his face and figure were attractive. Not being able to conquer her passion, Cécile resolved to satisfy it. She attracted the page to her house, loaded him with caresses, supplied him with sweetmeats and finally did as she wished with him.

"Now one day, as they were together in the jeweller's bed, Master Nicolas came home sooner than he was expected. He found the bolt drawn, and heard his wife on the other side of the door exclaiming, 'My heart! my angel! my love!' Then suspecting that she was shut up with a gallant, he struck great blows upon the door and began to shout: 'Slut! hussy!

wanton! open so that I may cut off your nose and ears!' In this peril, the jeweller's wife besought St. Orberosia, and vowed her a large candle if she helped her and the little page, who was dying of fear beside the bed, out of their difficulty.

"The saint heard the prayer. She immediately changed Jean Violle into a girl. Seeing this, Cécile was completely reassured, and began to call out to her husband: 'Oh! you brutal villain, you jealous wretch! Speak gently if you want the door to be opened.' And scolding in this way, she ran to the wardrobe and took out of it an old hood, a pair of stays, and a long grey petticoat, in which she hastily wrapped the transformed page. Then when this was done, 'Catherine, dear Catherine,' said she, loudly, 'open the door for your uncle; he is more fool than knave, and won't do you any harm.' The boy who had become a girl, obeyed. Master Nicolas entered the room and found in it a young maid whom he did not know, and his wife in bed. 'Big booby,' said the latter to him, 'don't stand gaping at what you see. Just as I had come to bed because I had a stomach ache, I received a visit from Catherine, the daughter of my sister Jeanne de Palaiseau, with whom we quarrelled fifteen years ago. Kiss your niece. She is well worth the trouble.' The jeweller gave Violle a hug, and from that moment he wanted nothing so much as to be alone with her a moment, so that he might embrace her as much as he liked. For this reason he led her without any delay down to the kitchen, under the pretext of giving her some walnuts and wine, and he was no sooner there with her than he began to caress her very affectionately. He would not have stopped at that if St. Orberosia had not inspired his good wife with the idea of seeing what he was about. She found him with the pretended niece sitting on his knee. She called him a debauched creature, boxed his ears, and forced him to beg her pardon. The next day Violle resumed his previous form."

Having heard this story the venerable Canon Monnoyer thanked Pierre Mille for having told it, and, taking up his pen, began to write out a list of horses that would win at the next race meeting. For he was a book-maker's clerk.

In the mean time Penguinia gloried in its wealth. Those who produced the things necessary for life, wanted them; those who did not produce them had more than enough. "But these," as a member of the Institute said, "are necessary economic fatalities." The great Penguin people had no longer either traditions, intellectual culture, or arts. The progress of civilization manifested itself among them by murderous industry, infamous speculation, and hideous luxury. Its capital assumed, as did all the great cities of the time, a cosmopolitan and financial character. An immense and regular ugliness reigned within it. The country enjoyed perfect tranquillity. It had reached its zenith.

BOOK VIII

FUTURE TIMES

THE ENDLESS HISTORY

Alca is becoming Americanised.— *M. Daniset.*

And he overthrew those cities, and all the plain, and all the inhabitants of the cities, and that which grew upon the ground.—*Genesis xix. 25.*

Τῇ Ἑλλάδι πενίη μὲν ἀεὶ κοτε σύντροφός ἐστι, ἀρετὴ δὲ ἔπακτός ἐστι, ἀπό τε σοφίης κατεργασμένη καὶ νόμου ἰσχυροῦ.*—(Herodotus, Histories, VII. cii.)

You have not seen angels then.—*Liber Terribilis.*

Bqsfttfusftpvtuse jufbmbb b up sjufef tspjtfucftfnqfsfvstbqsftbnpjsqsp dmbmbnfuspsjtghjttd-mjcfsufnbgsbodftftutpbnjtfbeftdpnqb   hojtt-gjobo — djfsfttr — vjejtqpteoueftsjdifttftevqbzt fuqbsmfn Pzfoevofqsf ttfbdifuffejsjhfboumpq-jojno

                                Voufnpjoxfsiejrvf

We are now beginning to study a chemistry which will deal with effects produced by bodies containing a quantity of concentrated energy the like of which we have not yet had at our disposal.—*Sir William Ramsay.*

---

* Poverty has ever been familiar to Greece, but virtue has been acquired, having been accomplished by wisdom and firm laws.
                                —Henry Cary's Translation.

THE houses were never high enough to satisfy them; they kept on making them still higher and built them of thirty or forty storeys with offices, shops, banks, societies one above another; they dug cellars and tunnels ever deeper downwards.

Fifteen millions of men laboured in a giant town by the light of beacons which shed forth their glare both day and night. No light of heaven pierced through the smoke of the factories with which the town was girt, but sometimes the red disk of a rayless sun might be seen riding in the black firmament through which iron bridges ploughed their way, and from which there descended a continual shower of soot and cinders. It was the most industrial of all the cities in the world and the richest. Its organization seemed perfect. None of the ancient aristocratic or democratic forms remained; everything was subordinated to the interests of the trusts. This environment gave rise to what anthropologists called the multi-millionaire type. The men of this type were at once energetic and frail, capable of great activity in forming mental combinations and of prolonged labour in offices, but men whose nervous irritability suffered from hereditary troubles which increased as time went on.

Like all true aristocrats, like the patricians of republican Rome or the squires of old England, these powerful men affected a great severity in their habits and customs. They were the ascetics of wealth. At the meetings of the trusts an observer would have noticed their smooth and puffy faces, their lantern cheeks, their sunken eyes and wrinkled brows. With bodies more withered, complexions yellower, lips drier, and eyes filled with a more burning fanaticism than those of the old Spanish monks, these multi-millionaires gave themselves up with inextinguishable ardour to the austerities of banking and industry. Several, denying themselves all happiness, all pleasure, and all rest, spent their miserable lives in rooms without light or air, furnished only with electrical apparatus, living on eggs and milk, and sleeping on camp beds. By doing nothing except pressing nickel buttons with their fingers, these mystics heaped up riches of which they never even saw the signs, and acquired the vain possibility of gratifying desires that they never experienced.

The worship of wealth had its martyrs. One of these multi-millionaires, the famous Samuel Box, preferred to die rather than surrender the smallest atom of his property. One of his workmen, the victim of an accident while at work, being refused any indemnity by his employer, obtained a verdict in the courts, but repelled by innumerable obstacles of procedure, he fell into the direst poverty. Being thus reduced to despair, he succeeded by dint of cunning and audacity in confronting his employer with a loaded revolver in his hand, and threatened to blow out his brains if he did not give him some assistance. Samuel Box gave nothing, and let himself be killed for the sake of principle.

Examples that come from high quarters are followed. Those who possessed some small capital (and they were necessarily the greater number), affected the ideas and habits of the multi-millionaires, in order that they might be classed among them. All passions which injured the increase or the preservation of wealth, were regarded as dishonourable; neither indolence, nor idleness, nor the taste for disinterested study, nor love of the arts, nor, above all, extravagance, was ever forgiven; pity was condemned as a dangerous weakness. Whilst every inclination to licentiousness excited public reprobation, the violent and brutal satisfaction of an appetite was, on the contrary, excused; violence, in truth, was regarded as less injurious to morality, since it manifested a form of social energy. The State was firmly based on two great public virtues: respect for the rich and contempt for the poor. Feeble spirits who were still moved by human suffering had no othei resource than to take refuge in a hypocrisy which it was im-possible to blame, since it contributed to the maintenance of order and the solidity of institutions.

Thus, among the rich, all were devoted to the social order, or seemed to be so; all gave good examples, if all did not fol-low them. Some felt the severity of their position cruelly; but they endured it either from pride or from duty. Some attempted, in secret and by subterfuge, to escape from it for a moment. One of these, Edward Martin, the President of the Steel Trust, sometimes dressed himself as a poor man, went forth to beg his bread, and allowed himself to be jostled by the passers-by. One day, as he asked alms on a bridge, he engaged in a quarrel with a real beggar, and filled with a fury of envy, he strangled him.

As they devoted their whole intelligence to business, they sought no intellectual pleasures. The theatre, which had for-merly been very flourishing among them, was now reduced to pantomimes and comic dances. Even the pieces in which women acted were given up; the taste for pretty forms and brilliant toilettes had been lost; the somersaults of clowns and the music of negroes were preferred above them, and what roused enthusiasm was the sight of women upon the stage whose necks were bedizened with diamonds, or proces-sions carrying golden bars in triumph. Ladies of wealth were as much compelled as the men to lead a respectable life. According to a tendency common to all civilizations, public feeling set them up as symbols; they were, by their austere magnificence, to represent both the splendour of wealth and its intangibility. The old habits of gallantry had been re-formed, but fashionable lovers were now secretly replaced by muscular labourers or stray grooms. Nevertheless, scandals were rare, a foreign journey concealed nearly all of them, and the Princesses of the Trusts remained objects of universal esteem.

The rich formed only a small minority, but their collab-

orators, who composed the entire people, had been completely
won over or completely subjugated by them. They formed
two classes, the agents of commerce or banking, and workers
in the factories. The former contributed an immense amount
of work and received large salaries. Some of them succeeded
in founding establishments of their own; for in the constant
increase of the public wealth the more intelligent and audacious could hope for anything. Doubtless it would have been
possible to find a certain number of discontented and rebellious
persons among the immense crowd of engineers and accountants, but this powerful society had imprinted its firm discipline
even on the minds of its opponents. The very anarchists were
laborious and regular.

As for the workmen who toiled in the factories that surrounded the town, their decadence, both physical and moral,
was terrible; they were examples of the type of poverty as it
is set forth by anthropology. Although the development
among them of certain muscles, due to the particular nature
of their work, might give a false idea of their strength, they
presented sure signs of morbid debility. Of low stature, with
small heads and narrow chests, they were further distinguished
from the comfortable classes by a multitude of physiological
anomalies, and, in particular, by a common want of symmetry between the head and the limbs. And they were destined to a gradual and continuous degeneration, for the State
made soldiers of the more robust among them, and the health
of these did not long withstand the brothels and the drink-
shops that sprang up around their barracks. The proletarians
became more and more feeble in mind. The continued weakening of their intellectual faculties was not entirely due to
their manner of life; it resulted also from a methodical selec-
tion carried out by the employers. The latter, fearing that
workmen of too great ability might be inclined to put forward
legitimate demands, took care to eliminate them by every
possible means, and preferred to engage ignorant and stupid
labourers, who were incapable of defending their rights,

but were yet intelligent enough to perform their toils, which highly perfected machines rendered extremely simple. Thus the proletarians were unable to do anything to improve their lot. With difficulty did they succeed by means of strikes in maintaining the rate of their wages. Even this means began to fail them. The alternations of production inherent in the capitalist system caused such cessations of work that, in several branches of industry, as soon as a strike was declared, the accumulation of products allowed the employers to dispense with the strikers. In a word, these miserable employés were plunged in a gloomy apathy that nothing enlightened and nothing exasperated. They were necessary instruments for the social order and well adapted to their purpose.

Upon the whole, this social order seemed the most firmly established that had yet been seen, at least among mankind, for that of bees and ants is incomparably more stable. Nothing could foreshadow the ruin of a system founded on what is strongest in human nature, pride and cupidity. However, keen observers discovered several grounds for uneasiness. The most certain, although the least apparent, were of an economic order, and consisted in the continually increasing amount of over-production, which entailed long and cruel interruption of labour, though these were, it is true, utilized by the manufacturers as a means of breaking the power of the workmen, by facing them with the prospect of a lock-out. A more obvious peril resulted from the physiological state of almost the entire population. "The health of the poor is what it must be," said the experts in hygiene, "but that of the rich leaves much to be desired." It was not difficult to find the causes of this. The supply of oxygen necessary for life was insufficient in the city, and men breathed in an artificial air. The food trusts, by means of the most daring chemical syntheses, produced artificial wines, meat, milk, fruit, and vegetables, and the diet thus imposed gave rise to stomach and brain troubles. The multi-millionaires were bald at the age of eighteen; some showed from time to time a dangerous weakness of mind. Over-strung and enfeebled, they gave enormous sums to ignorant charlatans; and it was a common thing for some trumpery bath-attendant or other who turned healer or prophet, to make a rapid fortune by the practice of medicine or theology. The number of lunatics increased continually; suicides multiplied in the world of wealth, and many of them were accompanied by atrocious and extraordinary circumstances, which bore witness to an unheard of perversion of intelligence and sensibility.

Another fatal symptom created a strong impression upon average minds. Terrible accidents, henceforth periodical and regular, entered into people's calculations, and kept mounting higher and higher in statistical tables. Every day, machines burst into fragments, houses fell down, trains laded with merchandise fell on to the streets, demolishing entire buildings and crushing hundreds of passers-by. Through the ground, honey-combed with tunnels, two or three storeys of work-shops would often crash, engulfing all those who worked in them.

§ 2

In the southwestern district of the city, on an eminence which had preserved its ancient name of Fort Saint-Michel, there stretched a square where some old trees still spread their exhausted arms above the greensward. Landscape gardeners had constructed a cascade, grottos, a torrent, a lake, and an island, on its northern slope. From this side one could see the whole town with its streets, its boulevards, its squares, the multitude of its roofs and domes, its air-passages, and its crowds of men, covered with a veil of silence, and seemingly enchanted by the distance. This square was the healthiest place in the capital; here no smoke obscured the sky, and children were brought here to play. In summer some employés from the neighbouring offices and laboratories used to resort to it for a moment after their luncheons, but they did not disturb its solitude and peace.

It was owing to this custom that, one day in June, about mid-day, a telegraph clerk, Caroline Meslier, came and sat down on a bench at the end of a terrace. In order to refresh her eyes by the sight of a little green, she turned her back to the town. Dark, with brown eyes, robust and placid, Caroline appeared to be from twenty-five to twenty-eight years of age. Almost immediately, a clerk in the Electricity Trust, George Clair, took his place beside her. Fair, thin, and supple, he had features of a feminine delicacy; he was scarcely older than she, and looked still younger. As they met almost every day in this place, a comradeship had sprung up between them, and they enjoyed chatting together. But their conversation had never been tender, affectionate, or even intimate. Caroline, although it had happened to her in the past to repent of her confidence, might perhaps have been less reserved had not George Clair always shown himself extremely restrained in his expressions and behaviour. He always gave a purely intellectual character to the conversation, keeping it within the realm of general ideas, and, moreover, expressing himself on all subjects with the greatest freedom. He spoke frequently of the organization of society, and the conditions of labour.

"Wealth," said he, "is one of the means of living happily; but people have made it the sole end of existence."

And this state of things seemed monstrous to both of them.

They returned continually to various scientific subjects with which they were both familiar.

On that day they discussed the evolution of chemistry.

"From the moment," said Clair, "that radium was seen to be transformed into helium, people ceased to affirm the immutability of simple bodies; in this way all those old laws about simple relations and about the indestructibility of matter were abolished."

"However," said she, "chemical laws exist."

For, being a woman, she had need of belief.

He resumed carelessly:

"Now that we can procure radium in sufficient quantities,

science possesses incomparable means of analysis; even at present we get glimpses, within what are called simple bodies, of extremely diversified complex ones, and we discover energies in matter which seem to increase even by reason of its tenuity."

As they talked, they threw bits of bread to the birds, and some children played around them.

Passing from one subject to another:

"This hill, in the quaternary epoch," said Clair, "was inhabited by wild horses. Last year, as they were tunnelling for the water mains, they found a layer of the bones of primeval horses."

She was anxious to know whether, at that distant epoch, man had yet appeared.

He told her that man used to hunt the primeval horse long before he tried to domesticate him.

"Man," he added, "was at first a hunter, then he became a shepherd, a cultivator, a manufacturer . . . and these diverse civilizations succeeded each other at intervals of time that the mind cannot conceive."

He took out his watch.

Caroline asked if it was already time to go back to the office.

He said it was not, that it was scarcely half-past twelve.

A little girl was making mud pies at the foot of their bench; a little boy of seven or eight years was playing in front of them. Whilst his mother was sewing on an adjoining bench, he played all alone at being a run-away horse, and with that power of illusion, of which children are capable, he imagined that he was at the same time the horse, and those who ran after him, and those who fled in terror before him. He kept struggling with himself and shouting: "Stop him, Hi! Hi! This is an awful horse, he has got the bit between his teeth."

Caroline asked the question:

"Do you think that men were happy formerly?"

Her companion answered:

"They suffered less when they were younger. They acted like that little boy: they played; they played at arts, at virtues, at vices, at heroism, at beliefs, at pleasures; they had illusions; which entertained them; they made a noise, they amused themselves. But now . . ."

He interrupted himself, and looked again at his watch.

The child, who was running, struck his foot against the little girl's pail, and fell his full length on the gravel. He remained a moment stretched out motionless, then raised himself up on the palms of his hands. His forehead puckered, his mouth opened, and he burst into tears. His mother ran up but Caroline had lifted him from the ground and was wiping his eyes and mouth with her handkerchief. The child kept on sobbing and Clair took him in his arms.

"Come, don't cry, my little man! I am going to tell you a story.

"A fisherman once threw his net into the sea and drew out a little, sealed, copper pot, which he opened with his knife. Smoke came out of it, and as it mounted up to the clouds the smoke grew thicker and thicker and became a giant who gave such a terrible yawn that the whole world was blown to dust. . . ."

Clair stopped himself, gave a dry laugh, and handed the child back to his mother. Then he took out his watch again, and kneeling on the bench with his elbows resting on its back he gazed at the town. As far as the eye could reach, the multitude of houses stood out in their tiny immensity.

Caroline turned her eyes in the same direction.

"What splendid weather it is!" said she. "The sun's rays change the smoke on the horizon into gold. The worst thing about civilization is that it deprives one of the light of day."

He did not answer; his looks remained fixed on a place in the town.

After some seconds of silence they saw about half a mile away, in the richer district on the other side of the river, a sort of tragic fog rearing itself upwards. A moment afterwards an explosion was heard even where they were sitting, and an immense tree of smoke mounted towards the pure sky. Little by little the air was filled with an imperceptible murmur caused by the shouts of thousands of men. Cries burst forth quite close to the square.

"What has been blown up?"

The bewilderment was great, for although accidents were common, such a violent explosion as this one had never been seen, and everybody perceived that something terribly strange had happened.

Attempts were made to locate the place of the accident; districts, streets, different buildings, clubs, theatres, and shops were mentioned. Information gradually became more precise and at last the truth was known.

"The Steel Trust has just been blown up."

Clair put his watch back into his pocket.

Caroline looked at him closely and her eyes filled with astonishment.

At last she whispered in his ear:

"Did you know it? Were you expecting it? Was it you ..."

He answered very calmly:

"That town ought to be destroyed."

She replied in a gentle and thoughtful tone:

"I think so too."

And both of them returned quietly to their work.

§ 3

From that day onward, anarchist attempts followed one another every week without interruption. The victims were numerous, and almost all of them belonged to the poorer classes. These crimes roused public resentment. It was among domestic servants, hotel-keepers, and the employés of such small shops as the Trusts still allowed to exist, that indignation burst forth most vehemently. In popular districts women might be heard demanding unusual punishments for the dynamitards. (They were called by this old name, although it was hardly appropriate to them, since, to these unknown chemists, dynamite was an innocent material only fit to destroy ant-hills, and they considered it mere child's play to explode nitro-glycerine with a cartridge made of fulminate of mercury.) Business ceased suddenly, and those who were least rich were the first to feel the effects. They spoke of doing justice themselves to the anarchists. In the mean time the factory workers remained hostile or indifferent to violent action. They were threatened, as a result of the decline of business, with a likelihood of losing their work, or even a lock-out in all the factories. The Federation of Trade Unions proposed a general strike as the most powerful means of influencing the employers, and the best aid that could be given to the revolutionists, but all the trades with the exception of the gilders refused to cease work.

The police made numerous arrests. Troops summoned from all parts of the National Federation protected the offices of the Trusts, the houses of the multi-millionaires, the public halls, the banks, and the big shops. A fortnight passed without a single explosion, and it was concluded that the dynamitards, in all probability but a handful of persons, perhaps even still fewer, had all been killed or captured, or that they were in hiding, or had taken flight. Confidence returned; it returned at first among the poorer classes. Two or three hundred thousand soldiers, who had been lodged in the most closely populated districts, stimulated trade, and people began to cry out: "Hurrah for the army!"

The rich, who had not been so quick to take alarm, were reassured more slowly. But at the Stock Exchange a group of "bulls" spread optimistic rumours and by a powerful effort put a brake upon the fall in prices. Business improved. Newspapers with big circulations supported the movement. With patriotic eloquence they depicted capital as laughing in its impregnable position at the assaults of a few dastardly criminals, and public wealth maintaining its serene ascendency in

spite of the vain threats made against it. They were sincere
in their attitude, though at the same time they found it bene-
fited them. Outrages were forgotten or their occurrence denied.
On Sundays, at the race-meetings, the stands were adorned
by women covered with pearls and diamonds. It was observed
with joy that the capitalists had not suffered. Cheers were
given for the multi-millionaires in the saddling rooms.

On the following day the Southern Railway Station, the
Petroleum Trust, and the huge church built at the expense
of Thomas Morcellet were all blown up. Thirty houses were
in flames, and the beginning of a fire was discovered at the
docks. The firemen showed amazing intrepidity and zeal.
They managed their tall fire-escapes with automatic precision,
and climbed as high as thirty storeys to rescue the luckless
inhabitants from the flames. The soldiers performed their
duties with spirit, and were given a double ration of coffee.
But these fresh casualties started a panic. Millions of people,
who wanted to take their money with them and leave the
town at once, crowded the great banking houses. These establishments, after paying out money for three days, closed their
doors amid mutterings of a riot. A crowd of fugitives, laden
with their baggage, besieged the railway stations and took
the town by storm. Many who were anxious to lay in a stock
of provisions and take refuge in the cellars, attacked the gro-
cery stores, although they were guarded by soldiers with
fixed bayonets. The public authorities displayed energy.
Numerous arrests were made and thousands of warrants issued
against suspected persons.

During the three weeks that followed no outrage was committed. There was a rumour that bombs had been found in
the Opera House, in the cellars of the Town Hall, and beside
one of the pillars of the Stock Exchange. But it was soon
known that these were boxes of sweets that had been put in
those places by practical jokers or lunatics. One of the accused, when questioned by a magistrate, declared that he was
the chief author of the explosions, and said that all his accom-

plices had lost their lives. These confessions were published
by the newspapers and helped to reassure public opinion. It
was only towards the close of the examination that the magistrates saw they had to deal with a pretender who was in
no way connected with any of the crimes.

The experts chosen by the courts discovered nothing that
enabled them to determine the engine employed in the work
of destruction. According to their conjectures the new explosion emanated from a gas which radium evolves, and it
was supposed that electric waves, produced by a special type
of oscillator, were propagated through space and thus caused
the explosion. But even the ablest chemist could say nothing
precise or certain. At last two policemen, who were passing
in front of the Hôtel Meyer, found on the pavement, close to
a ventilator, an egg made of white metal and provided with a
capsule at each end. They picked it up carefully, and, on the
orders of their chief, carried it to the municipal laboratory.
Scarcely had the experts assembled to examine it, than the
egg burst and blew up the amphitheatre and the dome. All
the experts perished, and with them Collin, the General of
Artillery, and the famous Professor Tigre.

The capitalist society did not allow itself to be daunted
by this fresh disaster. The great banks re-opened their doors,
declaring that they would meet demands partly in bullion and
partly in paper money guaranteed by the State. The Stock
Exchange and the Trade Exchange, in spite of the complete
cessation of business, decided not to suspend their sittings.

In the meantime the magisterial investigation into the case
of those who had been first accused had come to an end. Perhaps the evidence brought against them might have appeared
insufficient under other circumstances, but the zeal both of the
magistrates and the public made up for this insufficiency.
On the eve of the day fixed for the trial the Courts of Justice
were blown up and eight hundred people were killed, the
greater number of them being judges and lawyers. A furious
crowd broke into the prison and lynched the prisoners. The

troops sent to restore order were received with showers of stones and revolver shots; several soldiers being dragged from their horses and trampled underfoot. The soldiers fired on the mob and many persons were killed. At last the public authorities succeeded in establishing tranquillity. Next day the Bank was blown up.

From that time onwards unheard-of things took place. The factory workers, who had refused to strike, rushed in crowds into the town and set fire to the houses. Entire regiments, led by their officers, joined the workmen, went with them through the town singing revolutionary hymns, and took barrels of petroleum from the docks with which to feed the fires. Explosions were continual. One morning a monstrous tree of smoke, like the ghost of a huge palm tree half a mile in height, rose above the giant Telegraph Hall which suddenly fell into a complete ruin.

Whilst half the town was in flames, the other half pursued its accustomed life. In the mornings, milk pails could be heard jingling in the dairy carts. In a deserted avenue some old navvy might be seen seated against a wall slowly eating hunks of bread with perhaps a little meat. Almost all the presidents of the trusts remained at their posts. Some of them performed their duty with heroic simplicity. Raphael Box, the son of a martyred multi-millionaire, was blown up as he was presiding at the general meeting of the Sugar Trust. He was given a magnificent funeral and the procession on its way to the cemetery had to climb six times over piles of ruins or cross upon planks over the uprooted roads.

The ordinary helpers of the rich, the clerks, employés, brokers, and agents, preserved an unshaken fidelity. The surviving clerks of the Bank that had been blown up, made their way along the ruined streets through the midst of smoking houses to hand in their bills of exchange, and several were swallowed up in the flames while endeavouring to present their receipts.

Nevertheless, any illusion concerning the state of affairs

was impossible. The enemy was master of the town. Instead of
silence the noise of explosions was now continuous and produced an insurmountable feeling of horror. The lighting apparatus having been destroyed, the city was plunged in darkness
all through the night, and appalling crimes were committed.
The populous districts alone, having suffered the least, still
preserved measures of protection. They were paraded by
patrols of volunteers who shot the robbers, and at every street
corner one stumbled over a body lying in a pool of blood, the
hands bound behind the back, a handkerchief over the face,
and a placard pinned upon the breast.

It became impossible to clear away the ruins or to bury
the dead. Soon the stench from the corpses became intolerable.
Epidemics raged and caused innumerable deaths, while they
also rendered the survivors feeble and listless. Famine carried
off almost all who were left. A hundred and one days after the
first outrage, whilst six army corps with field artillery and
siege artillery were marching, at night, into the poorest quarter of the city, Caroline and Clair, holding each other's hands,
were watching from the roof of a lofty house, the only one
still left standing, but now surrounded by smoke and flame.
Joyous songs ascended from the street, where the crowd was
dancing in delirium.

"To-morrow it will be ended," said the man, "and it will
be better."

The young woman, her hair loosened and her face shining
with the reflection of the flames, gazed with a pious joy at
the circle of fire that was growing closer around them.

"It will be better," said she also.

And throwing herself into the destroyer's arms she pressed
a passionate kiss upon his lips.

§ 4

The other towns of the federation also suffered from dis-
turbances and outbreaks. and then order was restored. Re-

forms were introduced into institutions and great changes took place in habits and customs, but the country never recovered the loss of its capital, and never regained its former prosperity. Commerce and industry dwindled away, and civilization abandoned those countries which for so long it had preferred to all others. They became insalubrious and sterile; the territory that had supported so many millions of men became nothing more than a desert. On the hill of Fort St. Michel wild horses cropped the coarse grass.

Days flowed by like water from the fountains, and the centuries passed like drops falling from the ends of stalactites. Hunters came to chase the bears upon the hills that covered the forgotten city; shepherds led their flocks upon them; labourers turned up the soil with their ploughs; gardeners cultivated their lettuces and grafted their pear trees. They were not rich, and they had no arts. The walls of their cabins were covered with old vines and roses. A goat-skin clothed their tanned limbs, while their wives dressed themselves with the wool that they themselves had spun. The goat-herds moulded little figures of men and animals out of clay, or sang songs about the young girl who follows her lover through woods or among the browsing goats while the pine trees whisper together and the water utters its murmuring sound. The master of the house grew angry with the beetles who devoured his figs; he planned snares to protect his fowls from the velvet-tailed fox, and he poured out wine for his neighbours saying:

"Drink! The flies have not spoilt my vintage; the vines were dry before they came."

Then in the course of ages the wealth of the villages and the corn that filled the fields were pillaged by barbarian invaders. The country changed its masters several times. The conquerors built castles upon the hills; cultivation increased; mills, forges, tanneries, and looms were established; roads were opened through the woods and over the marshes; the river was covered with boats. The hamlets became large villages and joining together formed a town which protected itself by deep trenches and lofty walls. Later, becoming the capital of a great State, it found itself straitened within its now useless ramparts, and it converted them into grass-covered walks.

It grew very rich and large beyond measure. The houses were never high enough to satisfy the people; they kept on making them still higher and built them of thirty or forty storeys, with offices, shops, banks, societies one above another; they dug cellars and tunnels ever deeper downwards. Fifteen millions of men laboured in the giant town.

THE END

About The Author

ANATOLE FRANCE was the *nom de plume* of Jacques Anatole Thibault, who was born in Paris in 1844. He attended the Jesuit Collège Stanislas and began his literary career working for a publisher and writing weekly articles for the *Univers Illustré*. His first book of poems, *Les poèmes dorés,* was published in 1875, and his first successful novel, *Le Crime de Sylvestre Bonnard,* appeared in 1881 and won a prize from the French Academy. Much of his work appeared in periodicals and newspapers, and after the Dreyfus case (in which he supported Zola), it was slanted toward political satire. His other works include *Le Livre de mon ami* (1885), the first of a series of autobiographical novels, *Thaïs* (1890), *La Rôtisserie de la reine Pédauque* (1893), *Le Lys rouge* (1894), *L'Île des pingouins* (1908, *Penguin Island*), *Les Dieux ont soif* (1912), and *La Révolte des anges* (1914). The most prominent French man of letters of his time, he was elected to the French Academy in 1896, and received the Nobel Prize in Literature in 1921 for "the most remarkable literary work of idealistic stamp." He died at Tours in 1924.